# MURPHY'S SLAW

# MURPHY'S SLAW

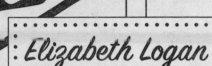

## Elizabeth Logan

BERKLEY PRIME CRIME
New York

BERKLEY PRIME CRIME
Published by Berkley
An imprint of Penguin Random House LLC
penguinrandomhouse.com

ISBN: 9780593100486

First Edition: June 2021

Printed in the United States of America
1   3   5   7   9   10   8   6   4   2

Book design by George Towne

*To our first responders, suppliers, and medical professionals, working constantly to keep us safe during challenging times.*

# One

MY BFF, ANNIE JENSEN, AND I SEIZED THE MOMENT, relaxing on the patio of her inn with fruity summer drinks. One of those long, hot August days in Elkview, Alaska, was before us. We were reveling in the six a.m. sunlight that would persist for more than fifteen hours—and even better, sharing stories about our cats.

Benny, an orange tabby, was the hero of my stories. I imagined him curled up on the top level of his plush cat condo in my home, a short drive away. Yulie was Annie's main character, a flame-point Siamese, now perched in front of a window, apparently eyeing us from inside the air-conditioned comfort of the inn's lobby. More likely, though, he was eyeing the red squirrel just out of reach on a tree branch close to the grand main building of the inn Annie's family had left her.

Annie and I had just waved goodbye to the tail end of two blue and gold "See Alaska" tour buses. Theirs was an ambitious tour, starting in Anchorage and making its way through Elkview and north to Fairbanks to see the northern lights. If the rest of the trip went well, the timing would be just right for the tourists to enjoy a view of the amazing green sweep of the aurora borealis.

Our waves and smiles had been accompanied by big sighs of relief as the two twenty-four-passenger buses pulled out of the inn's driveway. The lively and generous passengers had added significantly to the coffers of Annie's Inn and my Bear Claw Diner, but the work had taken its toll on us and our respective staffs.

I was lucky that many of my staff had been hired by the diner's previous owner, my mom, Evelyn Cooke, who'd passed both the diner and her precious cat on to me.

"It's great that our little town of Elkview is a stop on so many tours," Annie said. "My cabins have been pretty much at capacity all summer. Thanks for making the Bear Claw the perfect dining spot."

I nodded, indicating how pleased I was that my diner was the go-to place for meals for Annie's tourists.

"I agree. It's been a boon to be on the tour schedule. But it's also great that we have a break before the next buses," I added. "My suppliers could barely keep up. I had to request double orders of everything from almonds for the bear claws to cabbage for the coleslaw."

"They loved your slaw," Annie said. "I wouldn't have thought it could be so good without mayo."

"And your new afghans on the beds were a huge hit. It's great that you've taken up knitting again."

She smiled. "So what if I used size fifteen needles," said the returning knitter.

A passerby could always count on overhearing these post-tour reviews, during which Annie and I complimented each other on our work. Somebody had to do it. We'd practiced this supportive banter all through school, and even though we went to different colleges in the lower forty-eight, we maintained the tradition across the miles and picked it up again when we'd both made our way back to our hometown.

This week our guests had arrived in Alaska in time to

enjoy two days at the state fair, about an hour and a half south of where Annie and I sat chatting. By the time they'd arrived in Elkview, they'd accumulated enough souvenirs to take up an extra seat each on their bus. We were treated to displays of hoodies, T-shirts, baby bibs, tumblers, even flash drives with multicolored moose or bear visages.

"I have a good one, Charlotte," Annie said, getting back to our cat stories and using my full name to emphasize the seriousness of the joke, if that could be a thing. "It's not exactly a joke, but kind of a saying that I saw on Twitter."

"I'm ready."

"I mean, it doesn't have a punch line or anything, but it's hilarious."

As usual, it would be a while before Annie got to the point. Especially when she thought something was hilarious.

"Okay, here I go," she said, and cleared her throat. "If the world was flat, cats would have knocked everything off it by now."

She followed the meme with an over-the-top laugh. I granted Annie the pleasure of a reasonably loud guffaw myself and admitted it was a line worthy to be shared with my mom when we FaceTimed.

We sat quietly for a while, the only sounds being those of a finch in a nearby tree and the corresponding scratching from Yulie, who apparently had dreams of making contact.

While telling our feline stories and sipping our drinks, we'd both been flipping through local newspapers and flyers that had piled up during our double-booked tour groups. I was checking out a promotional postcard from the Alaska Veterans Museum in Anchorage, featuring a new navy exhibit I knew my dad would like. I thought of the two of them, Mom and Dad, currently spending a week in Oregon, attending a wedding anniversary party for friends who used to live in Elkview. Mom had been her friend's maid of honor. One thing was certain: my mom was keeping her resolution to travel during retirement. Dad still did some management consulting work but would drop it with little notice to join in the fun.

Annie gave out a sudden little squeal. "It's tomorrow," she said, waving a colorful postcard at me. "I forgot all about it. Good thing we're still free tomorrow."

I gave her a quizzical look. "What are we talking about?"

"The knitting workshop at the fair. It's new this year. I know we haven't gone to the fair in ages, but this year there's a special group teaching knitting techniques, and then all the items go to shelters, or the military, or some other charity." She screwed up her face into a familiar annoyed expression. "This postcard is so late. What if I'd missed this?"

I felt a tightness in my jaw. *And what if we did miss it?*

I let out an almost-audible growl. I'd worked the fair one summer at a small cotton-candy booth. My whole job had been about the monstrous pink stuff. When I wasn't making cones from flimsy paper, I was twirling one of them around the giant tub of flying sugar. As I remembered the gig, it was well into the school year before I got all the sugar out of my hair. If it had been up to me, I'd have tossed out every shirt I'd worn as hopelessly sticky no matter how many wash cycles I put them through. I'd begged my parents to never again force me to work outside the diner during school breaks. Only later did it occur to me that this might have been their plan all along.

As an adult, my experience of the fair was mostly negative for other reasons. Increased traffic on the George Parks Highway, crowds around the otherwise peaceful Eklutna Lake, roadblocks for the accompanying parade. Add to those twelve days of questionable music and entertainment, loud noise from every booth, and unpleasant odors from the countless animal pens.

And one other reason, if I was being honest. There was that year that I took my now ex-fiancé to the fair. Ryan

Jamison, attorney-at-law. I'd been more or less successful in pushing him out of my mind, but now and then, he popped in.

Annie took her turn with her view of the events, as if she'd been privy to my thoughts. "I love all the noise and the music, the animals. And the parade, especially. Let's go. We missed it the last couple of years."

"We didn't miss it. We skipped it."

"Same thing."

Not really. "I thought you told me you didn't even have time for a movie this week. You said you'd be busy cleaning up after this last tour." I pointed to the now-invisible trail left by the buses. "Remaking the beds in all the cottages, catching up on the bookkeeping, arranging the scheduling for your staff . . ." I trailed off, figuring she got my point and not wanting to spoil our break.

"You're right. I'm barely going to have everything cleaned before the next tour shows up. Or is it 'barely going to be cleaned up after the tour groups'? I know how much you love the right grammar. Not ending a sentence with a preposition and all." This was one observation she did not mean as a compliment.

Since it was only a small grammatical error, I was willing to let it pass. Besides, the preposition rule was pretty much passé. "More or less correct, Annie."

"But I want to go anyway."

"Anyway what?" I asked to possibly throw her off track. No such luck.

"It's only an hour or so down there, and we can leave early, be there when it opens, and be back before the Bear Claw's dinner crowd."

I couldn't continue to push the "We're busy" thread, since we both had staffs who were perfectly competent and always willing to give us the occasional day off. "It's more like an hour and a half."

"Please, Charlie."

Now she wasn't being fair, making me feel like a wicked mommy.

"I don't know, Annie. I have so much to do."

But I wasn't fooling her.

"I'll get my things together," she said.

"We're going early and leaving there right after lunch," I said. "I am not driving back here at the height of Parks Highway traffic."

On that I was firm.

Not that she heard me.

# Two

I LEFT ANNIE'S SUNNY PATIO AND HEADED BACK TO MY Bear Claw Diner in a less than great mood. I informed my staff that I'd be out the next day. They responded with a flurry of positive words.

"I'll make some extra snack packs." That was Victor Fiore, my head chef, who made a mean elk jerky for those packs. "I know there's a ton of food at the fair, but you might need some for the road."

Victor had added significantly to our menu without losing what we liked to call the "classic" diner fare: open-faced sandwiches, grilled cheese, burgers, fries, malts. I was getting hungry thinking of the choices, though my early breakfast wasn't that long ago. Victor's younger sister, Nina, our head waitress, liked to play with desserts, specifically my favorite, silky chocolate pie. Again, adding to, but not replacing, the traditional strawberry shortcake and apple and rhubarb pies that were more than just decoration for our refrigerated shelves and tiered cake holders.

"I'll be able to take an extra shift tomorrow afternoon," Rachel said.

"There's not another tour bus coming through here until next week, so you don't have to worry about a thing," Nina added.

And so it went, encouragement from even the part-timers who were tying their aprons on for the lunch rush. My dedicated and generous staff seemed a little too eager to have me absent for a day.

"I'll be back before dinner prep," I said. "We're not going to stay all day."

"It doesn't hurt to be prepared," said Ginny, a new girl, a high schooler eager to learn restaurant work.

"Would you all like to go in my place? I'll spring for the tickets."

"Well—" Nina began.

"No, no. You need to go, boss." Victor's face, his dark curls hiding under a red bandana, appeared in the through-window. "Try to connect with that farmer who grew a one-hundred-fifty-pound cabbage. I need it for that new slaw recipe I want to try."

Victor always went for a laugh, something I needed today.

"That's a joke, right?" Rachel, who'd only recently moved to Alaska from Los Angeles, looked confused. "You don't really mean one hundred and fifty pounds? One cabbage?"

"You're telling us you haven't noticed the nearly twenty hours of daylight since May?" Nina asked.

Rachel looked sheepish. "I guess I didn't put two and two together. About how things would grow bigger, I mean."

Nina turned to me. "Check on our suppliers while you're there. If they're just hanging around doing nothing or riding the Ferris wheel, tell them we need lettuce!"

"Will do."

"You might have a really fun time," Ginny said. The newbie who didn't know me that well.

"A fun time? Not likely," I said.

Were they that eager to get rid of me? Should I worry about what they did when they were in charge? I trusted them completely with the cash register and the inventory, and more than once they'd bailed me out when I was called away. If they happened to be holding a dance contest as soon as I left the parking lot, so what? As long as customers were well taken care of—and I had every reason to believe they would be—I shouldn't care.

I knew that Tammy and Bert, two college students who had the graveyard shift, starting at one in the morning, used most of the time to do their homework, unless I left them a long to-do list. I was only too happy for that win-win situation.

I took a breath. I really needed to lose the attitude. My staff should not have to suffer my foul mood just because I'd caved to Annie and was not looking forward to walking on uneven surfaces, some gravelly, some grassy, and suffering the host of unpleasant odors, whether from food or animals.

I managed a smile. "At least I can visit the cooking booths. Who knows? I might find some recipes we can adopt for our menu."

"Now you're talking," Victor said.

"Okay, then," I said. "I'll bring you back some souvenirs."

SINCE I'D BE SKIPPING MY MORE OR LESS STANDARD dinner shift, I thought it only right that I help my staff with lunch. I smiled and tied on my Bear Claw apron. *Big of me.* After serving a couple of dozen grilled cheese sandwiches, some with tomato and some without, and about the same number of ice teas, I packed up and made my way home to my cat.

I found Benny sleeping on the chair by my bed. So much for the pricey multistory tower I'd bought him, with scratching posts, hanging toys, and plush sleeping areas on every level. I wanted to wake Benny to complain to him that I'd be going to the Alaska State Fair the next day, to garner some real sympathy. He'd hate the commotion; he was happy to stay home. He knew he wouldn't have to worry, since there was always a neighbor or a friend or an employee to check on him in case his automatic feeder didn't work or some other calamity befell him. Of course, I had Benny apps on my phone and could communicate with him throughout the day, no matter where I was.

I lived only a short drive from my parents' home, aka the home I grew up in, where Benny had spent his youth being pampered by my mom. We didn't overlap as residents of the house, since Benny had arrived in the family while I was slogging through one school or another. His full name? Eggs Benedict, or Eggs Benedict Cooke, if I wanted to be formal. When my mom handed him off to me, along with the Bear Claw Diner, she had me promise not to change his name.

"He'd be traumatized," she predicted.

As soon as Benny stirred now, I scooped him up. I settled in the rocker with a purring cat in my lap and prepared to FaceTime with my parents. I'd gotten a postcard in the mail from those traveling Cookes, with Mom's handwriting, of course. The card was oversize, with a collage of photos from a diner in Portland—a train car–style room with green and blue stools and booths. I read the two main points to her message: "The hash browns are great" and "Why don't we have postcards made up?" Mom didn't run the Bear Claw anymore, but she still had good ideas. We had business cards at the cash register, but nothing as colorful as postcards. I made a note to bring it up at the next staff meeting.

It was a tie between Benny and my mom as to who was the better listener, although, of course, I never told her that. FaceTiming into my parents' travels was always a treat, usually including a brief appearance by my dad at halftime, or during seventh inning, or whatever sports break was on TV.

"Hi, sweetie," Mom said now. Then, "You, too, Charlie. Not just Benny."

"Love you, too, Mom. And thanks for the postcard." This back-and-forth was becoming our standard greeting now that Mom and Dad traveled so often. "How was the anniversary party last night?" I asked. This question was to assuage my guilt over what was coming: whining about having to go to the fair.

"The party was wonderful, really. There's nothing like old friends and live music to add to a vacation trip."

"We should start planning a party for you and dad."

"I prefer other people in the spotlight, but thanks anyway."

The "thanks" was facetious, as it always was when I offered to do something that would showcase her.

"I'm glad you called," she said. "I can show you where we are right now." Mom had developed a constant happy, relaxed tone since her retirement from management of the Bear Claw. She held her phone to face a Victorian-looking mansion with extensive grounds. "One of Dad's friends took us here. It's the Pittock Mansion, outside of Portland," she said. "It's been used in lots of movies and television shows."

"It looks magnificent," I said.

When my mom's face came back on the screen, Benny stood up on my lap and rubbed his face on the corner of my phone.

Mom smiled. "He's all over your cell phone, right? I can just see one ear and an eye. Whenever I was using my tablet, he insisted on sitting on it. Hi, Benny! It's Mom!"

I pulled the phone back so she could see him perched on my lap.

Her smile grew wistful. "How is he?"

"Fat and sassy, Mom. He gets all the salmon he wants and more. Don't worry about him. Just enjoy Oregon."

Benny settled back down in my lap, and his purrs grew softer. I scratched him gently behind one ear and gazed at the flower-filled garden that filled the screen behind my mom. "The grounds of the mansion look beautiful. I wouldn't mind being there myself."

"You should see the inside. There's an amazing central stairway with a banister you wouldn't believe, with bronze grillwork. The floors are marble, and the ceilings are— Wait, you wish you were here? What's wrong there?"

*Now I've done it.* I hadn't meant to interrupt mom's excitement. No one was more deserving of these retirement travels she'd worked out for herself and my dad, after years and years of managing the Bear Claw twenty-four-seven while dealing with an often recalcitrant child. (That child would be me.)

"I'm going to the fair tomorrow," I said, trying not to sound disgruntled.

"You hate the fair. It must be Annie's idea."

"Uh-huh. But I shouldn't complain. Maybe I'll pick up a new recipe or two. As long as I can keep Annie off the kiddie rides, we'll be fine."

"I remember the year she twisted an ankle getting out of the bumper cars." Mom laughed. "I know it's not funny, but—"

"It kind of was, then."

"Take some photos of the produce, okay?"

Once a diner owner, always a diner owner.

I HATED TO WAKE BENNY, WHO'D FALLEN ASLEEP ON my lap during my FaceTime with my mom. I sat there enjoying his comforting warmth and watching his paws twitch as he chased something through his cat version of dreamland. Assuming cats dreamed. Annie thought they did. She'd read an article about the dream life of rats and decided cats must have them, too. Apparently, with nothing better to do, scientists had compared the brain activity of rats both running around and sleeping and found no difference.

"I don't know why it wouldn't be the same for cats," she'd concluded.

"Neither do I," I'd said.

It was now evening, and my stomach rumbled, reminding me that even though the sun was still high, it was dinnertime. I shifted in the chair, waking Benny. He jumped down and wandered with me into the dining room, his tail swishing in its happy mode. If he'd had pleasant dreams, he wasn't talking about it.

I'd left the diner with food for tonight's dinner for me and Benny. Victor had prepared enough salmon and rice to cover all bases at home and away, with added snacks for both of us for tomorrow.

"You know there's food every three feet at the fair," I'd reminded him.

He gave me a look that needed no interpretation: there was nothing like his food anywhere outside the Bear Claw.

The least I could do now was leave Nina's special brownies sealed up for the road trip and check out my freezer for tonight's dessert.

I was almost in the clear with a large slice of Dutch apple pie to finish off my meal when my front doorbell rang.

If Benny was alert to my mom's voice, Alaska State Trooper Cody Graham had a sixth sense for arriving when dessert was on the table. Sure enough, I opened the door to a tall, lanky officer of the law, in a blue suit with a gold stripe down his pant leg. The wrinkles in the uniform told me he hadn't spent the day primping before a mirror, or even sitting comfortably behind a desk.

I came close to remarking on how worn-out he looked, but instead, I invited him to join me at the table.

"What do you know? My favorite pie," he said. His

smile was weak, I hoped only from low blood sugar and a need for pie.

"Every pie is your favorite."

"That, too."

I pushed the large slice I'd cut toward him while I stepped into the kitchen to cut another, smaller, slice of pie for myself and start a pot of coffee. I'd known Trooper, as a few of us were allowed to call him, since I was a kid doing my homework on a Bear Claw Diner stool. I knew when there was something troubling on his mind.

"A body," he said, by way of welcoming me back to the dining room table, and convincing me once again that he had perfect pitch when it came to reading the minds and answering the unspoken questions of those who loved and revered him.

"I'm sorry," I said.

"I have to ask you a favor," he said, between bites of Dutch apple pie. "I'm due up in Petersville. I just got back from a quick trip there, and need to return. That's where the big law enforcement conference is this year. And you know the drill. If you don't show up, your name and station might just slip off the budget allocation sheet."

From years of knowing Trooper, and something of politics, I knew what he meant.

I straightened up. And there was "a body," as he'd put it, somewhere.

I placed mugs of coffee at our two places and sat to listen.

I assumed Trooper needed me to represent him in what might be a homicide case. In the past, he'd made me and Annie, whom he'd known for practically our entire lifetimes, informal deputies. We'd conduct interviews and otherwise assist in an investigation and report to him. Chris Doucette, Elkview's best and only full-time journalist, was also included on this team. Chris and I were still working out to what extent our relationship went beyond working together. If at all. But that was for another day. Now I was thinking how great it would be if this so-called favor for Trooper also got me out of a trip to the fair. I held my breath.

"I need you to go down to Palmer," Trooper said.

I let out a groan that I hoped wasn't too loud and sensed a frown that I hoped wasn't too deep. "Palmer? To the—"

"Yes," Trooper said. "To the fair."

I swallowed hard. "How can I help?"

TROOPER HAD FINISHED OFF HIS PIE AND MINE, THEN confessed that he hadn't had lunch or dinner, and he wouldn't say no to a grilled cheese and tomato, with maybe a little ham on the side.

"No problem," I'd said and served it all up.

When you've grown up in a diner and now owned one, there wasn't much you hadn't seen by way of eating habits, whether it was kids asking for a mayo sandwich on white bread ("Yes, just mayo, please"), or grown-ups, like Trooper, eating dessert first.

On the chance that I'd say yes to his request, Trooper had brought along his file, skimpy as it was, on the body that had been discovered at the fair.

"Technically, just off the fairgrounds, on a bordering street, and close enough that we start there for answers."

At his fourth consecutive wide yawn, I suggested that I read the file on my own tonight and call him in the morning if I had any questions.

He smiled. "If you insist," he said, donning his tall blue hat.

Benny, who was a fan of Trooper's, walked him to the door, then sprinted back to find my lap, which I'd moved to the rocker in the family room. As much as I wanted to dive into Trooper's folder, I felt I owed Benny a little playtime. I let him choose the game and found myself watching as he chased his pop-up mouse toy from one opening in the base to another. The only challenge I could provide was to turn the small console every now and then.

Benny followed me as I made my way to my bedroom, laptop and Trooper's FAIR folder in hand. In a change of heart, now I was eager to get on the road tomorrow.

I could hardly wait to tell Annie.

# THREE

I GOT SETTLED IN BED WITH A MUG OF TEA, MY LAPTOP, and, most interesting, Trooper's FAIR folder. Benny had chosen the soft cat bed on the floor, one that had started out in front of my night table, but had somehow made its way to the narrow space between the table and my bed. I never doubted Benny's ability to move furniture.

I found it interesting that Trooper had chosen to label the folder not BODY, as he'd said when he'd described his day verbally, but the more positive-sounding FAIR.

No sooner had I opened the folder than my cell phone rang.

Chris Doucette's name popped up on the screen. Coincidence? I thought not, since Trooper and Chris were buddies and Trooper often paired us up as "deputies," though we'd had no formal training and carried no badge or gun. My mom called us Keystone Deputies, having to explain more than once how her parents had loved a group of slapstick comic policemen from old silent films. I smiled thinking of the day Trooper had asked us to raise our right hands and take the oath in the middle of the Bear Claw Diner.

Chris and I had solemnly sworn to uphold the laws of Matanuska-Susitna Borough in the state of Alaska.

"I didn't know that was a thing," Chris had said.

Trooper smiled. "It isn't."

We laughed at ourselves and then laughed again later, when Trooper pulled the same trick on Annie and my mom.

"I hear we have a project," Chris said now on the phone. "Or maybe 'assignment' is a better word?"

Of course Trooper would marshal all the forces he could. When my call with Chris was interrupted by one from Annie, I knew the full complement of three quarters of the team was in place. At least he hadn't called my mom to come back home to join us in the investigation—if he had, she would have told me.

"Who's driving?" I asked.

Chris chuckled. "As if you didn't know."

I did know that Chris was enamored of my vehicle, and I'd falsely assumed it was only during winter months, when my Outback's heated steering wheel served an important purpose. Come to find out, my car's excellent cooling system was also an attraction.

I added Annie to the call, figuring she'd have a teasing remark about me and the fair, and she didn't disappoint.

She could hardly speak through her giggles. "Gee, Charlie, are you sure you don't want to skip the fair again this year?"

I decided to let her win that round.

"The fair opens at ten on Sundays," I said.

"The vendors will be there around nine," Annie said.

"We should get there as soon before that as we can. So we leave Elkview at—"

"No later than seven thirty," was the cruel answer from Annie, who never slept past the crack of dawn. You'd think she was a farmer, rather than an innkeeper.

"Oh no," Chris said—at the early hour, I was sure.

"I'll bring food," I said, almost positive I saw Benny's tail swish out of the corner of my eye.

AFTER I CLICKED OFF THE PHONE, MY EYELIDS WERE approaching half-mast, but I wanted to get a head start on the case. I figured I could read the whole file out loud tomorrow on the way to the fair, since Chris would be driving. Too bad that Mom, who loved reading whodunits, wasn't in on this trip. I wouldn't rule out that she might know the victim, since she had run the diner for nearly thirty years and had lived in Elkview most of her life. I'd call her first thing and let her know, as soon as I checked on her time zone in Portland, Oregon, something I always had trouble remembering. I told myself it was because she'd traveled in at least four zones over the past few months.

I opened the blue police folder with the seal of Alaska on the front to the first sheet, the crime report, and read through various identification numbers for the incident, still with Mom in mind.

It hadn't occurred to me that I'd be the one who knew the victim.

But I did.

Under LAST NAME, FIRST NAME, MIDDLE INITIAL, I read: Carson, Kelly A.

I held my breath, then made up a story. There was more than one Kelly Carson. It wasn't that unusual a name. Sure, there was a Kelly Carson who'd been two years ahead of me in my small high school and was now one of my produce suppliers, a woman who regularly attended the state fair as a vendor. But that didn't mean there wasn't another Kelly Carson, someone much older, perhaps, who'd had heatstroke this hot August month that simply mimicked a homicide.

I shut the folder, then opened it again, as if that might

alter the entries. When the text didn't change and realization dawned, my moan was so loud it woke Benny, who hopped on the bed and slunk onto my lap.

"Thanks, Benny," I said and stroked his back, more for my comfort than his.

I could hardly bring myself to read the rest of the page, which had dozens of boxes, some filled out or checked—like the X next to the box labeled HOMICIDE—some not. I skimmed the information, finding it unbearable to study it closely.

The next bits of data were the victim's address, on M Street in Elkview, and her vehicle, an old Ford truck, which together removed all doubt that it was the Kelly I knew.

I thought back to the last time I had seen her. Not for the most recent delivery, when I wasn't at the diner. It might have been a month since KC and I met at the Bear Claw. Had I been kind? Friendly? Asked her how she was, how the business was doing, whether she planned to compete at the fair? Or had I simply waved from my desk and let Victor and other staff do all the schmoozing?

I didn't want to hear my answer.

Sleep was impossible now, so I went in search of a cracker or two and offered Benny a treat from his side of the cupboard. I returned to my bed so Benny would follow me and go back to sleep. There was no sense in having two of us tossing and turning all night.

In our small Mat-Su Borough school, all our early grades had been grouped together, making Kelly, Annie, and me classmates for most days. When I told Annie who the victim was, in the car the next morning, and she broke down, I was glad I hadn't awakened her with the news when I had first looked at the folder. It had been hard enough to report the news to my mom, who knew KC's mom, as well as all the other parents of my classmates.

"I'm really sorry about this," Chris said, at the wheel of my Outback. "It's tough to lose someone you've known that long. I don't remember her at all. I guess I was long gone by then."

To the army, he meant. Chris was a little older, and had left for Fairbanks soon after his graduation.

It was a good thing our driver had no personal connection with Kelly. One of us had to remain as objective and unemotional as possible. Trooper's team needed our wits about us if we were going to bring Kelly's murderer to justice.

I did my best to read the report to Annie and Chris without choking up, citing details like the date and time of day when Kelly had been discovered—in the northeast corner of the property, close to a bordering residential street and the cabbage display that was featured in her booth in the produce section.

"She was stabbed," I said, as quietly as possible.

Annie shivered in the back seat.

I cleared my throat and pulled myself together as much as I could manage, summarizing details from the chronological record Trooper had provided.

KC had been found by a member of the fairgrounds security crew who was on her way to her vehicle after her shift. The time recorded was 11:05 p.m., approximately an hour after the fair had closed. The record provided other specific times, such as the coroner's arrival at 11:40, and who was interviewed and at what time.

At the end of the chronology were spaces for AR-RESTED and CASE PRESENTED TO DA. I wondered how long it would take to fill in those blocks.

I scanned the report for something I might have missed—Trooper hadn't given me the original copy, and the font was small to begin with, the fine print being truly fine. At least, that was my excuse for missing a box that asked for LOCATION OF OCCURRENCE.

"This has the location at Spruce Street between Pierce and Main," I said.

"Then why are we going to the fair?" Annie asked.

"Trooper said they found her just at the edge of the fairgrounds, technically not on the grounds itself, and a group of volunteers worked all night to clear the area so the fair wouldn't have to be shut down." This from Chris, who'd gotten more information from Trooper than I had.

I constructed a scenario where Trooper visited Chris first, since he lived closer to the highway, then moved on to me when he realized that my home was more likely to have food that didn't come in a can.

"Here it is," Annie said, rotating her map. "I see where that part of Spruce is. Right off the northeast corner."

"Still," I said. "It doesn't seem right to have fun and games going on right next to where someone was stabbed to death."

"Did you think we were going to a shut-down fair?" Chris asked.

I hadn't given it any thought, was the real answer. And as to the separate question of how come Chris knew so much more about the state of affairs than I did, I threw in the theory that Chris got a scoop from old Wally Bean, his boss at the *Bugle*. He and Trooper went way back, and I could see why Trooper would want the correct news to reach Wally before the rumor mill got in gear.

I looked across at Chris, his fitness, shaved head, and excellent posture reminding me of his military training. With his US ARMY baseball cap balanced on his knee, the whole picture sent out vibes of self-confidence and trustworthiness.

"I wasn't thinking," I admitted. "Anyway, it certainly makes sense to start at the fair, with all the principals still there."

"If he is," Annie said.

"He?"

"You know. The killer. If the killer's still there."

Annie had unwittingly brought on another period of silence in my car.

According to the report, the last person to see Kelly at her stall was her mom, Laurie Patterson, who ran a hardware store near Talkeetna with her new husband. Annie and I remembered when Kelly's dad died, casting a pall over the events of her senior year. It was unlikely that Laurie or her husband would be at the fair today. We'd have to build in a time to talk to them in their home later.

It was too early in the morning for summer traffic to have kicked in. What should have been a scenic drive through deep patches of spruce and a beautiful blue sky, maybe accompanied by some sing-along music on the car radio or a CD of oldies from the turn of the century, when we were all new high school graduates, was instead somber, the only chatter directed toward whom to interview, where, and when.

Back when Annie had been anticipating a day of fun for the two of us, neither of us knowing about our deputy detail, she'd downloaded pages from the fairgrounds website and added color-coding for food and entertainment locations. She'd also inserted bits of interesting information, such as John F. Kennedy's visit to the fair in 1960.

We used the printouts now to plan an interview schedule, deciding to split up to cover more ground.

The fair was spread over a vast area, three hundred acres according to the literature, and while we didn't need to examine every inch, we needed to put a dent in the square footage. The big question was, Would we be spinning our wheels? It was as likely as not that whoever killed Kelly had done the deed and split for parts unknown. Alaska was a big state, with lots of places to hide.

There was another page to the sheaf in the folder Trooper had given me. One that I was putting off looking at. Doc Sherman, acting as the medical examiner in KC's case, had filled out his report. The text was not surprising, listing the vital statistics of the deceased, from eye color to a description of her hair (both brown) to whether or not she was clothed (yes).

It was the sketch in the right-hand column that was hard to look at. A generic diagram took up about a third of the page, with a front and a back view of a body.

On the diagram for KC's report, Doc Sherman had filled in an image of a stab wound on her back, between her shoulder blades. A simple vertical red line, but it was enough to make me gag. I decided not to reveal this page to my two companions until we were safely out of the car. If ever.

Halfway into our trip, around the town of Willow—not my attorney friend, Willow Yazzie, but a Census Designated Place, like Elkview—we stopped for a break to stretch our legs and dip into the snacks.

No one had had time for breakfast, so we lingered awhile at the rest stop parking lot and ate bear claws from my diner. Annie had brought a large thermos and ceramic mugs, plus cream, sugar, and utensils, and I had brought the special cookie of the month, snickerdoodles—made by my Bear Claw staff, of course. I'd also brought the snack packs that included Victor's tasty elk jerky and handed them out for an emergency hunger pang. Chris, who'd come empty-handed—because "How can I compete with a diner owner and an innkeeper?"—offered to treat us to dinner at a restaurant in town.

The second leg of the trip was less somber as we checked the map of the fairgrounds and carved out sections of it. I'd take the area that included the cabbage display near which KC had been found and which may or may not have been the crime scene. Annie would head for the row of craft booths, where she would feel at home asking questions, and Chris suggested he take the outermost tents and make his way into the food concourse. We'd be in radio contact—that is, on our cell phones—at all times. It felt good to have a plan. Once the expected thousands of attendees arrived, we'd be glad we had a lifeline connecting us to one another.

Trooper had arranged for us to pick up passes at one of the check-in points, and we were able to enter the grounds early, with the vendors. This Sunday was the fourth day of the fair, and the vendors were already showing signs of wear, with eight days still to go. They trudged in, most pulling dollies with boxes of supplies spilling over. I knew some would have had a much longer trip than my group had and that it was a challenge to make the journey several days in a row. Staying at a motel or even a B and B would eat into the profits unacceptably for many.

Once inside the gate, I found myself viewing everyone as a suspect with the exception of children under twelve years old—clearly vendors' kids, so not scary. And if a vendor had a kid with him or her, wouldn't that exclude the person as the killer? This being my desperate attempt to narrow the suspect pool.

I wanted to query the men and women I had entered the grounds with, but thought I should wait until they were at least partially set up. I realized how ill prepared I was for this task.

Did I want to interrogate at random? What if I happened on the killer?

Maybe it wasn't such a good idea for Trooper's team to split up. I was sure I'd have felt better if our entire car pool were walking around the site together. I made a move for my cell phone to see if Annie and Chris were amenable to changing the plan and getting together for the interviews.

"Horrible, isn't it?"

The booming voice behind me sent me off balance. My phone fell to the ground, fortunately onto a grassy knoll. I turned to see one of my produce vendors, Roland Hortenson, as large a man as I was likely to run into today. Roland was taller than my above-average height, and considerably wider than I was, too.

"Sorry, Charlie. I didn't mean to scare you."

"I guess everyone is on edge today," I said.

Roland nodded, then shook his head, as if in disbelief. "So awful what happened to KC."

"It is. Horrible."

"I've been coming here for more years than I care to count, and I don't ever remember something like this happening," he said.

"I don't think it has."

"I guess we'll just have to make do today, as best we can. Does the Bear Claw have a booth here?" Roland asked.

*Uh-oh.* I hadn't thought about a cover story. Though we hadn't spelled it out this time, Annie, Chris, and I usually worked unofficially, not announcing our connection to Trooper's official investigation. I smiled as I recalled how the three of us had explained it to ourselves.

"It works out better this way, since we don't have badges or guns," one of us said at one time, and the other two agreed.

I cleared my throat and came up with a story for Roland. "The Bear Claw doesn't have its own booth this year. I'll be helping out some friends." I paused, but not long enough for Roland to ask for specifics. "In fact, I'd better get moving, or they'll think I'm flaking."

I gave Roland a brief wave and hurried on. *Close call,* I thought.

It was going to be a long day.

# Four

FARMER ROLAND'S BOOMING VOICE AND ACKNOWL-
edgment of Kelly's murder made everything more real. Roland's calling her KC, our nickname for her, established
years ago, brought home a sober fact. It seemed like yesterday when we thought of using her initials and then laughed
when we realized they were attached to a popular singing
group.

The murder victim was indeed one of my old school
friends and currently a business colleague. It was not a rumor, not an error in the police report, not a wild-goose
chase, that had brought me to the fairgrounds on a mission
for an Alaska State Trooper.

I chided myself for not keeping up with an old friend.
More often than not, it was Victor or Nina who was there
to accept the deliveries for the diner. Lately, I tended to
show up for the dinner crowd and stay until Tammy and
Bert arrived at one in the morning. That way, I could sneak
in a few hours in the kitchen when it was slow to try new
recipes or whip up my favorites for a late dinner for myself.

My crazy hours didn't excuse me from calling KC to see

how she was doing and suggesting we meet for coffee to catch up instead of mindlessly writing the monthly check for sacks of greens.

My braver self kicked in, and I decided not to call in the troops I'd driven down with and claim I wasn't feeling well and needed to go home. I had to start acting like an investigator. In fact, why hadn't I chatted more with Roland? I supposed it would have been awkward for me to have blurted out a detective's typical first question: "Where were you after hours on Friday night?" In the middle of a rush of his fellow vendors, no less.

I'd catch up with Roland later, at his booth. I hadn't decided whether it would be better to start with people I knew or with strangers. I hadn't had much time to think it through, having mostly focused on memories.

I hoped Annie and Chris were doing better than I was.

After I walked around awhile and chatted with a couple of growers who seemed not to have known KC, I allowed myself "How's it going?" calls to Annie and Chris.

"This is hard," Annie said.

"Kelly's mom sent a substitute here," Chris said, "one of Kelly's employees, Donna, to staff her booth. I was able to get a little insight into the relationships Kelly had at her farm. Which didn't really get me anywhere, but at least it was a start to eliminating situations, meaning there was no bad blood in the group working on the farm."

"Nice work," I said, wondering how Chris had gotten to KC's booth before I had, when it was supposed to be my turf.

"I ran into Donna as I was walking toward my section," Chris said, as if he knew my question. "She was wearing a badge with Kelly's label. How's it going with you?"

"It's going fine," I said, then pretended to lose the connection and hung up before he could ask for details.

I reminded myself how lucky we were to have at least one professional investigator on the team Trooper had sent here. So what if he only worked for the *Elkview Bugle*, a small-town newspaper? He was only a couple of years older than me—still young enough to win a Pulitzer someday.

On my own, heading for the cabbage booth, my brain was still switching back and forth from investigator to victim, feeling oddly vulnerable, as if I might be the next one to be taken down as KC had been. I knew the feeling was groundless. Of all the write-ups of the fair over the years, I could not remember a single homicide. One year, a woman died from a fall from the Ferris wheel, and another time a man lost his life in a car accident close to the entrance. There might have been a tussle or two over the years among the many thousands of people who crowded the area, but nothing as newsworthy, or heart-wrenching, as a homicide.

Until now.

Would the killer come back today, madly wielding a knife, to pick off another fairgoer? I tried not to think of serial killers through history, ones that kept showing up in different locations. I couldn't help thinking about a book my mom had read during her true crime phase about a serial killer who had roamed loose in Chicago during a world's fair there. The same one where the Ferris wheel was introduced, if I remembered correctly. But that was more than a century ago, I was sure. Still, I moved my shoulder bag around and clutched it to my chest, as if it could serve as a bulletproof vest.

It was still chilly, and I had on a Denali National Park hoodie. I pulled the gray hood over my head. Another great layer of protection from a knife or gun, I mumbled to myself.

A welcome lighthearted moment came when I passed the canvas tent where a young woman in coveralls was adjusting the ribbon on Big Bertha, a thirty-nine-inch-long green bean that had won first prize. I'd forgotten that produce exhibitors gave their products names, especially when the item was large enough to enter into the contests. Looking around at all the spectacular veggies, it was hard to believe that only five percent of the food consumed in Alaska is grown in Alaska. I hoped what I'd read was true, that there was renewed interest in farming in the state, and that we wouldn't lose all our best soil to developers.

It occurred to me that Annie and I could help this cause by talking up farm visits to the tour companies that came through. There was enough promotion of the usual Alaska attractions on the way to the northern lights, but what if we came up with information, maybe flyers, advertising the many local tours that highlighted farms and food? Maybe I was channeling my mom and her Portland tours, but so what? What was good for farms along the Parks Highway was good for the Bear Claw Diner.

I turned to see Posh Squash being laid out on a make-shift wooden counter and Scouts' Sprouts on another, with, sure enough, a young boy sporting a green Boy Scouts of America cap. He stood proudly next to a light purple ribbon, signifying a grand champion win for the squash. I thought it was a little too early for him to be taking up his post and wondered how long he'd be able to stand at attention, as he was now.

The spurt of levity gave me the impetus to check in with Benny. Why not continue with ways to boost my spirits? Not that it had been that long since I'd left my cat, but I needed one more lift besides what the fun-loving farming population had to offer.

I clicked on the Bennycam app on my phone and got a look at an empty family room. I willed Benny to leave his comfy tower in the back bedroom and come out to greet me. No such luck. I clicked over to the Notes app and jotted a few words to remind me to check into installing a second camera in the guest bedroom, aka Benny's condo address.

A blast from the loudspeaker sent my phone to the ground again. Familiar carousel music took over the air-waves this time. That started a cacophony of sounds, in-cluding a mic test, which sounded like a group of teenagers testing a bull horn with various degrees of laughter. I could have sworn I heard cattle sounds also, but that may have been my awareness of the environs playing tricks on me.

If this year was like all the others, upwards of six dozen food vendors were scheduled to drive their tasty morsels to the fair. We could expect staples like hot dogs, pizza, burgers, and all kinds of food on a stick, plus more exotic Alaskan seafood selections. I passed a sign advertising "the world's largest prawns" and another for wild octopus, including tentacles, arms, and body meat. Dessert offerings were also varied, from ice cream to cream puffs and more. Then there was the dreaded cotton candy, purple this year. I hoped I wouldn't inadvertently step on a discarded cone and send sticky sugar coursing up my ankle.

As far as I knew, my mom had never attended the fair as a vendor. I wondered why not, other than that it would be a lot of work to transport Bear Claw Diner food and the means of keeping it hot or cold, or simply safe to eat.

Maybe she would have considered it if I hadn't borne a grudge against cotton candy all these years. Mom and Annie were the only ones who knew about the embarrassing trauma involving sugar and pink food coloring, although I always suspected that my mom had told my dad, since I knew the two of them shared everything they knew about me, one way or another.

I wondered if I would ever have the kind of relationship my parents had. But I couldn't linger on that question now. I had work to do.

I checked the map I'd picked up at the entrance and saw that I was still far from the edge of the property where KC's body had been found.

"Charlie, over here," I heard.

I turned. This time the sound was a reasonable one, and I did not drop my phone. Aly Morgan, from Aly's Café in Elkview, waved at me from where she was setting up her booth. Aly had made the most of her small space, squeezing in narrow stools in front of a countertop, the closest she could come to assembling a real café. And just in time for my second cup of coffee. I cast a longing glance at the fresh blueberry muffins she'd arranged on a tray, but couldn't convince my stomach to absorb a second breakfast. Not with the potential for lunch I'd seen all around me.

"Charlie, how about what happened to KC? Isn't she your supplier, too? She is—was—one of my best vendors. I almost didn't come today, but I need these days to stay alive." She stopped, realizing what she'd said. "Sorry, what a horrible thing to say."

I shook my head as if to excuse her. Aly fixed my coffee while she talked, slowly, relying on years of serving me the same thing in her café to get it right.

"I can't get over it, either," I said.

"I keep thinking of poor Milo and what will happen to him," Aly said.

Milo. KC's teenage son. I used to ask about him every time I saw her. But once he was older, it didn't seem to come up anymore. KC had adopted Milo, her nephew, when his parents—KC's sister and brother-in-law—were both killed in a bush plane crash coming back from watching a sled dog race as it passed through a checkpoint. Milo had been a toddler at the time. All four on board, including another local couple, had been killed. There had been questions about the pilot's choice to take off in bad weather, but nothing had ever come of it as far as I knew. I hadn't followed the incident in any detail, but I recalled that KC left college to take over Milo's care, as well as the farm his parents had run.

"KC had it rough," I said. "I remember when her dad died, when we were in high school," I said.

"Right. And then her sister, Milo's mom, in that plane crash. And now KC, too. I can't imagine what Laurie is going through."

Laurie. KC's mom. Neither could I. That was a lot of grief for one family to bear.

"Laurie spent a few hours helping out here with KC at the booth. In fact, she stayed to help KC pack up on Friday night at closing. She might have been the last person to see KC before . . . you know."

Aly and I went silent, both looking down at the ground, mourning the three great losses KC's mom had suffered. I decided I might as well start here. I tamped down my emotions and assumed the role of the pseudo-deputy I was expected to be.

"I know you kept in touch with KC," I said. "Did she ever talk about being afraid of someone? Anything like that?"

"Not to me, Charlie. Just the usual complaints, you know. People who were late paying her, or changing the order at the last minute." Aly let out a long sigh. "Like me, sometimes. We're all devastated, the whole staff at the café. I'll bet yours is, too."

My staff. I hadn't thought to tell them. Did I need one more reminder that I was never going to win Manager of the Year? I was sure that by now the word of KC's murder had spread throughout Elkview, but I confessed my failure to Aly anyway and pulled out my phone.

"I need to call Victor," I said.

Aly was kind enough not to give me a judgmental look. I stepped away to contact Victor. As I had suspected, he'd already heard about KC's murder, and he offered to scope out where to send flowers. I knew he'd pass the job on to his sister, but that still made him a better boss than I was.

I hung up with Victor and was ready to move on when Aly called after me.

"Would you mind taking some pictures today, Charlie? Before the crowds come and everything is a mess? I promised Wally at the *Bugle* that I'd send him photos, but I left my cell phone in my car, and my niece won't be here to cover while I get it for another hour or so. Besides, it's a mile away in the parking lot."

I nodded. "I know what you mean. I feel like I walked at least a mile to get this far. I'll take some photos with my phone and send them to you."

"Perfect. Thanks, Charlie."

I scrolled to my camera app and pointed the phone at Aly. "I'll start with you."

"I'm not in the best mood for a photo, but okay."

I could see what she meant as I tried to capture a hint of joy in her face, but couldn't find one. I gave her a minute to remove her sun hat, straighten her dark brown hair, and replace the hat. I took a few photos of her and her setup and promised to email them to her by the end of the day. While I was at it, I texted Annie and Chris and asked them to take photos also. You never knew what might be captured on candid camera.

I had the feeling that chatting with me, a mutual classmate, was an unfortunate reminder to Aly of the friend she'd lost. I hoped the day would get better for her. It was possible, since the fair was probably going to get very busy, and very soon, she'd be too distracted dealing with the crowds to dwell on KC. The fair drew people from all over the state and then some. They might bring some cheer to the event and to Aly.

Not so much to those of us who were here to find a killer.

I CONTINUED PAST ENDLESSLY SUNNED VEGGIES. Broccoli, cauliflower, radishes, turnips, potatoes, beets, carrots, spinach, and lettuce all grew very well with the nearly twenty hours a day of summer sunshine. I saw prize ribbons everywhere and remembered that the items had been judged before the fair officially opened.

I stopped short. A few yards ahead of me, three men in

the telltale shirts of civilian volunteers, the lifeblood of an overworked law enforcement system, were taking down the black and yellow crime scene tape on the street bordering the fair. The street where KC's body had been found. The cordoned area was off the beaten track, so it made sense that the entire fairgrounds hadn't been shut down.

I mustered my courage and stepped between trash containers, making my way to the volunteers—three men, one of whom looked like a rookie. I approached him first, introducing myself as one of Trooper Cody Graham's informal deputies.

"What do you mean 'informal'?" he asked, lifting his baseball cap from his head and giving his forehead a swipe with a bandana.

Not as much of a rookie as I'd hoped. *Note to self: don't use the word "informal" again in this context.*

"I mean that he sent a team of us deputies here to investigate." I tried to camouflage the word "investigate" with a slight clearing of my throat, in case he asked for a card with that designation.

"Where's the rest of the team?" he asked.

Now he was annoying me. Was I really going to let a guy barely out of his teens get the best of me?

"We've carved up the grounds into sections. You're in mine." I took out my phone. "I'll call Graham right now so you can check it out. What's your name?" I asked, tilting my head to read the patch on his shirtsleeve. Which, by the way, was a meaningless gesture, since there was no mark identifying the wearer, just the seal of the great state of Alaska, featuring its snow-capped mountains.

I was surprised that my bravado worked. I figured it didn't hurt that I was several inches taller than him and more than a couple of years older. But even though my don't-mess-with-deputies attitude worked for today, it was time that Trooper issued cards or some form of ID to me and his team. I put it on my mental agenda for our next briefing. I'd volunteer to order logo shirts or jackets, too. The Denali hoodie I was wearing wasn't always the right clothing for the job. The best thing would be to have a choice of what to wear.

It was always a trade-off—wear something casual and be more relatable to an interviewee, or wear something official and have more standing when asking questions. I'd offer to sponsor the signature clothing I had in mind, as my contribution to our first responders. Or was that "informal responders"?

I dug a notebook from my satchel and made a show in front of the rookie, all official in spite of my touristy sweatshirt, entering information, mumbling the date and time.

"Your name?" I asked.

"Bill. Uh, William Mason, ma'am."

Way to make me feel old—but that's what I wanted in this case. I was glad the others in Bill's crew weren't paying any attention to me.

"How long have you been on duty here, Bill?"

"Most of the night. We're on the three to eleven shift."

"So the victim had already been transported when you arrived."

"Oh, yeah, we're just cleaning up."

"Did you find anything the forensics team might have missed?"

"Yes, ma'am. We were told to put things aside that might be useful to the investigation."

I gave him a look that silently asked why he didn't rush me over there now. The look worked, and he did just that.

I was beginning to enjoy being at the top of the chain of command. It didn't go over so well in diner management. Unlike my relationship to this rookie civilian volunteer, I wanted mine with my staff to be one of mutual respect.

Bill led me to a random collection of items that might have been related to the crime scene, or might have simply represented a couple of days' worth of whatever had been tossed from the windows of passing cars. A button of some thickness, with a rounded brass top. The wrapper from a stick of gum. A juice box. A pocket comb. Did I really want to carry these items to Trooper?

I took out several sealable plastic bags that I always carried in my tote. I meant them for leftover food, but Bill didn't need to know that. They had an opaque block for labeling with a marker, and I did that as I inserted each item into a separate bag.

Several cars and trucks were parked on the street just outside the designated crime scene area. I glanced at the license plates that were visible, all from Alaska. I assumed the vehicles that were here when KC's body was found had been catalogued. A flash of light fell on a new SUV, the tires of which had thick, well-defined indentations. I tried to determine the source of the reflection and saw that something was embedded in the grooves of the tires.

I walked over for a closer look and saw that it was a watch. I snapped a photo and then used tweezers to dig it out. It wasn't the first vehicle in the row, so its plate might not have been recorded, I reasoned, as I snapped another photo.

"What are you doing?" Bill shouted over to me.

"Nothing you need to worry about," I said.

That seemed to satisfy both Bill and his two shift mates, who didn't further question the fact that I was studying the scene and removing potential evidence. Either I'd played my role well or they didn't care. In any case, an informal deputy outranked a civilian crime scene cleanup crew member. That was my story and I was sticking to it.

One last question for Bill as I walked back toward him: "Has there been much traffic since you got here?"

He shook his head. "An occasional vehicle."

"So these items aren't from random cars or trucks driving by?"

"No, the stuff was here when we got here."

And yet the official crime scene folks hadn't thought they were worth the trouble to collect. I wondered who they were. We were close enough to Anchorage here to enlist the services of their crime scene techs, but I wasn't sure how taxed that staff was. And I wasn't about to ask Bill.

Besides, it was possible the button, et cetera, might have blown onto the scene during the night, well after the crime took place. Thinking of a generic crime that had taken place was easier to swallow than dwelling on the murder of my friend.

I decided it was time to cut my losses and head away from the site before the more senior members of the crew decided to investigate the alleged investigator. Not that I was acting illegitimately, but why trouble Trooper with having to justify my being here?

Looking a little more closely at the other two men, I could see that they weren't exactly veterans, any more than Bill was. I figured Trooper saved the more seasoned volunteers for something more than cleanup.

Still, it was time for me to leave. I could always come back later, after eleven o'clock, when I was sure these guys would waste no time heading home for breakfast and a long nap.

"If you'll just give me your contact information," I said to Bill, "I'll be on my way and you can get back to work."

He screwed up his mouth and grudgingly read off his cell phone number as I entered it into my contacts.

I turned and left before he could turn the tables and interview me.

My phone read ten a.m., the official opening time. Fairgoers were streaming onto the grounds. Men, women, and children hurried in, talking excitedly about rides, concerts, and exhibits from arts and crafts to baked goods and livestock. Happy talk was everywhere—hard for me to listen to while KC was probably on Doc Sherman's table being prepared for a burial service.

In past years, the fair had drawn more than three hundred thousand visitors over the course of twelve days. That would make about twenty-five thousand of them headed my way now.

Was one of them a killer?

# FIVE

I WAS AWARE I'D LULLED MYSELF INTO A FALSE SENSE
of accomplishment. I had a satchel full of meaningless cast-
offs that trained crime scene technicians had left behind.
The truth was I'd hardly begun the job Trooper had sent me
here to do, which was to interview KC's colleagues. And
now the fairgrounds were open for business.

So much for approaching vendors before they got busy.

But it was only slightly after ten, and some vendors were
still setting up. I wanted to search out Donna, whom Chris
had named as KC's employee handling the booth today. I
consulted the map and found a listing for a Donna Madsen as one of the vendors for booth sixty-four, which was
called Kelly Carson's Cart, located not that far from where
I was.

Someone had thought it was a good idea to have pseudo-
benches along all the walkways. They were made of bales
of straw—not the most comfortable material, but good
enough for a phone call or two, or better yet, a session with
my cat via our Bennycam. I took a seat and saw a laser dot
game with my feline housemate in my future.

I found myself glancing at the produce at times, once to admire a pumpkin with a label reading 938 POUNDS. Not even a record, as I recalled. I checked the documentation with the display and, sure enough, the largest pumpkin ever recorded in the fair's Great Pumpkin Weigh-Off was in 2016. That giant squash had tipped the scales at 1,469 pounds. *Now, that would make a lot of pumpkin pies,* I thought, always with the Bear Claw Diner in mind. How did they even weigh such a veggie? I was sure I had known at one time.

It was worth standing to take a closer look at the photos tacked to the posts to see the crane-like apparatus used to hoist the pumpkin onto an industrial flat-bed scale for the weigh-off.

A smile of sadness came for a stand-alone bulletin board, like the one at the elementary school where KC and I had shared classes and friends. This board held photos of men and women in orange and green costumes near their gigantic winning pumpkin. Other growers pictured wore yellow with their ears of corn or red with their enormous apples. Celebrations of pride in their farming skills. A twenty-pound carrot had inspired a costume that reminded me of third grade performances and I shook away the embarrassing possibility that I might once have dressed up like a carrot. I smiled and decided it must have been Annie. It also gave me the idea to make a carrot cake the next time I had access to a kitchen.

I raised my head, my eyes scanning the horizon beyond the giant produce, looking to the enormous looming mountains. Who knew how big around they were, how much they weighed? Majesty on a large scale. I was grateful to live where there was such beauty.

I recalled an observation that had come from a little girl wandering through Denali National Park, where I'd occasionally worked as a kid on school breaks.

She'd looked up, wide-eyed, and given her tourist parents her evaluation of their trip. "Nature is big in Alaska," she'd said.

Everyone around her had laughed, but we all knew she was right.

SOME OF THE VENDORS WORE THEIR COSTUMES TO-day, probably expecting more photo ops. I decided that the getups might provide a way for me to engage them while sneaking in some interview questions.

I approached a young woman, a high schooler, probably, in a bright yellow sundress in the sweet corn booth. The low-sixties weather didn't seem to bother her bare arms. A true Alaskan.

"Okay if I take your picture?" I asked her. "I'm helping out a friend with an article for the *Bugle*, and you look great in that corn-colored dress."

The lovely blonde put her hand against her forehead. "Oh, please no, my grandmother is making me wear this ridiculous outfit." She pointed to her canvas shoes, also yellow. A sunshiny bow in her hair completed the picture. I was fairly sure she didn't want people to remember the name on her badge: STEPH.

"I'll bet your friends are envious, Steph."

"Yeah, right."

I clicked off a few photos. "They should be envious of your prizewinning work here. I'll take a dozen of the yellow and a dozen white before they're snapped up. Did you have anything to do with this crop?"

She nodded and swung her arm around to encompass other booths before she got to the work of bagging my corn. "Just about everyone working here helps out on one or another of the farms. It's about the only game in town if you're in school and want spending money."

"That's interesting." I didn't have to lie about that. "Did any of your friends work for the poor woman who died the other day?" That was a bit of a lie, not outing my relationship with KC and the reason for my visit.

"Some of them, I'm sure. Not me, though." We exchanged money for corn, while she continued her report. "We all fill in wherever we're needed when we're not in school. Depends what crop needs us. I'm lucky, at least, because all of this"—she indicated the neat rows of corn in front of her—"is greenhouse grown. It's too cold in the fields for corn." She turned to a table of turnips and radishes behind her. "These are the cool-weather veggies."

Steph stopped talking and gave me a quizzical look. "You must not be from around here?"

*Uh-oh. Way to get busted, Charlie.* Although I hadn't worked on local farms during school breaks—I had a permanent gig at the Bear Claw Diner for that—many of my friends, like KC herself, did count on farms and ranches for employment, and I was familiar with the practice of rotation among the various fields.

Steph checked my outfit, up and down, to find a clue, it seemed. Maybe she'd decided she wasn't going to waste her time on a tourist who'd never become a regular customer. Good thing I'd worn my Denali hoodie and not the one from San Diego that my dad had brought back from his last business trip.

"Born and raised in Elkview, and still living there," I said. I laughed and waved in the general direction of my aging face. "But as you see, it was a long time ago that I was looking for work on school breaks." I spoke as if I'd been out of school forever, which wasn't too far off from her fifteen- or sixteen-year-old perspective.

She shot me a more welcoming grin. "Then you do know. But it's much harder now than when you were growing up. That's what my mom says, anyway." I gulped. Was I in her mom's generation? Could be. At thirty-six, it was not biologically out of the question that I'd have a teenage daughter. "There's so much competition for the jobs, and also for the prize money." She seemed forlorn, as if she was the sole source of income for her family. I had no reason to think otherwise.

Before I left Miss Sunshine, I managed to eke out a couple of names of her friends who'd worked rotation and had probably landed on KC's acreage this summer. I made a concerted effort not to write the names and booths down, so she wouldn't suspect—that is, uncover—my motive for seeming so interested.

As soon as I was clear of the corn, I took a seat on a bale, parked the heavy bags of corn on the ground, and took out my phone. I typed from memory, as quickly as I could:

Zach—raspberries

Hildy—beans

Cecilia—rhubarb pie (with the winner)

I could hardly wait for that pie booth.

And I almost pumped my fist in the air at the feeling of usefulness that came over me at last.

As IT TURNED OUT, THE RHUBARB BOOTH WAS NEXT on my way to booth sixty-four, KC's assigned location.

When I admired the selections but mentioned to the vendor that I could hardly carry much more, the maroon-and-green-clad matron reached down and pulled a stack of oversize canvas bags from a box.

"We have just the thing," she said. "Just arrived this morning." She displayed the image of herself and two other matronly women screened onto the canvas, their prize ribbons included.

"This is perfect," I said. "I'll take one rhubarb and one strawberry-rhubarb." I slipped my hand into my pants pocket, and out came a few bills and one wristwatch, which I managed to extract from its bag. "By the way, can you point me to Lost and Found? I found this watch not far from here and would like to drop it off. I don't suppose you recognize it?"

The woman screwed up her face while I watched for signs of recollection and guilt. Nothing.

She pulled out her enlarged map and opened it to the section with the southwest corner of the property showing, near the entrance we'd used earlier. I could have located it myself, but she didn't have to know that.

"Here," she said, her pen touching the image of the security building. "But who wears a watch anymore?"

It was worth a shot.

"One more thing," I said. "Is Cecilia around today?"

Another screwed-up facial expression. "No." From her expression, I gathered she'd rather not talk about Cecilia, so I let it go and thanked her for my pies.

Another shot that missed by a mile.

WHEN I REACHED BOOTH SIXTY-FOUR, I SAW A WOMAN, presumably Donna Madsen, dusting the gigantic leaves of a cabbage that had won a yellow ribbon in the cabbage weigh-off. In fact, as I'd covered the grounds, I saw that there was hardly a piece of produce on display without a ribbon of some color, and I started to think the losers had packed up and gone home.

"Hi, Charlie," Donna said, seeming out of breath. She was a short, stocky woman, my age, give or take a couple of years. The gymnastics of navigating the ladder needed to reach the cabbage leaves might have taken the wind out of her. "Chris said you'd be coming around."

Donna was way ahead of me, knowing who I was when I didn't recognize her. I figured she'd made some deliveries to the Bear Claw and seen me there, hovering like a boss.

I felt a twinge of annoyance that Chris would alert her that I was on the way. Wouldn't it have been better if Donna hadn't had time to come up with a story, if she needed one? This was a constant, if mild, tug-of-war between Chris and me. He sometimes got scoops from Trooper simply because he had the police beat, a term I'd heard used in San Francisco that didn't quite fit Elkview, but it was the same idea. Reporters everywhere tried to cultivate sources of news, and who had more news than cops? Or, in this case, Alaska State Troopers?

I had to admit that most of the time Chris was well-meaning.

I couldn't fault him for doing his job. It wasn't as though I were his boss. We'd been deputized simultaneously. I needed to forget anything that resembled a competition between us and get to work.

"Anything I can do to help set up here?" I asked Donna.

"Anything but move that cabbage."

She laughed. "Isn't it a great one? We're lucky not to have a long trip from the farm to here. The cabbages lose a lot of water weight in this weather, so the poor farmers who come from far away have to be more careful, cut the cabbage as close as possible to the fair date."

"Interesting," I said, half meaning it.

Donna took a seat on a bale of straw, real or fake, and motioned me to do the same on the one next to her.

"Help will be arriving soon," she said. "I enlisted my friend's daughter. We're all trying to adjust to what happened. But we can't really give up the booth. The fair represents a significant part of our income. Plus the contacts we make, and so on." She sniffled, trying to be unobtrusive. "Maybe it doesn't matter anymore. It's hard."

I didn't want to cause any further distress. "I'm so sorry," I said, realizing that until now, I hadn't given any thought to the financial repercussions of KC's death. "KC and I were in high school together. We shared a lot of classes." I paused. "But I haven't really talked to her in a while. You worked closely with her. Were you aware of any problems she was experiencing lately?"

"Not at all," Donna said. Too quickly? Or was I all too eager to build a suspect list and bring this investigation to a speedy resolution.

"No sticky business issues?"

Donna shook her head. "Not that I'm aware of."

I hesitated to use the word "personal," so I went a circuitous route. "And she and Milo were doing all right?"

Donna stood and moved over to a table in the middle of the booth. She made, or pretended to make, adjustments to a scale—the normal kind, for produce of a reasonable size for the family dinner table—that sat in one corner of the surface, then straightened an already neat pile of sacks.

"Yup."

*Okay, then.* Maybe I should have told Chris to hang around Donna for a while. He might have a different approach.

"Bye for now, Donna. I may be coming around again to see if you've thought of anything else." *Or anything at all,* I meant.

"Okay, sure," she said, and retrieved a stack of bags from below the counter.

I took out my phone. "Don't mind me," I said. "I promised to take some photos for the *Bugle*, to help Chris out."

She gave me a smile. I'd have preferred more information, but the day had just begun.

I WAS SEVERAL YARDS AWAY FROM DONNA'S BOOTH when I thought of more questions. For one thing, I should have asked what might happen to Milo now. I could find out other ways, of course, but it would have been useful to see how Donna responded.

Before I forgot, I took a seat on a second bale of straw, now grateful for what I had once ridiculed, opened the Notes app on my phone, and entered:

KC involved with anyone special? Dating?

Where does Milo go now? Other relatives? Interview
    THEM.

*Major progress,* I told myself.

Not really.

It was time for a discussion with Benny. I needed to figure out my next steps, and I needed his help. I didn't know what made me think I could simply walk up and down the pathways stopping at each booth to ask a well-defined set of questions as if I were doing a report on the state fair for my fifth grade teacher.

I seemed to be on a roller coaster as big and hilly as the one on the grounds behind me, feeling elated at progress one minute and depressed at the lack of it the next.

At one point, I'd even considered staying overnight nearby so I could finish up interviews with the last few vendors on the grounds.

I'd spoken to less than a handful of sellers, even if you counted bumping into Roland, and one newbie volunteer with a pickup tool.

I knew I could count on my cat, who appeared to be waiting for me in front of the camera in the family room this time. I sat on the neat pile of straw and watched Benny. He'd managed to pull off a new trick lately. He'd climb onto the seat of a straight-back chair and then hoist himself somehow and straddle the back section, with half his body on each side of the chair back so his belly was in contact along the top of the chair. This was different from his former practice of nestling on top of open doors and pouncing when anyone came through.

The first time he caught me off guard with the old trick, he'd been waiting on top of my open garage door and pounced on the hood of my car when I drove in. I'd been so startled, I hit the accelerator and nearly drove through the wall and into the house.

*Thanks, Benny.*

More than once I tried to catch him in the act of reaching any of these perches worthy of an Olympic gymnast, but no such luck. Like a magician, he wasn't about to reveal the secrets to his tricks.

Today I opened the app for the laser dot game, hoping to

see how he got down from the chair back perch, perhaps giving me a clue as to how he got up there in the first place. I couldn't fool this cat, however. I'd hardly blinked and he was on the floor in a flash, chasing the bright red dot.

Maybe next time.

For now, I used the touch screen on my phone to move the laser dot around, sending it up the wall now and then and back to the floor. I'd adopted a pattern of leaving the dot on the floor for a few minutes at a time so Benny could have the satisfaction of landing a paw on it and batting it back and forth. Or so he thought.

"I'll be home this evening," I told him. I waited in case he wanted to indicate that I should stay at the fair, that there was a lot to be accomplished by going booth to booth asking each vendor what they knew about KC and her interactions—specifically, which interaction or relationship might have gotten her killed. But even if I did manage to stop at each produce stall, who was to say the killer wasn't the Ferris wheel operator, or the teenager who handed out the teddy bear prizes at the pop-the-balloon booth, or the guy who served tacos from his truck on Mexican Food Day, one of the themes the fair organizers listed? Or someone not associated with the fair at all?

I played with Benny awhile longer, letting my mind settle down from its deputized interactions. As always, I was able to focus with Benny, more so than with any other calming technique. I took him to be saying I needed to quiet myself and plod through the steps of the investigation in an orderly, unrushed way.

No one said a murder could reasonably be solved in a day at the fair.

# SIX

I WAS EAGER TO FIND OUT WHAT ANNIE AND CHRIS HAD accomplished during their trek through the fairgrounds. For all I knew, they'd spent the time riding the bumper cars or throwing darts at balloons and cardboard cutouts of caribou. Or maybe they had stuck with the investigation and had a better sense than I did of whether they were gazing into the eyes of a killer or just another vendor hoping to make the rent.

Our meetup at noon was at a table in the one open area that served as a food court, a large covered clearing with metal tables and chairs, surrounded by food trucks and other stands with tasty treats in both temporary and permanent setups. Chris and Annie were already there, checking out the menus and laughing about something. I hoped it meant they'd cracked the case, but I doubted it.

I brought out the diner snack packs, which we'd broken into during our drive from Elkview. We took turns holding our places at the table and scouting for something more interesting than Victor's elk jerky, which, although quite good, we could have any day of the week. The fair prided itself on having dishes from many different regions of the country and the world.

Chris brought back a seafood gumbo pizza. Annie went with shrimp and fried rice served in a hollowed out pineapple. I settled on a sourdough bread bowl filled with creamy chowder, a dish I'd gotten hooked on during my time in San Francisco, although this bowl was filled with Alaskan razor clams.

I'd alerted my friends ahead of time that I had dessert in my canvas tote, but Annie still returned with a moose hoof—a version of a local pastry consisting of deep-fried batter smothered in powdered sugar, cinnamon, honey, and berries. Messier to eat than a bear claw, and equally delicious. Chris risked a hot fudge sundae on a cone and then had the problem of which to eat first, his cooling pizza or his melting ice cream.

"I don't get why you chose to get pizza here," Annie told him. "You can get that anywhere."

"Exactly," he said. "Low risk."

Chris also sprang for a family-size serving of oysters to share with us, fresh from Prince William Sound.

Looking at our team and our table, one might have thought we'd come to the fair for the food.

Once we'd sampled everything, passing around paper plates and bottles of water and soda, we got down to business. It was hard to contain Annie's and Chris's enthusiasm, which was fine with me, since I was in a downward swing.

Annie edged Chris out, taking the floor first with her newfound knowledge of the murder weapon—a knife that had not been recovered, according to the report Trooper had supplied us.

"I had a little time before anyone came to open up the craft booths," she said. "So I was reading about what you can and cannot bring in here. You're not supposed to bring firearms, knives, or any weapons."

"There were definitely knives around, for vendors' use,"

Chris said. "But I did notice they were out of the reach of the rest of us."

"And where they were for sale," Annie said, "they had to be preapproved and in a secure case that couldn't be opened until the buyer was off the fairgrounds property, or they'd be confiscated. Maybe a fine, too. They don't do that if you buy a knife in a store, like a kitchenware store."

"So, with all that security, how did a knife come to be in the hands of KC's killer?" I asked. I was secretly trying to overcome my growing despondency, and perhaps have some of my friends' fervor rub off on me.

"I guess this must mean the killer either had to be a vendor, with access to a knife, like to cut up cabbage, or he stole it from a booth?" Annie concluded, but it was nothing we could take to the bank. Or to Trooper.

Chris had been leafing through literature he'd picked up from one of the mailbox-like stations for such reading material, located about every three feet around the grounds. The flyers provided maps of the grounds plus a schedule of concerts and other special events. One item caught his eye, and he interrupted with an excited observation. "Hey, today is Military Appreciation Day, for active and retired military. I could have gotten in for five dollars."

"You got in for free," Annie reminded him.

"I have my military ID with me, so I could have gotten both of you in at the discount, too."

"But we all got in for free," Annie pointed out. But it was clear Chris had his own logic.

"Still, there's something you got to love about a discount."

Annie and I shook our heads.

"I forgot how many categories there are for contests," she said. "You can win a prize for almost anything."

"Did you see that zucchini cheesecake?" Chris asked.

We both uttered a form of *eeuw*, accompanied by shaking heads: *No, thanks.*

"I bought some corn," I said.

"Not the prizewinning two-foot one?" Annie asked.

"Hardly."

"What about that rhubarb pie contest? Wouldn't you like to be the judge for that one?" Chris asked.

"Now that you mention it," I began. I took the rhubarb pie from my newly acquired canvas tote.

Annie clapped. It took Chris less than three minutes to reach a vendor and come back with extra napkins and plastic utensils, plus three bags of homemade potato chips. He added a bag to each place setting.

"I didn't want to just grab their supplies," he said.

"Mister Nice Guy," Annie said.

Was that a blush on the face of Army Sergeant (or whatever) Christopher Doucette? I decided not to call him on it.

We dug into our pie, exclaiming over its perfection.

"Shall we take some food back to the folks in Elkview?" Annie asked.

"You can," I said. "But I'm thinking I'm going to give my staff a day to come here themselves, all expenses paid. Even though it's not my number one go-to place for fun, I know they love it."

"Good idea. Me, too," Annie said.

"Wow," Chris said. "That's even better than a military discount."

We agreed.

I THOUGHT AFTER FILLING OURSELVES TO CAPACITY, speaking for myself at least, we'd be ready to focus on the case for more than two minutes at a time, but not so.

Annie wanted to share the research she'd done for next year's fair. "I checked out the knitting booth when they finally opened and read through the rules. Just about anything is acceptable as far as submitting to a competition. There's even a machine-knit category, as long as you operate the machine yourself, but I'm going to submit things I make by hand, like a sweater-vest. I think that would be cool, and I have all year to practice."

"Good idea," I said. "Count me in for the items that don't work out."

After a few minutes of silent eating I broached the topic of why we'd come.

"Shall we talk more about what we accomplished so far, by way of the murder investigation?"

"You mean the reason we're here?" Chris asked. He shook his head in an unpromising way. I took it as a message that he hadn't made out much better than I had.

Annie plopped her chubby forearms on the table and uttered a loud sigh. "I talked to so many people. The bead people. The clay people. The macramé people."

"People still do macramé?" I asked.

"Uh-huh. The wreath people. The fur hat people. The—"

"We get it, Annie. Lots of crafts," Chris said.

"—feathers people," she said, determined to finish.

She sat back, crossed her arms, and smiled.

"I found a watch at the crime scene," I said, scrolling through my phone to find the photo, and showing it to them.

"Pretty fancy," Chris said. "It's one of those with Bluetooth. It can measure your blood pressure, your oxygen level, your heart rate. It can even perform an ECG on you."

"You're kidding," Annie said.

Chris shook his head no.

"Wow, that could be a breakthrough," Annie said. "They'll be able to get DNA and all that health information. Maybe it's the killer's."

"The license plate is clear, too. They'll find out who owns the vehicle. Nice work, Charlie," Chris said, flashing a smile that could have been interpreted as more personal than business, but it was impossible to tell. And, for the moment, I let it go.

"Or maybe it has nothing to do with the crime. It could

be from a trip that SUV took to the Rainbird Trail a month ago," I said, pointing to what I remembered as a new sticker on the back bumper.

"I hiked that trail," Chris said. "In Ketchikan. Really beautiful."

Annie sighed again, seeming frustrated. "Only one person I talked to, in all that walking I did, even knew KC, and she just met her standing in line to get in one day. She was one of the leather people."

Chris nearly choked laughing, but Annie continued, unfazed. "She said KC came over to her booth later and got a personalized key holder made. The leather people do it on the spot. You tell them what you want and, depending on the crowd, you come back in, like, an hour, and it's ready."

"What did she have put on it?" I asked.

"Huh?"

"You said it was personalized. What was on it?"

Annie gasped. "I should have asked. It could be a clue, right?"

"Most people use a personalization as a gift." I shrugged. "So far, we don't know if KC was involved with anyone. That might tell us."

Annie stood and gathered up all our trash, which was legion. "I'm going to go over there right now and ask them."

"Looks like I'm the only one who struck out," Chris said, when it was just the two of us plus a young couple who asked if they could sit at the other end of our table. "I wandered over to the Diaper Derby by mistake and got stuck holding some mother's diaper bag."

I suppressed a laugh. "Your good deed for today."

"Have you ever watched a bunch of one-year-olds race to a goal post when they don't always know which direction they're supposed to be headed?" He paused, but wasn't through. "That's even though the goal post is their parents, waiting across the grass?"

"Can't say that I've ever seen that." This time I did

laugh, and I gave his shoulder a pat. "Better luck in round two," I said. "For both of us."

By NOW IT WAS AFTER TWO O'CLOCK, AND THE FIRST shift of families, with little kids like the ones in Chris's Diaper Derby, were about to go home. They'd be replaced by teens, those without jobs in the fair's ticket booths, food concessions, or vendor stands. They were either lucky or unlucky, depending on their circumstances.

I took Chris up on his offer to take my load of produce and extra pie out to the car. I'd picked up a few other sacks besides the corn, mostly at the stands of growers I knew. As I walked and waved at acquaintances, I planned my next stops on the way to the crime scene—a first for Alaska State Fair history, I would have been willing to bet.

Like Annie, I had decided to backtrack. I wanted to examine the crime scene area without the distraction of the cleanup crew. I looked at the map to see if I could find a different route there. *Why not cover as much ground as possible?* I thought. The first route hadn't been all that productive.

The new path took me by some of the crafts Annie had mentioned, plus games of skill like Frog Fishing, Pop a Balloon, and a host of others where you could take away an unidentified furry object as a prize. I froze for a few seconds as a little boy rushed past me, his face dripping with blood. His delighted screams convinced me he'd just come from a session with the Paint-a-Monster-Face Lady.

I made a quick stop at the souvenir stand and picked up a woolen hat with the fair logo for my mom and a long-sleeved T-shirt for my dad, the kind he liked, with raglan sleeves. I knew they'd come back from Oregon with similar items for me.

I zipped past the honey products and the quilts, stopped for a minute at the photography booth, thinking what fun some people were having with these activities. Maybe it was being around all the arts and crafts, but I felt I should come up with a hobby. *As soon as KC's killer is behind bars,* I told myself, and started a list of possibilities in my head. Nothing related to sewing. Not pottery or photography, or anything else that required a lot of space and supplies or machinery.

I took out my phone and snapped a few photos of happy faces on the rides—mostly kids shrieking as they let themselves be flung through the air at various angles, without much more than a seat belt, all of them making the Ferris wheel look tame and the Merry-Go-Round look no more thrilling than the Diaper Derby. One thing was sure: once you were up there, whether sitting, standing, or spinning, you had one of the most beautiful views in the world, with mountains, lakes, and rivers as far as you could see.

I overheard a few comments, smiling at one from an astute teenager lying on her stomach, strapped to something like a gym mat: "I don't like this. It's unnatural." From another teen, who was standing nearby, strapped to the same kind of rectangular pad, I heard, "I could do this all day." Though no one asked, I came down on the side of the first young woman.

It was impossible to capture some of the attractions with my phone camera, like the bicycle gymnastics that had bike and rider doing Olympic-style flips in the air or the train-like contraption that I feared was going to propel its riders upside down on the end of an enormous metal lever, to dire consequences. I turned my head and walked away before that could come about.

I was impressed at how neat and orderly the grounds looked, in spite of bags of popcorn and other treats being in the hands of two out of every three people and a variety of brightly colored condiments scattered on tables. No one slid in puddles of spilled soda or ketchup; no paper or plastic trash littered the grass. An unobtrusive cleaning crew must have been working nonstop, constantly vigilant.

I didn't remember ever getting caught up in the energy

of the fair like this when I was expected to, as a kid. Why now? I had to admit to the possibility that I was stalling now, not looking forward to revisiting the place where my friend had been murdered. Because I wished there were still a chance to call her to reminisce about the day the ancient Mrs. Hiller tripped coming into our classroom, spilling the bottle of ink she'd been carrying all over our final history exams. Or to chat about the class picnic that had seemed to be perfect until a sudden downpour had us running for the shelter of the restrooms.

I felt a chill, though the temperature had risen significantly, and pulled the hood of my sweatshirt over my head. I lowered my eyes and picked up my pace, heading straight for Spruce Street and the area I'd photographed earlier.

Now or never.

I needed to do my job and get away from the rollicking good time that was the Alaska State Fair.

Hᴇʏ, CHARLIE. YOU STILL HERE?" ALY HAD COME UP BE-hind me. "I was going to email you, but here you are. I thought of something."

Aly was carrying what looked like lunch—a rather plain hot dog that I figured was the fastest thing she could pick up. I looked over at her booth, where a line had formed in front of a young woman who was probably mealtime help.

"Do you need to go back to your booth?" I asked.

She pointed to the seats of straw near us. "That's okay. I can take five."

"What is it that you thought of?"

She took a small bite, covered her delicate mouth, swallowed and started in. "You'd have to check this, but I'm sure Trooper would be able to do it quickly. Heck, I'll bet you can do it yourself now that you're a deputy for him. Anyway, I'm pretty sure KC was in a legal dispute over some property."

I sat up straighter, really wishing I had that pie for her. I dug into my tote and pulled out a package of Victor's elk jerky, wondering why I hadn't thought of it right away.

"Try this," I said. "It might be fresher than that hot dog."

"Bless you," she said. "I've had this and I love it."

That done, I felt I could continue querying. "Do you remember whose property KC was having a problem with?"

She shrugged. "I'm not exactly clear. It's a lot, a pretty big one, I believe, an area next to hers, and there's something about it that's squirrelly. I think it's supposed to go to Milo when he reaches a certain age, which I think is soon. And the neighbors are saying it's really theirs. Like I said, you'd have to check with the borough offices. When I tried to bring it up again with KC after the first time she mentioned it, she sort of clammed up. I had the feeling lawyers got involved and she couldn't discuss it anymore."

"Thanks, Aly. This could be very important."

"It could also just be nothing, but I thought I'd tell you. I appreciate all you're doing to clear this up." Aly stood and tossed her wrappers, along with the remains of the hot dog, in a nearby trash container. "Maybe she could have used some support or something from me," she said, her voice cracking. "I'm just sorry I didn't pay more attention, you know? I mean when KC was around."

"I understand."

*More than you know,* I thought.

Instead, now that our friend was dead, we'd have to do whatever we could to help find her killer.

# Seven

I WALKED THE REST OF THE WAY TO THE CRIME SCENE without interruption. The SUV was still in its spot. The houses along the street were vintage, probably dating from the 1950s, with small one-car garages, so it made sense that, even if it did belong to a neighborhood resident, the SUV would be parked on the street. I took a seat on one of the ubiquitous straw bales at the edge of the fairgrounds and punched in Trooper's number.

Just as I expected to hear his voicemail greeting, he picked up.

"How's it going, Charlie?"

"I suppose you'd have called me if you'd found KC's killer."

"I thought that was why you were calling."

"Touché." What made me think I could best Trooper? I pictured his lanky frame, feet up on his desk at the station, wide-brimmed blue uniform hat on a rack behind him. As the sun bore down on my back, I wished I were with him in the somewhat shabby but air-conditioned room that was his office, though I knew he was probably still out of town.

I'd long since pushed the hood of my sweatshirt off my head. "I have something I need you to check."

"Shoot."

"Can you look up who owns a license plate?"

"Let me have it."

"Papa, Uniform, Tango," I said, then rattled off the number above the designation, "The Last Frontier." I felt so professional, using the alphabetic codes I'd heard on TV.

A few seconds later, Trooper responded. "What are you, psychic or something?"

"Maybe. I'm not sure what you mean."

"That vehicle was reported stolen on Friday evening around seven thirty. It's still listed as missing."

"I guess I found it."

Trooper laughed. "Looks like I sent you there to find a stolen car. I'll have someone pick it up. Text me the exact location."

"Whose vehicle is it?"

"Old man Jessup."

"Shoe repair, et cetera, on Main, right?"

"Yup. His wife just convinced him to get rid of his ancient clunker, and this happens. All he can say now, of course, is that the old jalopy never would have been taken."

"He's got a point."

I remembered my dad claiming that he was happy when our cars got their first dent.

"No one will steal it now," he'd say. "And I'll get to go first when there's a stalemate at a stop sign."

"Where was the car when it was taken?" I asked Trooper.

"He left it in front of his shop, since his wife picked him up to go out to dinner. When they came back, the car was gone."

Very efficient car thieves. Successfully capturing a vehicle in a brief window of opportunity—the time it took for one dinner. I kept the thought to myself.

"I wonder why the security people at the fair didn't find

the vehicle? I know they're located on the west side of the grounds and the car is on the east side, but wouldn't they have gotten the report?"

"They can't be expected to pay attention to reports like this from Elkview. Not for a stolen car, anyway. They have enough to do within the grounds without patrolling outside the limits."

I was sorry I brought it up. I should have known that Trooper would come to the defense of another arm of law enforcement, public or private. Once in a while he complained about being overworked, but then, so did I. An added benefit of his solution to the problem of understaffing was to give me a chance to contribute to the welfare of my community—besides my work managing, sometimes satisfactorily, the great contribution of the Bear Claw Diner to the health and well-being of its patrons.

"I get it," I said.

"We're grateful for the help they gave us in this case, identifying Kelly and alerting us quickly. That company provides all the services on the grounds, from taking tickets to crowd control. They even operate the information booths."

"A couple of other things," I told Trooper, pivoting from the quality of security on the grounds.

"You found a duffel bag full of cash."

My turn to laugh. "I won't keep you guessing."

I described Aly's mention of a possible property dispute and, by the way, wondered to myself why Donna, KC's employee, hadn't mentioned it.

I told Trooper about the watch that had been wedged in the grooves of one of the SUV's brand-new tires.

"I don't suppose it has an engraving on the back, like, 'To KC with love from Bobby Smith,' for example. Or 'To Bobby Smith with love from KC.'"

"No, but Annie's working on something like that." I went on to describe the personalized leather key case Annie was tracking down.

"We have a lot to check out, thanks to all of you. Not bad for a morning's work," Trooper said.

Just the boost I needed.

BENNY DESERVED TO HEAR SOMETHING POSITIVE FOR a change, too. I accessed the Bennycam and found him sprawled flat on his back in the family room, forepaws curled to his chest, back legs splayed. Uh-oh, was our house too warm for him? I'd been thinking about getting a smart thermostat, and now might be the time. Summer temperatures aren't usually that severe along the Anchorage-Fairbanks corridor, seldom exceeding eighty degrees. Still, weather was unpredictable anywhere, and I hated the idea of Benny being uncomfortable if it could be helped. If my mom were around, she'd be reminding me that cats love the warmer temperatures and Benny was most likely enjoying himself.

I knew he had enough food and water, so I let him be and hoped he guessed that I'd be heading home soon.

I took another turn around the area where my new friend Bill had been cleaning today, but saw nothing more on the street or in the gutter. Now that I knew the owner of the SUV, I thought I'd step up for a closer look. Maybe whoever had taken the vehicle from Main Street in Elkview to the state fair had left a clue—besides the one stuck in its tire. I walked around the car and saw no scrapes or dents. Not vandals, then, seeking pleasure in destruction for its own sake. But who steals a vehicle just for transportation to the bumper cars or the spinning hurricane at the fair? A twelve-year-old without a car of his own? I doubted it.

It was handy to be tall at a time like this, and I thanked my dad for bestowing his genes on his only child. My mom would have needed a boost to climb inside. The vehicle was locked—nice of the thief to ensure its safety from other thieves. I saw a six-pack on the seat, but didn't recognize the label, my familiarity with brews being limited. For all I knew, it was a multivitamin drink.

The windows were tinted, or dirty, or both, and I couldn't make out anything as subtle as a drop of blood.

I decided to leave the area, so as not to get in the way of whomever Trooper had contacted to move the vehicle. I knew I'd be able to answer questions back home if Trooper's car retrievers had any for me.

I hated to leave the fairgrounds knowing I hadn't covered all possible avenues. The one track I'd simply skimmed in my conversation with Trooper that might be important was about the property dispute Aly had suggested as recently troubling KC. I told him I'd do some digging when I got back to Elkview, and he'd agreed that the legalities of land ownership weren't as easy to divine as those of car registration.

I needed to check in with the rest of our team. I set up a conference call for quick reports and to determine our departure time. We had the long ride home to discuss what, if anything, we had found out that could help solve KC's murder. I had to remind myself that we weren't sent here to solve a crime but simply to gather information that might help Trooper and his real deputy do the hard work of putting it all together.

I began the three-way conversation with the topic of the stolen SUV that was butt up against the place where KC's body had been found.

"That's unfortunate for the Jessups, but do you think it's related to our case?" Chris asked.

"Maybe," was my erudite response.

"I have news," Annie said. I had to plug one ear as a noisy group of teens walked by. At times it was hard to remember that their fun, and not attempting to solve a murder, was the main point of the Alaska State Fair. Annie continued, "KC bought a key case for Milo. His eighteenth birthday is coming up. The leather lady said it sounded as though KC had in mind giving him a car to go with it."

We all went silent, not for the first time today. For me, I was touched by what KC had planned for Milo's coming of age. I wondered if he knew yet what she had been planning to arrange.

"There's more," Annie said.

Sometimes Annie liked to stretch out the attention she felt she was due. I wished this wasn't one of those times, but I played along.

"What is it, Annie?"

"KC ordered two of those key cases, but she came back later and canceled the other one." Annie paused. "Aha, right?" she asked.

"Does she remember who the other one was for?"

Annie let out an exasperated breath. "No, and she tore up the order, which went out with the trash."

"It was worth a shot," Chris said, echoing what we'd said often today. "But it does sound like there was someone, then suddenly there wasn't. It could be significant."

"Or not," I said, for some curmudgeonly reason.

Chris had a more interesting report, making up for his unproductive morning with baby wipes, as he put it.

"I decided to go to the security building, since it was a security person who found KC's body. Interesting people over there. These guys, and some girls, take care of everything from parking and traffic to what they call 'alcohol management.'"

"They're overworked, just like our troopers. Trooper told me as much when I asked why no one in security noticed that the SUV had been reported stolen."

"I'll show you the security company's report when I see you. One of the guys gave me a printout for Friday. A lot of it has to do with loud noises or disturbances, and things like"—I heard the rattling of paper as Chris read off an entry—"'suspicious activity by the Viking Ship ride. Personnel provided assistance.'"

"Does that mean that finding KC's body is in a report?"

"Not in this report, since technically it—I mean she—wasn't on fairgrounds property. The big thing to me is that earlier, she was involved in a quote 'altercation' unquote just before the fair closed at ten."

"Altercation with whom?"

"Doesn't say."

"Should we try to find out?" Annie asked.

"I have the name of the guy who responded, but he's not at work today."

"Shall we come back tomorrow?" Annie asked, a bit too eagerly to suit me.

To my relief, the vote was two to one against returning to the fair. "We can talk to him at his house," Chris said.

"Or I can have Victor look him up tomorrow," I said, offering my staff.

"We can talk more when we're driving back."

"Which will be when?" I asked.

"Now?" Chris suggested.

Once again, the vote was two to one, against Annie.

I promised Annie, the two-time loser, that we'd stop on the way home and I'd buy her a fresh café au lait.

It seemed some of us had had enough fun for one day.

# Eight

I CAN'T BELIEVE HOW MUCH WE MISSED," ANNIE SAID as we drove home to Elkview. "Like the equestrian arena and all the exhibit halls. I remember great flower displays in past years."

"As well as large items like pool tables and patio furniture and home spas for sale," I said, to add a little commercial perspective.

"Don't forget the animal pens," Chris said. "Aren't you sorry we passed up the odors of pigs, cows, chickens? What am I leaving out?"

"Goats," I said. "And those smells are part of the reason I didn't want to go back this year."

"Oh, yes, the goats. We used to feed the baby goats," Annie said, skipping over the comments about the sales floors and the animal smells. "I wonder where we got the bottles of milk?"

"My guess? Your parents bought them on the fairgrounds," I said. "They sold those little cones of food for the animals, too."

"You think there might have been clues in those other areas?" Chris asked. "With the flowers and the piglets?"

"Maybe," Annie said.

"You can go back tomorrow," I said. Meaning without me.

Then I also remembered Roland Hortenson, whom I'd bumped into on the way into the fairgrounds. I'd meant to follow up with him at his booth but forgotten all about it.

In spite of all we'd skipped or forgotten, I was of the mind that there would be more to learn in Elkview than at the fair, spending more time wandering around, hoping for a lead. My reasoning wasn't foolproof, but it seemed that even though KC had been killed at the fair, the motive was homegrown. It was hard to imagine she'd aggravated a fellow vendor or attendee at the fair to such an extent that she'd be killed for it. And it was unlikely that she'd won a ribbon someone else had been hoping to earn. Or that she'd cheated someone out of a sale. Or any number of other fair-related offenses.

I hoped we'd learn more from Doc Sherman about the knife that had been used as a weapon. If it was a "fair knife," so to speak, that might make premeditation less likely.

Chris handed over the fair's security reports for me to read aloud while he drove us home. I wondered if we'd all ever get back to nice, relaxing drives on the Parks Highway, with beautiful trees on either side, Denali in the distance, and nothing to watch for but a stray elk or moose ambling down the center line.

Most of the items in the report were one-liners that Chris had already described to us over the phone on our conference call, such as "Medical aid needed in front of Sharks." We'd laughed at that, the entry making it sound as though real sharks had been present, whereas it was simply the name of a ride. We laughed again at "Unwanted person on Zombie Train."

The incident of interest to us was an "Altercation at cabbage booth" at nine in the evening on Friday, the night of

KC's murder. Fair hours on Friday were noon to ten. According to Aly, KC had closed her booth on time, with her mother's help, so she had been alive after this altercation. At some point, KC's mom left, and shortly after that, KC's killer arrived. A shaky timeline, but better than nothing.

"So, the altercation person came back?" Annie asked from the back. She'd scooted to the edge of the seat, stretching the limit of the seat belt so she could lean forward, the better to hear us.

"Could be," Chris said. "It would be nice to know that person's name. The one KC fought with. I think we should talk to the person who broke up the fight as soon as we can. The guy in the security building gave me his number." He pointed to the sheaf of papers I had on my lap. "I wrote the info in the margin of the page where the incident is described."

I rifled through the sheets. "Got it. Lee Hadley. We might as well try him now." I pulled out my phone and punched in the number, which looked vaguely familiar.

A somewhat gravelly woman's voice came on. "Firehouse Number Three Thirteen."

No wonder the number looked familiar. It was on my list of emergency contacts by the phone in the kitchen at the Bear Claw. Had I dialed it by mistake just now? I held the phone away from my ear, at almost arm's length, and gave it a questioning look, as if the device could explain itself and answer my question.

"Excuse me. I thought I was calling Lee Hadley?"

"This is Lee. Are you calling from the fair?"

Female Lee, not male Lee, as we had supposed. I was a little ashamed of myself for the assumption. "Yes, from the fair." *Sort of.* I gave her my name.

"I figured someone would be contacting me soon. I'm a new firefighter for the region, but I moonlight with the company that services events like the fair. When I heard that woman was killed, I wondered who'd be handling it."

"I'm going to put you on speaker if you don't mind."

While Chris maneuvered my car into a parking lot in front of a combination gas station and convenience store, I gave firefighter Lee a brief description of our status with Trooper Graham.

"We were hoping you could provide a few more details about the incident you wrote up on Friday night."

Lee groaned. Without the road noise, it was easier to hear her, but only slightly. The noise from her firehouse predominated in the background, as if the resident professionals were testing their alarm systems. More likely cooking dinner, if there was any truth to firehouse lore that they were great cooks and cuter than cops.

"I wish I could tell you more," Lee said. "But, you know, I almost didn't write it up at all, because the guy split as soon as he saw me. The uniform will do that sometimes. I guess they're meant to scare people off. We wear those orange sweater-vests that no one else in their right mind would wear during the summer."

"Can you tell me who sent for you and what you saw when you got there?"

"A call came in to the security building, a panicky woman's voice. An older person, I thought. Around nine o'clock, I think. I can look at the logbook to be sure. She wouldn't give her name, but she sounded frantic. She said that two people, a man and a woman, were having it out by the cabbage patch." Lee cleared her throat. "Sorry, I didn't mean that to be funny."

"It's a tense time," I said. It occurred to me that the anonymous caller might have been KC's mother, since she would have been there right up to ten o'clock. But I couldn't imagine why Laurie Patterson wouldn't identify herself and stay around, perhaps even trying to assist her daughter. I imagined my mom picking up a skillet if someone were attacking me in the Bear Claw—or, in Laurie's case in the fair booth, the heaviest cabbage she could find to fend off someone going after her daughter.

"The caller said she was afraid the man was going to knock the woman out or something. I couldn't raise any officer closer to the site, so I grabbed one of our scooters and rode it out there. And, as you probably know, our building is at the other end of the fairground from where the incident took place."

"About as far away as it could be," I said. I pictured a woman in an orange vest, on a motorized scooter, maneuvering through oblivious fairgoers as they scattered out of her way in a panic.

"As I approached, I heard raised voices, but couldn't make out any words. The guy was about the same height as Kelly—I saw her name on the booth before I talked to her. He had on a regular shirt that was more dressy than fairgoing wear. Not a T-shirt, I mean. As soon as he saw me, he turned, got on a motorbike of his own, and rode off the property. I stayed behind to make sure Kelly was okay. Anyway, his bike was bigger than mine, and I never would have caught him. Ours are made for the grounds, not the streets."

"Had Kelly been hurt?"

"It didn't look it. Anyway, she wasn't interested in pursuing the matter."

"And the caller?" I asked.

"Nowhere to be found."

"We were led to believe that KC's, the victim's, mother was with her at the booth until ten o'clock, when the fair was closing. Could she have been the caller?" I had to double-check.

"I honestly can't say, but if so, why wouldn't she have been there when I got there?"

My question exactly. "So you didn't meet the victim's mother?"

"I didn't. Only the victim-to-be, I guess you'd call her, was there, and the attacker, who fled."

Chris mouthed, *Other witnesses?*

I nodded and asked Lee, "Did anyone else see anything? Any witnesses at all, next to the booth or on the path?"

"No. I asked around, of course. To tell you the truth, at that time of night, not many people are at the fair for the produce, which is more or less all there is in that sector. It's the kids who arrive and congregate at that hour, the groups of teenagers and other young people, you know, crowding the rides, the concerts, playing all the games to win those ugly prizes." She paused. "Sorry, I guess I'm already a little jaded, and there are still many more nights to go."

"That's okay. I get it," I said, being truthful.

"I wish I could give you more."

"Thanks, Lee. We might call you back after we've digested this and reported to the state trooper who's in charge."

"No problem. Let me give you my personal cell number."

I took her number, thanked her again, and clicked the phone off.

"Well, since he rode off on a motorbike, we can assume he didn't steal Jessup's car."

"That's something," Annie said.

*Not much,* I thought.

WE AGREED THAT WE NEEDED TO LOOP TROOPER IN on everything as soon as possible. Annie set the schedule.

"First, we go home and get out of these sweaty clothes."

"Are you looking at me?" Chris asked.

"You know what I mean. And Charlie and I need to feed our cats. Well, I know Benny has his own feeder, but he's spoiled." She laughed. A good thing, lest I take her comment as a slur toward Eggs Benedict. "Then maybe we can have dinner at the Bear Claw with Trooper. I can text him. Does that work for you guys?"

I nodded in agreement. "It's almost four o'clock now. That puts us at the diner around seven," I said.

"I don't have a cat to go home to," Chris said. "And I don't feel like making the round trip. So I might take myself and my sweaty clothes straight to the diner."

"You can come to the inn," Annie said. "The lobby's pretty comfy, as you know."

I had mixed feelings about Annie beating me to the invitation. I kept quiet while they continued to banter about whether Chris should take a shower in one of the many cabins at Annie's Inn. At one point she joked that he might want to throw his sweaty clothes in the trash and change into some fresh ones from her Lost and Found Department, which was a box under the registration desk.

It was true that the inn's lobby was more conducive to relaxing than the booths and stools at the Bear Claw. Plus, invariably as I read the newspaper, I found a story I wanted to share with Benny, and Chris might think that was weird. Reading aloud to my cat. Not that I cared, but why bother explaining?

It turned out not to matter what I thought, since Annie and Chris seemed to be working it out, sallying back and forth about whether Chris could give Yulie, her cat, a rubdown or just stretch out on the couch or check the next guests in.

Chris ended the round with "As long as you don't light the fire and make me sweat even more."

I slid down in the front seat and pretended to take a nap.

BACK HOME, BENNY WAS VERY RECEPTIVE TO SITTING on my lap in the rocking chair while I got caught up with papers and magazines. I also had a new cat book my mom had given me. I could hardly count the number of cat books I owned, one of my favorites being a collection of cat quotes in Shakespeare.

"He mentions cats more than forty times," my high school English teacher was fond of telling us. I'd never been to her home, but I had a feeling more than one cat was being cared for on the premises.

But it was Mom who encouraged me to read aloud for Benny. "He'll like the sound of your voice. Trust me."

I always trusted my mom.

In today's *Elkview Bugle*, there was a human interest story by a popular animal advocate who often wrote features. A stray cat appeared in the writer's yard with three kittens, all four looking very hungry. The author put out a bowl of food and watched as the mother brought food to her kittens before taking a bite for herself. Eventually, of course, the whole family of cats moved in with the owner.

Purring, Benny didn't move while I read the story, stroking his back whenever I could free a hand. He left his perch on my lap only when I read "The End," leaving me to believe that Mom was right—he liked the sound of my voice and was going to stay until the story was finished. At least, that was my theory, and I didn't much care if anyone else believed it. Benny and I—and Mom—had an understanding.

This time, in fact, instead of jumping down to the floor, Benny made his way over my shoulder and behind me. It was possible that, besides the sound of my voice, he liked the lavender scent from my soap and shampoo. He stretched across the back of the chair, providing me with a quite decent orange and white furry striped pillow, as long as I didn't press on it. The configuration made it impossible for me to nap, however, since I was afraid of trapping my cat between the chair and my neck.

As long as I was forgoing a nap, I managed to pull my laptop over and start a search of property records in our Mat-Su Borough. Whatever made me think the records would be readily available, it wasn't the one painful year I'd spent in law school. I needed to open an account at a minimum, and at a maximum offer my firstborn should there ever be one. Not only that, but the office where there might be staff to help me through the process was closed, not just today, which was understandable, but also tomorrow, Monday.

Had I missed a holiday? As far as I knew August was free of holidays, with no celebration coming between the Fourth of July and Labor Day.

There was nothing to do but show up for dinner at the Bear Claw, where, hopefully, Trooper would appear and help us gain entry to vital statistics about KC's property, among other things.

Since Benny had already marched off to his condo in the guest bedroom, I made sure his feeder was replenished, toys within reach, and headed for the diner to reconnect with my staff.

The upbeat sounds of the fair were still in my head— screams of delight from adventuresome riders, familiar organ music from the carousel, hawkers beckoning anyone who wanted to swap a few dollars for a stuffed creature of an unlikely color.

The reverberations almost drowned out the awful reality of a friend who was murdered and what she might have heard at the end of her life, what her last minutes might have been like.

Almost, but not quite, drowned out.

# Nine

Dinner at the Bear Claw was set for seven o'clock. I was early enough to give everyone in the kitchen an update and announce that anyone who wished was free to spend a day of their choosing at the fair, as long as everyone didn't take the same day.

"There are still eight more days of the fair left. I don't trust myself all alone here, in case an all-nighter tour bus arrives, but I can spare half of you at a time. Figure out when and with whom you'd like to go and get thee to a fair."

"Have you been reading about Shakespeare's cats again?" Nina asked, grinning, just after she let out a mild cheer.

"Yeah, boss?" Victor asked, the widest grin taking over his face. "We'll keep an eye out for recipes we might want to try here, and you can call it a business expense."

"That would be great, but not necessary. Just have a good time."

I'd stopped at the fair's ticket booth on the way out to the parking lot and picked up enough flyers, maps, and day passes for everyone. I spread them on the table in a corner of the kitchen I sometimes called my office.

I felt I was channeling my mom, who was always thinking up perks and ways to keep her employees happy.

The whooping and high-fiving was measured, since there were a few patrons in the booths, serious hikers from the way they were dressed. It was generally easy to distinguish the tourists from the locals or from those who came to experience the inherent challenges of Alaskan terrain. Some tourists wanted to observe the wilder part of the Last Frontier, but from a safe, comfortable distance. Annie provided for them by maintaining a set of cabins to the east of the main house that were furnished with hotel-level amenities, like running hot water. Their often brand-new outdoor clothing and unscuffed hiking boots were also a giveaway.

The men and women in the two booths this evening were the hardier types. My guess was that they'd either sleep in their vehicles or pile into one bare-bones cabin on the west side of the Annie's Inn property. Their talk was of navigation tools and first aid kits. I sat on a stool and eavesdropped for a few minutes about an updated version of a personal locator beacon, a gadget that could be used to alert emergency personnel when regular cell phone service might be spotty or nonexistent. The PLB, as it was called, would determine a hiker's position using GPS and send a message via satellite.

The arts and crafts at the fair had once again inspired me to take up a hobby. I'd already given some consideration to photography, and now I turned to hiking—or a combination of the two. I'd hiked some as a kid, as nearly everyone in my school had. We were in Alaska, after all, photogenic to its core. When I worked summers at the National Park Service's visitor centers, I knew exactly how many trails were in or close to Denali National Park. Now, thanks to the literature tourists brought to the Bear Claw, I'd learned about an app claiming more than one hundred thousand trails in the state, some wide enough for only one person at a time

I didn't have an abundance of free time, but I'd joined a

hiking group during my stay in San Francisco. We tended to stay close to the shoreline, trekking along the cliffs bordering the Pacific Ocean, exploring historic gun batteries, seeps, and springs, always with stunning views. It was time I got back to my own local trails and views.

I wondered if I'd be able to find my old hiking clothes or if I'd have to buy some shiny new ones.

Clattering from the Bear Claw kitchen brought me back to my reason for being here this evening in particular. I knew Victor was eager to get dinner ready for Trooper and our team. He knew what each of us liked and was happy to prepare meals to order. Except for the dessert, which he promised would be something new and special tonight, and a surprise.

That was fine with me. I couldn't think of a dessert I'd pass up if it came from the Bear Claw kitchen.

I moved off the stool and commandeered a back booth. Nina brought me a fresh cup of coffee and a small appetizer plate of mozzarella sticks and potato skins with cheese and bacon bits. Not that I let my staff spoil me.

I opened my laptop and worked on an agenda of sorts for when the others arrived. I had a lot of questions and only a few answers. I typed everything out, nibbling on the appetizers now and then.

- The SUV. *Picked up? Forensics analysis?*

- The watch. *Give to Trooper for forensics. Registered?*

- Other bagged items?

- The crime scene. *Any video from surrounding neighbors? (Wishful thinking.)*

- The property lines for KC and neighbor. *Key players? Legal proceedings in motion?*

- The key chain. *To Milo yet? Follow-up? Milo of age? Will? (see prop. lines)*

- The nine o'clock argument. *Video footage from fair security? Where was KC's mom?*

- Photos. *Decide how to organize from all three phones.*

- Other possible interviews: *Roland, teens*

- Other items?

That would do to start. I printed four copies to the equipment in the back of the diner and, with some degree of guilt, finished up the appetizers. Such a small plate, I told myself, and planned to ask Nina for a refill for the rest of the team when we were assembled.

CHRIS AND ANNIE ARRIVED TOGETHER AT SEVEN o'clock sharp. I'd noticed earlier that Annie had revived her timetable of seasonal hair coloring. The only time I fooled around with my hair that way was when I worked as a chef, wearing the same white uniform jacket every day. I'd decided I needed a little color and had my beautician add highlights, the shade of her choice, which meant the colors of the rainbow over the course of a few months.

Annie's newly blond summer locks were wet now and her clothes different from our trip clothes. Chris, of course, shaved his whole head on a regular basis, a habit he'd picked up during his time in the army. There was no way to tell— not until we got closer, anyway—whether he'd showered.

Victor took their orders and got to work on two different seafood dishes involving Alaskan salmon.

"I'm going out on a limb here and making enough for Trooper," he said, a wise young man.

I had to admit that I'd polished off a whole plate of appetizers, so I wasn't ready for a regular meal.

I heard a familiar noise from the kitchen—the sound of dice rolling on the stainless steel table. Apparently, Victor and friends had vandalized a board game from the shelf of toys and activity books we kept for kids, and had devised a way to assign Alaska State Fair days. My softer side prevailed and I decided that they should all go together. Victor and Nina were siblings; Tammy and Bert were dating; Victor and Rachel were another couple. Ginny was assimilating well. They all got along, a plus for me, and it wouldn't hurt to give them a day off together. I'd call it a team-building exercise and bring in temporary workers.

I asked Nina to spread the word, and this time there was no holding back on the cheering. I sent a quick text to the service I used for ad hoc help. The small business was run by college students who were available night and day at a reasonable rate. Most of them were delighted to work the graveyard shift, knowing they'd have lots of time for doing homework or playing games on their computers.

Trooper came in a few minutes after seven. I noticed he'd been dropped off by another man in blue. Two Alaska State Troopers in the same patch of Elkview was a rare sight, and I mentioned it to our resident one.

"Ran into an old buddy of mine at the conference," Trooper said. "Wayne is from up north and hasn't been down here for a while, so I said he could use my wheels to look around while I'm at this meeting. We only spent about an hour together on the way over, catching up."

Trooper seemed apologetic, and I regretted calling attention to what was probably his longest vacation in years—an hour with an old friend.

For me, I felt I'd let KC down by relaxing at home with Benny for too long. I got to it and distributed the ad hoc agenda I'd created. Trooper seemed to sense my agitation.

"Take it easy, Charlie," he said. "I know you want to find

your friend's killer, but there's not always a quick solution. We need you in this for the long haul."

I knew he was right, but I couldn't slow down for long. "I *am* taking it easy," I said. "Has the SUV been picked up? Are the techs going over it?"

Trooper laughed, as did the whole team. Even me.

Between mouthfuls of salmon and potatoes au gratin and hollers of gratitude to the cooks, Trooper reported the SUV had been delivered to the station house, where techs were working on it.

"We should have a fingerprint report and any other analysis in the next day or so," he said. "There's no guarantee the prints will match anyone in the system, but we'll have them to compare if we do get a viable suspect."

"When," I said. "*When* we get a viable suspect."

Trooper nodded. "The Jessups are in no hurry to get their vehicle back. I think Sue Ann considers it bad luck and wishes she'd let her hubby keep the old jalopy."

"I'll be glad to take it off their hands," said Chris, the not-so-proud owner of a pickup of questionable worth, probably older than the Jessups' jalopy.

"So we might learn who stole it?" Annie asked, only a beat behind.

"If they're in the system, yes," Trooper clarified.

"The watch," I said, moving to item number two on my agenda. I pulled it out of my tote.

I'd put the watch in a plastic bag at the fair, one of the stack I always carried with me for food emergencies, then switched to a paper bag when I got home.

The rules about paper and plastic for evidence were mixed. Plastic was better for fingerprints, which the watch might have. But paper was preferable for textiles. Which the watchband could fall under.

I needed my mom to help me sort it out. She read every police procedural crime fiction she could get her hands on and kept track of these things. Without her, I had to guess.

"Paper," Trooper said. "I'm impressed."

"Mom," I said, and he nodded that he knew how my mom was always sharing tips she learned from fiction. Sometimes they were spot-on; other times not so much.

"It looked to me like the battery was dead, besides getting beat up on that tire," Chris said. "But I was wondering if the watch might be registered somewhere, given that it has all that data about someone's BP and so on."

"Like implants and things," Annie said, getting slight nods, but no verbal confirmation. "I meant like contact lenses and stuff," she added.

Chris volunteered to check on how that all worked. Before taking custody of it, Trooper pulled his own emergency kit from his pocket in the form of rubber gloves. He laid out the watch facedown, while Chris copied some numbers into his smartphone app.

I handed over the other items I'd taken from Bill and his cleanup crew at the crime scene, a little embarrassed that I'd thought they'd be useful.

Trooper looked at the gum wrapper, button, juice box, and comb. He didn't seem excited about the items, but neither did he refuse to take them.

The wishful-thinking item—video from neighbors on Spruce Street—proved to be just that, wishful thinking. Trooper had gotten the report from the people he had sent to canvas. I wondered if young Bill and the cleanup crew were included but decided not to ask, lest it be seen as a challenge to their competence, which in a way it was, and which Trooper was defensive about.

"A lot of people have those new video doorbells," Trooper said, "but they go out only so far. They're not designed to look at the neighborhood."

Watches, doorbells, TVs—everything was smart nowadays, except when it mattered.

"Give it a while," Chris said. "There'll be complete camera coverage on all of us twenty-four-seven."

"They've really come down in price," Annie said. This, like many of Annie's observations, had only a tenuous connection to the topic and did not immediately follow it.

Nina came by to clear our table. I was always impressed by her limitless energy. The small-framed woman had a spring in her step even at the end of a shift, like this evening. But then, she was young, I reminded myself, still in college, though I couldn't say I was similarly bouncy at that age. Sometimes Nina's feet seemed not to be hitting the floor even as she toted a loaded tray of dishes from the booths to the kitchen.

"Doggy bags?" she asked, barely containing her laughter, since there was not a crumb left on any plate. Nothing to bag. Not even from my plate, though I'd claimed to not be hungry enough for dinner.

Word came from the kitchen that dessert would take a few more minutes. A good thing, as we were all stuffed. A small group of patrons had arrived, two booths' worth. They weren't locals, but Nina apparently recognized them from another visit and addressed them by name, as if they were her best friends and she couldn't wait to serve them again. A day at the fair seemed not enough reward for such a great waitress.

We moved to a more difficult topic on the agenda: the property dispute Aly had told me about.

"We're not even sure it's a thing, are we?" Annie asked. "Didn't you say Aly wasn't sure?"

"And we both talked to Donna," Chris reminded me. "She worked with KC on the farm. Well, in the office, but still, on a daily basis, and she didn't mention it at all."

"All true," I said. "But I think it's still worth pursuing. Milo turns eighteen soon. We should find out exactly when, because that could matter in terms of property ownership. We should find out if there's a will, also. That might have something to do with it. If there are conflicting documents, for example."

"I'll get on that tomorrow," Trooper said. "Might as well put it to rest if there's nothing to it."

"The Recorder's Office is closed tomorrow," I said.

Trooper winked. "No matter. I have my ways."

"I'm glad to hear that."

We still had a couple more items to discuss, including the nine o'clock incident report from firefighter Lee Hadley. One perplexing issue was that the timing was off. If KC's mother was supposedly with her until ten, where was she when her daughter was in a fight at nine? Plus—

"Dessert is served," came the call from the kitchen, interrupting my thought.

Nina appeared at the head of a little parade of kitchen staff, carrying a dish that might have been heavier than her.

"It's Boston cream pie," Victor announced.

"But it's not really a pie. More of a cake," Nina said, depositing the appealing confection on our table.

"Created at a famous Boston hotel almost two hundred years ago," Victor said.

Nina took on the posture of a model at a car show, using graceful gestures to point to the three layers. A cake. Cream filling. A chocolate glaze.

"Triple delight," she said, playing the role beautifully.

"I'm so glad I ate light," I said.

# TEN

**W**ITH THE SURPRISE ARRIVAL OF THE BOSTON CREAM pie, it took some doing to get us back on track with the reporting and sharing we'd come together to accomplish this evening.

First, we had to hear from Victor that a twelve-foot-diameter Boston cream pie had been made a few years ago for a New England food fair.

"It weighed more than a ton," he told us. "I think we should try to make one for our Alaska State Fair next year."

"We can create a whole new category of a prize," Nina said.

"Why not an enormous bear claw?" Rachel suggested. "That's who we are," she added, in case we'd forgotten. Rachel, Victor's girlfriend, was the most recent full-time Bear Claw waitperson and was fitting in nicely. The others did tease her about her Los Angeles "valley girl" accent.

Lately, Victor had become interested in regional foods—not our Alaskan Mat-Su region, but others across the country. Thus the Boston cream pie. He'd hinted at tinkering with the menu to include dishes like Philly cheesesteak, Denver omelet, and Maryland crab cakes. Key lime pie was already a staple, but Victor wanted to substitute Persian limes for the lime juice he had been using.

Nina gave away his secret. "My brother is hooked on this website that gives the best dishes for every state or major city in the country. Wait until he asks to serve Spam because it's still a big hit in Hawaii."

"Not just any Spam," Victor said. "Spam musubi. You make a sandwich of spiced ham—otherwise known as Spam—and rice and wrap it in seaweed." He smacked his lips to emphasize the desirability of adding the dish to our menu.

I loved the enthusiasm of my staff. But I felt the need to add a word of caution. "As long as you check our budget before you start importing ingredients," I said.

"And as long as you don't remove Eggs Benedict Cooke's namesake dish from the menu," Annie added. "Even Yulie would be upset at that."

"Would that be Yulie Jensen?" Nina called out.

In a diner, there were no private conversations.

I appreciated the fact that the three of us civilians, and probably Trooper also, who'd contemplated more Boston pie, as he called it, were somewhat burned out from the intense focus and emotional toll of the past twenty-four hours. It seemed a lot more like twenty-four days, yet at this time yesterday, I had barely learned that Trooper needed help with a homicide, and it was only a little while after that when I discovered that the victim was one of my childhood friends.

With great effort, I brought us back to the phone call with Lee Hadley, firefighter by day, security officer by night. Or vice versa.

"We never asked if there was video footage of the incident she interrupted," I said, though I realized how unlikely that was. The lack of orderly aisles for the produce stands precluded a way to mount cameras with a meaningful view.

It was possible that the major rides or ticket kiosks had cameras, but those wouldn't help us.

"No harm in asking," Chris said. "We really don't know what resources the security people have."

"It does sound like another call to this firefighter might be useful," Trooper said. "Do you want me to make it?"

We all nodded, and poor Trooper was left writing in his notebook, undoubtedly adding to a long to-do list.

When it came to figuring out whether KC's mom had been around for the altercation that had brought Lee Hadley out to investigate, it seemed only right that we give Trooper a break and look into it ourselves.

"Maybe she just stepped away to go to the restroom," Annie suggested. Always the practical one.

"And at just that moment someone happened to pick a fight with her daughter?" Chris asked. "Isn't that a little too convenient?"

"He could have been lying in wait for KC to be alone in the booth," I said, mulling over a possibility.

"So we can just ask the mom when she went to the restroom," Chris said.

"Do you know her?" Annie asked.

Chris shook his head. "Can't say I've ever met her."

"So some strange guy shows up and asks her when she had to—" Annie began.

Chris laughed. "I was kidding." I couldn't tell whether his explanation was necessary. With Annie, it wasn't always clear.

"I think Annie and I should visit Laurie alone, since we have some history with her," I suggested.

"Good idea. I think this is a wrap for now," Trooper said, accepting a container of food to go from Rachel.

Annie looked at the agenda I'd printed out. She pointed to the last items on the list. "What about going through our cell phone photos? And interviewing Roland Hortenson, the other produce vendor? Plus all the teens who work on other farms during breaks, and maybe on KC's, too?"

"How about meeting again tomorrow?" I said. "We can each sift through our photos and eliminate duplicates or otherwise useless ones."

"And what about 'Other items'?" Annie asked. "Down at the bottom of your list of tasks, you wrote 'Other items.' Shouldn't we see what other items there are, from other people besides Charlie?"

Because it was Annie, there was no way I could take offense at her litany of "other." Besides, when put to a vote, my deal was accepted and the meeting broke up, with an agreement to meet for dinner again tomorrow, Monday evening.

When the rest of the team had left, all I wanted to do was put my head on the table and take a nap. Instead, I asked Rachel for a coffee refill.

"And another piece of Boston cream pie?" she asked.

I hesitated, weighing the pros and cons. I knew if I went home, I'd succumb to my comfy bed and pillow, with Benny included in the tableau. But I felt the need to do more with the evening. The sugar hit combined with caffeine would probably fire me up for a couple more hours. After that, I'd probably tank. But that might not be so bad. Maybe I'd get a good night's sleep out of it.

"Just a small one?" she offered.

"If you insist." I smiled, and so did Rachel.

I opened my laptop and accessed the agenda. I wanted to update it while the meeting resolutions were fresh in my mind. I set to editing.

- The SUV. *We'll have forensics analysis in the next day or two.*

- The watch. *Trooper has it. Chris took numbers to see if registered.*

- Other bagged items? *Trooper took them.*

- The crime scene, bordering on produce area. Video? *Not in produce area.*

- The property lines for KC and neighbor. *Trooper will check, even tho closed Monday.*

- The key chain. *To Milo yet? Follow-up? Milo of age? Legal will? See above re: prop.*

- The nine o'clock argument. *Security footage? KC's mom? Annie and I visit mom.*

- Photos. *Decide how to organize from all three phones. Go through before next mtg.*

- Other possible interviews: *Roland, teens. Discussion deferred.*

- Other items? *Discussion deferred.*

There was nothing like checking off items to feel productive, even if the tasks hadn't been completed.

My staff had been productive also. They'd decided to hit the fair midweek, having calculated that weekends plus a day or two on either side would be more crowded.

"People take long weekends," Nina reasoned. "But nobody takes Wednesdays off."

I wasn't about to argue, especially since that would give me a couple of days to line up temp help.

With all the notes on the agenda written out, only a smear of chocolate left of the Boston cream pie, and the staff due to work as usual on Monday and Tuesday, I was ready to close my laptop and head home.

I said a final word to Tammy and Bert, who'd agreed to arrive early, at eleven p.m., and would be on duty in the wee hours.

"I forgot to check with Annie," I told them. "Can you call in the morning around seven o'clock and ask her if she expects a group to come here for breakfast?"

"Sure thing," Bert said. "We can get extra bear claw dough ready just in case."

"Sleep well," Tammy said.

I wondered if I would.

BENNY WAS ASLEEP IN A SMALL CARPET-LINED CAVE on a middle level of his condo tower. I remembered when I'd bought the apartment building, as I liked to call it, for him. At the time, I'd struggled—my mom had said "obsessed"— over the size and color and whether to buy instead an elaborate house I'd seen in a magazine ad, much like a doghouse in shape. I'd scrolled through countless pages of houses that were more intricately designed and decorated than many dollhouses. One looked like a clock tower; another was in the shape of the famous Japanese wave painting. In the end I'd settled for a simple, plushy-carpeted, multilevel stack.

"Simple indeed," Mom had said, with a wide grin.

I'd learned that even the gentlest touch or stroke woke Benny up, so I let him be. If I needed to wake him up to be a sounding board, all I had to do was open a can of tuna and he'd be by my side in an instant, rubbing against my ankles.

However, instead of heading directly to bed, I made the mistake of pulling a dusty yearbook from a shelf in the family room. I took a mug of tea to the table by the rocker and opened the *Antlers*, as the book was called. The mistake was that I knew it would make me sad. As if the day hadn't been sad enough.

Whatever the reason, I couldn't go back. I did it anyway.

All *Antlers* yearbooks had a dark blue cover sprinkled with gold stars, reflecting the design of the Alaskan flag. The year was embossed in gold along the bottom edge. Elkview was small enough that all four high school classes were featured every year, with a couple of pages each for freshmen, sophomores, and juniors, and the rest of the book for seniors. In the formal part of the book, the senior girls wore a black drape and pearls; the boys were stuck (as they claimed) with black bow ties.

My fingers had landed on the edition that was produced the year Annie and I were sophomores and KC was a senior, the year KC's dad died. The *Antlers* had been issued before that turn of events for her.

I flipped through the pages with photos and long captions describing faculty, sports teams, clubs, and special activities, like our ski trips. Annie and I appeared together in several montages at different club meetings, both of us with long, straight hair purposefully curled at the ends. The boys wore their hair combed forward in various styles of bangs, which would now be considered silly. I smiled as I saw snapshot after snapshot of uncomfortable-looking boys. Not that the rest of us looked comfortable, with our smiles forced on us by the photographers.

I held the page open to reflect on David, always clowning around, and now Elkview's esteemed pharmacist; Richie, the nerd, currently a doctor at a hospital in Fairbanks; Elaine, another nerd, a geologist somewhere in the lower forty-eight.

There were more activities than students some years, so we all had a shot at being president at one time or another. Heading up the Ski Club meant nothing more than booking a lodge in Talkeetna and making sure there were enough cold-weather snacks. But we were told it would be good for our college applications if we could claim club officer status. It didn't matter either that we all knew how to ski almost as soon as we could walk and didn't need a club to get us to shop for skis or snowshoes.

The way I remembered those days, it had been about getting together outside of school and enjoying the Alaskan outdoors.

The senior section opened with a shot of KC flying through the air as she made the most of a giant trampoline set up in one of our larger parks. The big question was how she had managed the maneuver in the dead of winter, wearing heavy boots and many layers of clothes. I pictured her now, probably in Doc Sherman's basement morgue. I stayed with the *Antlers* in spite of the emotions it provoked, or maybe because I needed the release.

I couldn't remember why I was pictured sitting in a circle in the sunken living room of our student lounge. The caption read "Drama Club," but I'd never been a member. It was entirely possible that I and some other classmates had been recruited to fill slots of missing thespians.

The yearbook editors had put together a clever montage of various tickets—to movies that were popular then, to concerts. I found the page of top tens. Had we really voted Aerosmith the top artist? *Bridget Jones's Diary* and *Ocean's 11* the top movies?

KC and her science lab partner, a guy whose name I couldn't remember, earned a large spot in the honors section. She always claimed she was going to put her science to good use on the family farm. We all knew she was joking. Except that when her sister died, it turned out that it was not a joke.

My cell phone rang, startling me. Annie's name was on the screen. "Are you awake? I am," she said. We both laughed that I was awake now that the phone had rung.

When I told her what I'd been doing, she had the reaction I'd expected.

"Why didn't you call me? Don't look at the whole thing without me, okay?"

"I'll save signatures and dedications to read with you tomorrow. We can reminisce over all the promises to remember so-and-so forever."

"Oh, remember when we had to submit quotes when we were seniors?"

"A tradition for many years. I think I chose one from Pink Floyd. How embarrassing."

"Not as bad as mine. Dolly Samuels talked me into using one from Yogi Berra. I didn't know who he was at the time." She paused, and I could almost see her screw up her nose. "I was so easy to push around back then."

"Especially since Dolly was a cheerleader with her own fan club," I said, trying not to snipe about the classmate who had often dissed my best friend.

"I remember she said I talked like him. I thought it was a compliment." Annie sighed, humiliated all over again.

"Hey, Annie, my dad told me Yogi got a purple heart for heroism in World War II, and he's in the Baseball Hall of Fame now. How's Dolly doing?"

Annie giggled. "Right. Who knows? Thanks, Charlie. You always did stick up for me. And I can't even remember what the quote was."

I did, but I made sure we hung up before I reminded her of the Yogi saying under her photo: "You can observe a lot by just watching."

Before I closed the book, I looked up the quote under KC's photo.

"How far we travel in life matters far less than those we meet along the way."

An anonymous author, but a choice to be proud of.

After getting ready for bed and before turning off my bedside lamp, I spared a thought for KC, for all she'd hoped for and dreamed. I wondered who had attacked KC the last night of her life. Because whoever it was, they cut her life's journey short.

I couldn't let that horrible fact go unpunished.

# ELEVEN

ANNIE AND I PLANNED TO VISIT LAURIE, KC'S MOM,
around eleven in the morning on Monday. Before then, I
wanted to talk to my mom to see what advice she might
have. I hated to disrupt her fun visit with her friends in
Oregon with a problem, but I knew she'd be very willing to
listen and talk.

At nine in the morning in Elkview, it was ten o'clock in
Portland. My mom, who was as tied to her cell phone as
any millennial, answered immediately.

"I've been wondering how you are, sweetie. I knew
you'd get back to me if you needed anything. I sent a note
to Laurie, of course. The poor woman."

I was on my rocker, and Benny had climbed up onto my
lap. I switched to FaceTime so my mom could get her
Benny fix while we chatted. A mug of morning coffee and
the last of a bear claw were in reach on the table next to me.
All the comforts of home. Mom listened without comment
as I briefed her on the investigation so far.

When I'd finished, Mom chimed in with a vote of confidence. "I know you'll say the right things when you see her

today, if there is anything right in all this. Just be yourself and she'll know you're there to help."

I whispered my thanks, glad she had such faith in me—more than I had in myself.

Mom continued. "You might remember that Laurie met her husband, Spencer, at one of those grief support groups after Diedre and her husband, Milo's parents, died in that awful plane crash. Spencer's wife had died a couple of years before from a long illness. I forget what exactly. And of course you remember when Kelly's dad died."

I nodded. "I was a sophomore. I know Laurie and Spencer run Spencer's Hardware Store together now. Laurie was helping KC at her produce booth at the fair. It seems they were still very close."

"Imagine Milo essentially losing two mothers." I heard my mom's heavy sigh. "Or losing both your daughters."

My mom went silent. I waited, stroking Benny's fur, listening to his purrs. I had a good idea what Mom was thinking and wished I could assure her that Dad and I were going to be around for a long time.

Mom cleared her throat. "One thing to remember is that Laurie has already been through the five stages of grief, or the four tasks of facing loss, or whatever the psychologists' theories are now. Just let her take the lead. Ask if there's anything you can do, and let her answer."

"Thanks, Mom." I looked at her face on my iPhone screen. She looked so sad. I decided it was time to switch the topic to something more pleasant and get her away from talk of death, broken families, and broken people. "How's your trip going?"

"A lot of fun. Did you get my latest postcard?"

"Not yet. Another diner?"

"Yes. This one is very modern. I think you'd like it. Today we're going to do two food tours in Portland."

I smiled. "Of course you are."

"The first one is called the Food Carts and Restaurants

Tour, and it includes lunch. The other one, in the afternoon, is a walking tour of chocolate, with tastings, production sessions, and what they're calling chocolate education. The last stop on the tour pairs all kinds of chocolates with various fruits. Dipping a variety of fruits into chocolate fondues. Tasting a variety of chocolate-covered fruits—strawberries, blueberries, pineapple, orange slices." Mom appeared to be salivating already. "I wish you were here for that one especially."

"Me, too. Photos, please," I said.

"Absolutely. And I'd be surprised if they didn't have a fantastic gift shop, so I'll leave time for that. And space in my luggage," she added, with some excitement.

I was glad we could end on an upbeat, tasty note.

WHERE'S CHRIS TODAY?" ANNIE ASKED AS WE MADE our way to the home of Laurie and Spencer Patterson. "I've forgotten what he's supposed to be doing."

"Don't you have that new printout I gave you with the updated agenda?"

"That's right, I do." Annie took a tightly folded piece of paper from her tote. "Chris has to check on the watch you found in the Jessups' SUV tire tread to see if it's registered to anyone." She ran her finger down the page. "I guess that's all, but I'll bet he does something else. He needs a story, for one thing. And he's no slacker."

"I wouldn't be surprised if he goes back to the fair," I said. At which point my cell phone rang through my car's interface and we heard Chris's voice from the speakers.

"Hi, I'm at the fairgrounds."

It took a while for Annie and me to calm down from hearty laughter. It didn't hurt that we were all nervous about the day's agenda. So much seemed to be riding on that list. For now we needed the emotional release that hearing something funny brought.

I was driving my own vehicle for a change. Because Chris and I were the same height, I hadn't had to adjust the seat, the way I did when Annie or Mom or one of my staff took my car. I missed Chris, and not only because he did the driving.

In all our working together over the past year, we'd had only one trip that might be called a date. He'd been assigned a travel piece for the *Bugle* and asked me to join him on a sightseeing trip between Talkeetna and Anchorage. True, I'd had a chore to do in keeping notes as we stopped along the way, but, I told myself, he didn't really need an assistant, and it wasn't just because he liked my car better than his old pickup for a long trip, as well as all the Bear Claw snacks he knew I'd bring.

Those were the things I told myself.

I had no idea what he told himself.

On that journey, we'd enjoyed Eklutna Village, the oldest Athabaskan settlement; walked part of the Thunderbird Falls Trail; and trekked around the Eagle River Nature Center. That had been a couple of months ago. Nothing since.

I wasn't all that eager for a romantic relationship anyway, although I considered myself fully recovered from my failed engagement to a San Francisco attorney.

I blinked and brought myself back to the present. While I'd been working out these issues, Annie and Chris had been talking through my car's Bluetooth.

"I thought I might check on the high school kids who may have worked on KC's farm, but I don't have their names," Chris said. "I thought they'd be on that agenda you gave us, Charlie, but I don't see them. You just wrote 'teens.'"

Was that a critical tone I heard? I responded in as neutral a voice as I could muster. "Let me look through my phone and I can give you the names in a minute." *And, by the way, I hope that wasn't a criticism of the hard work I did putting together the agenda in the first place. And also, by the way, you're welcome.*

"Great. I'm really early," he said. "I forgot the fair doesn't open until noon on weekdays, so I'm sitting in the parking lot. Did you know there's a dry entrance and a wet entrance to the theater on the grounds where they hold the concerts and other performances?"

"You must be desperate, reading the fair literature," I said.

Chris laughed. "As I said, I'm early."

"So what's the difference?" Annie asked. "Alcohol and no alcohol?"

"Exactly. You have to be twenty-one to go directly into the alcohol area. I could tell you about the no-pets-except-for-service-animals rule and the warning that coolers will be inspected and how you can rent a stroller, but I'll spare you."

"Are you ready for the teens' names?" I asked.

"Shoot."

"Zach who did raspberry picking, Hildy on beans, and Cecilia on rhubarb. You might start with the sweet corn booth. A young woman named Steph, working there, is the one who gave me the names."

Rattling off the teens' names reminded me of other notes I'd taken after my visit to produce booths yesterday. I remembered typing into my Notes app:

KC involved with anyone special? Dating?

Where does Milo go now? Other relatives? Interview THEM.

These were questions for today at Laurie's. If only I could ask them in a way that wouldn't bring her to tears.

CONTINUING ALONG THE PARKS HIGHWAY TO LAURIE'S home, we passed Spencer's Hardware Store in a small strip mall on the outskirts of Elkview, close to the border of Talkeetna. I couldn't tell if the store was open, but I was pretty sure Spencer wouldn't be there in any case.

I couldn't remember a time when I had been less thrilled about arriving at my destination.

The Patterson home was large, with two stories and an expansive, well-manicured lawn. The front door spanned the entire height of the building, the top section an artistically designed dome shape with what was either stained or painted glass. An elaborate array of wooden garage doors ran along the front, one for a single car, one two-car size, and a third, the longest, that probably housed a shop, appropriate for the owner of a hardware store.

Annie and I exited my car, straightened our clothes, smoothed our hair, took deep breaths, and walked up a wide, smoothly paved driveway. The flowering bushes seemed too bright, the morning too sunny, for what I expected the mood in the house would be.

We were within a few feet of ringing the bell when the nicely finished door opened.

Laurie Patterson apparently had nothing better to do this morning but look out her foyer window. She managed to fall on both of us together, tearfully, breathlessly.

At least she was making our job easier.

We didn't have to do much more than whisper "Sorry, sorry" into her sagging shoulders.

IN A FEW MINUTES A RELATIVE CROWD WAS SEATED IN a large area that began as a tiled foyer, became a simply furnished dining room, and ended as a living room that overlooked a lovely patio. The stairway and banister off the foyer were of light wood and promised only the most comfortable of bedrooms upstairs.

Annie and I found ourselves on one beige couch, across from Laurie and Spencer on another, matching one, with Milo on a separate easy chair. I was glad Annie and I had discussed our wardrobes last night and decided on dignified business casual, with neat shells and our nicest jackets this side of dressy wedding outfits. Gold and green for Annie; complementing shades of burgundy for me. We both remembered Laurie as the kind of mother who never appeared in a housedress or an apron but always looked like she was ready for important company.

Milo, on the other hand, wore a black sleeveless T-shirt with a distinctly Goth vampire look, ruffled collar and all, though it was printed on.

Laurie looked slightly haggard, but I could tell she'd tried, with a neat, light gray pantsuit and her hair pulled back in a loose bun.

I had the greatest admiration for Laurie, who tried to make it as easy as possible for her guests, beginning with not forcing us to ring a doorbell and explain our presence at her home at a time of trauma and sadness. She introduced us to her husband and grandson, then asked us if we'd like a hot or a cold drink. We addressed our preferences to a quiet young woman who could have been a relative or friend or housekeeper.

Then Laurie told us why we were there. "Our friend Trooper Graham told us to expect you," she said to Annie and me, as if she were honored to have us. If this was how she greeted guests at a time of grief, I could only imagine how she behaved when she was happy.

Cheers to Trooper, also, for paving the way.

"Trooper explained that the sooner we got some questions and answers out of the way, the better it was for solving the case, and that you were kind enough to volunteer to help him out," Spencer said, his arm around the back of the couch, enclosing his wife. His words came out softer than one might expect from such a large man, who looked capable of building an entire home by himself. Maybe he had.

All talk ceased, and an uncomfortable silence enveloped us. I shifted on my end of the couch. Who was going to speak next in this emotionally charged gathering? Fortunately, it was none of us but the young woman, carrying a tray of drinks with ice, as requested all around, and a plate of French macarons in familiar pastels.

"Let me know if you need anything else at all," she said, and slipped away.

Spencer handed Laurie her lemonade. She took a sip, held her hand up to pass on the cookies, and cleared her throat. Spencer took the glass from her and placed it on the table. He appeared ready to pick it up again when she needed it. I couldn't imagine the stress the last few days had brought to the family.

"I'll never forgive myself," Laurie began haltingly. "We weren't that busy at the booth. It never is in the evening hours when most families have gone home—the young people aren't interested in produce. So around eight thirty I thought I'd take a little walk around the fairgrounds and catch up with some of the growers I hadn't seen in a while. And I guess that's when that man went at Kelly. If I'd stayed where I should have been—"

"Who knows what would have happened, Laurie?" Spencer asked, probably not for the first time since Friday night. "You could have been hurt. Or, worse, if he wanted to get to Kelly and you were in the way, and you both would have—"

Laurie shook her head. "And then I left before ten, before Kelly loaded her truck." She threw up her hands as if to chide herself all over again for leaving KC to close up alone.

"Did she pack everything away completely every night?" Annie asked. It seemed a strange question until I realized where she was headed.

"No, just the cash and the few things that need to be refrigerated overnight."

"So it wasn't a big job. It couldn't have taken her very long."

Laurie shook her head, catching Annie's meaning.

*Nice going, Annie. Take a little of the burden from Lau-*

*rie.* She hadn't left her daughter with very much to do before heading back home.

My turn. "Not that we're experts, Laurie, but we have some experience in this, and when someone is out to"—I paused, swallowed—"commit a crime, they'll find a way. Nothing you did or did not do would have made a difference in the long run."

Spencer nodded in agreement, probably grateful to have someone reiterate what he'd been telling his wife.

"Are you saying someone was looking to kill my mom?" The first words from Milo since "Hi" when we arrived, and I wasn't even sure he'd said that, since he'd mumbled his so-called greeting when we were introduced. He'd been sitting back with one leg across the other. Now he leaned forward, elbows on his knees. It was hard to read his face with his head down low. I hadn't seen him since he was in grade school, and now he was about to turn eighteen—or already had, for all I knew. He was a tall, thin young man, without his adoptive mother.

"I wish we knew, Milo," I said.

"That's what we're looking into," Annie said. "Any help you can give us. Any ideas you have, we'd welcome."

"For example, was Kelly seeing anyone right now?" I asked. Such a personal question. How did the cops do this all the time? Poor Trooper. The worst possible moment for a family to be talking about a private matter, with all that question implied.

"Yeah. A jerk," Milo said. "She was seeing a jerk."

Laurie and Spencer gave him sharp looks.

At the same time, the doorbell rang. I gathered from Laurie's and Spencer's startled expressions that this time, a visitor was *not* expected. Milo, on the other hand, jumped up.

"That's Shark. I have to go."

"Milo—" Laurie said.

But he was already halfway to the door.

I caught a glimpse of the man our server had opened the door to. He was much huskier than Milo, perhaps a little older, and he was also wearing a sleeveless black T-shirt. He'd chosen the same shaved-head style as Chris. Milo intercepted him before he got very far into the foyer, but I caught a glimpse of him as he waved, seemingly to Laurie and Spencer.

The two young men left the house. There were no introductions.

"Milo's still in shock," Laurie said, excusing a boy who had every right to be cut some slack.

"'Shark' is what they call Milo's friend Judd Waters," Spencer said. "Because of his last name. Plus he's won some swimming tournaments in Southern California, where he grew up. He's a nice young man."

Laurie put her hand on Spencer's thigh. "But he was born here, I think, dear, then his family moved to Santa Monica when he was just starting school. Not that it matters, I guess," Laurie said. "Kelly didn't especially like him. She tried several times to get Milo to stop hanging around with him."

"She found out he has a juvie record," Spencer said. "But a lot of teens, especially boys, I think, make mistakes and then turn out fine. That's why they seal those records."

"He's very polite," Laurie said, putting the final seal on Milo's friend.

"I think we were talking about the man KC was seeing?" Annie said.

I was pleasantly surprised that Annie was staying on track, which I'd seldom seen her do. She even passed on the cookies, which might have shifted her focus.

"Milo doesn't like him. Tony's my accountant at the store, though I'm not sure for how much longer. There's a chance that Tony—" Spencer began.

"It's hard for Milo to adjust," Laurie said. Much to my

dismay, Laurie interrupted what might have turned into a bit of useful information. "He's had Kelly to himself all these years. Milo was only a toddler and never really knew any parent other than Kelly. She held on to him and cared for him, even when there was so much to work through after the crash. She took over the child, the farm, the lawsuit, everything. I was a wreck and no help at all for a long time, I'm afraid." Her husband took her hand and stroked it, and Laurie continued. "And now there's Tony, another man in Kelly's life. Was, I mean." She ended in a deep breath.

"Tony was a poor choice in more ways than one. He—" Spencer started again, but Laurie pulled herself together to interrupt again.

"But, you know, Kelly has been there for Milo," Laurie said. I hoped eventually we'd know what Spencer was trying to say. "He's eighteen now. Just yesterday, in fact. An adult. She deserves—" Laurie choked up, seeming to realize that Kelly was no longer around to deserve anything.

So far, except for Spencer's aborted attempts otherwise, we were hearing about normal family dynamics, where the parent, KC, didn't like the guy her child was friends with, and the child, Milo, didn't like his mother's boyfriend. If those were motives for murder, I doubted there'd be an intact family on the planet.

We heard a phone in the distance. The young woman who'd delivered our drinks and opened the door to Shark appeared and whispered in Laurie's ear.

"It's the funeral home," Laurie said softly. "Will you excuse me?"

Annie and I both stood. "Of course," I said. "We're grateful for your time."

But I wasn't finished. Not nearly. My ears had perked up when I heard the offhand remark from Laurie in connection with the plane crash that killed her other daughter. Maybe because of the one misguided year I'd spent in law school, the word "lawsuit" always got my attention. I made a note to come back to that.

Spencer stood also, his gaze following his wife. "I think she needs to rest, if you don't mind."

We followed Spencer, walking toward the door. "We would love to talk to Milo sometime," Annie said. "Do you have any idea where he might be going, or when we could catch him later?"

"If it was an ordinary day, he'd be at the store," Spencer said. "But not today. He's off somewhere with Judd." *The "bad news" guy,* I said to myself. Spencer continued, "We'll tell Milo you want to talk to him."

"Is he staying here now?" Annie asked.

"Yes. At least, he's sleeping here. He goes back and forth to his house a lot," Spencer said. "Or maybe to Judd's."

"And what about your employee? Tony? You were about to tell us something?"

"It was nothing," he said, edging us all closer and closer to the door.

I didn't want to leave before learning about Tony and asking about the property dispute over the neighboring farms, but even Spencer was sounding more and more tired by the minute, and I knew he'd want to go and be with his wife.

I reminded myself that Trooper was following up with town management on the land issue. We'd have to get the family's take on it another day.

By the time we got to my car, I was ready to fall onto the seat, wishing more than ever that I didn't have to drive, but I knew Annie hated driving my Outback, claiming it did too much automatically that she wanted control over. When pressed for specifics, the only one she ever gave me was that the lights came on by themselves at dusk, whether she wanted them to or not.

We were back on the road, with Willie Nelson on the radio, bringing on another smile for driver and passenger.

"There's that strip mall," Annie said. "And there's an ice-cream shop in it. What do you say?"

I hit the brakes and turned in.

# TWELVE

THERE WAS NOTHING LIKE A CHOCOLATE MALT TO RE-
vive a woman's spirits. Annie and I considered sharing one,
since we were told that, yes, each order came with the tall
mixer container, too much for one standard shake glass. I
was the first to admit that I could drink a whole one—that
is, the full thirty ounces. After all, I'd let a plate of cookies
go to waste in front of me at the Pattersons'.

"Me, too," Annie said. "I'll have my own full one." The
implication in her tone was that it had better be really full.

In minutes, a young woman in a pink top that looked
like hospital scrubs served each of us a tall glass of shake
plus the extra ounces that were being kept chilled in the
stainless steel.

The little shop was all pink—tabletops, seat cushions,
menus, and uniforms—and surprisingly busy for a week-
day afternoon. But it was summer, after all, and only so
many people could be lured more than eighty miles south
to a fair in the hot outdoors. We took off our green and
burgundy jackets, respectively, and hung them over our
chairs, thus ruining the strawberry decor.

Working on the shakes kept us and our straws busy for a while before we launched into a debriefing of our visit with the Pattersons and Milo Carson.

"First, we need to tell Trooper about Judd's juvie record," I said, taking a much-needed break from my drink.

"I know. I caught that, too. Call him now," Annie said, excited.

"Good idea."

In a quick, ungrammatical text, I explained to Trooper that any fingerprints in the Jessups' car might belong to a Judd Waters, but that his record might be sealed. I knew there was a lot working against us, from the fact that Judd might not have been the Jessups' thief at all to the possibility that Judd had not left fingerprints if he was the one who stole the car.

A lot of "mights," but Trooper was willing to give it a try, and he decided to call me instead of putting all his comments in a text. He'd been doing his best lately to keep up with modern communication modes, but he was always concerned about security, especially when names were used. I agreed with him that it was tough to figure out which method was the least susceptible to being hacked.

I answered his call and spoke in low tones, as he did, most of the time saying only "Okay" and "Uh-huh."

When we clicked off, Annie was eager for a report.

"Does he think it's possible to open a juvie record?"

I nodded. "Apparently there are exceptions to the sealed-record laws. Trooper hasn't had occasion to read up on current regs, but he thinks they can be unsealed temporarily for traffic violations, like driving under the influence or driving with an expired or suspended license. It depends on the state or states where it all happened."

We both thought it made sense to consider "driving someone else's car without their permission" a traffic violation in any state, but neither of us was a lawyer, as we both acknowledged.

"About the alleged property dispute," I said. "Trooper's downloading pages and he'll send them to us."

"We're doing pretty well, don't you think? On all these leads we're following."

"I do."

"If the Jessups' car is connected to Milo's friend, that's something, isn't it?"

"I think so, yes."

I'd been trying to determine how to compliment Annie on her handling of the interview with Laurie and Spencer without sounding condescending. I decided we'd known each other long enough not to be stressed over potential hurt feelings.

"I think it went smoothly today, thanks to your keeping us on track."

"Really? You don't think I was too pushy?"

"Not at all." I took a sip of shake, then poured the extra into my glass. "You were just right."

"Thanks, Charlie."

The smile on Annie's face above her shiny gold sleeveless shell was enough to tell me there were no hurt feelings.

We had more to talk about. Whether Chris had found the teens who worked with KC. If Chris had cell phone photos revealing anything that would help identify who had assaulted KC. Our guesses as to where Milo might live now that KC was gone. What would turn up concerning Milo's friend Shark. What about Tony, Spencer's employee at the hardware store and KC's dating partner? And a complete review of our interview with Laurie and Spencer.

When the check came, I reached for it, since it was my turn to pay. Annie stopped me, however.

"I'll get this. I need to ask you something."

"You can ask me something without picking up the tab when it's my turn. Besides, we've been asking each other questions and guessing at answers since we got here."

"This is nothing to do with the case."

"Okay. But since when do we only talk about a case?"

We'd both lowered our voices, though we were sitting apart from the bulk of the patrons, and besides, I couldn't imagine that the rest of the ice-cream crowd would have found our conversation interesting. In fact, most of them seemed too young to care about us at all.

I quickly ran through possible topics Annie might want to bring up. Her excitement about knitting after visiting the crafts at the fair? Getting another cat as a companion to Yulie? Remodeling at the inn? None of these would merit a heavy introduction, or her paying out of turn for our ice cream.

"It's about you and Chris." She blurted this out. More exactly, the words seem to explode from her lips before she was ready to say them.

I took a large gulp of shake. "I'm not sure what you mean."

But, of course, within the next two seconds, I knew what she meant. Were Chris and I an item behind her back, so to speak? Going on dates without being up front about it? More specifically, did I want to go on dates with Chris?

I also knew why she was asking. Once I finished my chocolate gulp, I wiped my lips, carefully and slowly, stalling. My eyes landed on a poster behind the cash register, a large photo of a hot fudge sundae—an image that ordinarily would have brought a smile to my face. But now it was an uncomfortable sight, both because I was full and because I was sure this next topic was not going to end well in the long run.

It had become very clear what Annie was driving at: she was interested in Chris herself.

Annie waited patiently, in one of those moments we often made fun of, where she knew that I knew that she knew.

"There's no 'me and Chris,' if that's what you mean," I said finally, the truth as far as I knew it, though I hadn't made up my mind, or my heart, yet.

"Because, if there was . . ." she said, shaking her head.

Annie was back to Annie-ese, using broken sentences, usually eliminating nouns and ending before the verb. A sure sign of heavy emotional involvement.

She continued. ". . . I wouldn't, you know."

The rest of our conversation was full of code like this. If anyone was eavesdropping, they'd have thought we were spies. Or crazy.

My first option for a response was *Keep your hands off. I'm close to seriously dating him.* But recent experience did not support that, nor would I have done such a thing to my best friend.

"You should go for it," I said.

"I might, then, but I wouldn't if you . . ."

"Signs? Signals? Anything like that?"

"Nothing yet," she said. "Except."

We turned at the sound of a commotion behind us. A troop of children entered, girls and boys dressed in bright blue T-shirts with white stripes along the sides. Loose, non-uniform shorts of many different colors completed the look. Leading the team was a friend of ours, Daisy Morton, who taught grade school in town.

She recovered her balance after a youngster taller than she was bumped into her.

"Hi, Charlie. Hi, Annie," she said. She pointed to her charges. "Summer soccer camp is over."

A chorus of "We won, we won" broke out, and Daisy whispered to us behind her hand, "All the teams win, but don't tell anybody." We knew that, but laughed anyway.

Daisy directed a wave of children to a large circular booth in the corner. The shop would never be the same as the sounds of six or eight pairs of shoes knocking against the booth and screams for double scoops of bubble gum ice cream took over.

It was just as well, because Annie and I had talked out the

Annie-Chris topic, and this new sports arena atmosphere was a convenient excuse to pick up our jackets and leave.

ONCE WE WERE OUTSIDE THE ICE-CREAM SHOP, THE world seemed quiet again, and very warm. Annie had the same idea I had as she pointed surreptitiously to Spencer's Hardware Store a few doors down. There was a lot of stock out on the sidewalk, so we knew it was open.

"Shall we?" I asked, as we dropped our jackets into my car and headed for the hardware store.

"What shall we do?" Annie asked. "Pretend to be shopping?"

"The Bear Claw can always use some new kitchenware," I said.

Like every hardware store I've known, Spencer's inventory was legion. On the sidewalk out front were ladders and trash containers on one side and buckets with slats of wood of various sizes on the other. Rakes, brooms, and mops each had their own containers. The signs in the window and above the door promised PLUMBING, ELECTRICITY, PAINTS, LOCKSMITH, KITCHEN, AIR-CONDITIONING, JANITOR SUPPLIES, and REPAIR SERVICES.

The fonts were a mixed bag, but they got the point across: everything you need for your business, home, and garden was available here.

The narrow storefront had been misleading. Inside was a very long shop with two aisles and floor-to-ceiling goods. Annie and I were focused more on the name tags of the sales associates in bright red vests than on the cans of paint, some dustier than others, and the dozens of different-size wrenches, screwdrivers, nuts, and bolts.

There had been a rash of graffiti vandalism lately, and I figured that was the reason spray paint cans were under lock and key. Other items that could be picked off the shelf readily were also locked in a cabinet. The plethora of security cameras and mirrors, both for sale and mounted around Spencer's Hardware Store, were, I supposed, a sign of increased awareness.

At times like this I was glad the Bear Claw had only a small number of items that could be whisked away by a customer. I'd followed the guidelines of restaurant magazines that advised using very tiny salt and pepper shakers, for example, so we wouldn't be losing a lot of product if items were taken, or very large containers that couldn't be easily slid into a pocket or purse.

We walked past a young RILEY, an older VICKY, and a middle-aged FRANK, smiled at all of them and declined assistance, and then found ourselves near the back, where reels of cable lined the wall.

"No Tony," Annie whispered, patting her own label-less chest.

I stopped at a section with small furniture items and picked up a wooden magazine rack. "I can use this in my family room, next to my rocker," I said.

"Benny won't like it," Annie said. In response to my questioning look, she reminded me, "Doesn't he like to walk around on newspapers and magazines the way Yulie does, and hear the crinkle? He's not going to be happy if they're all neat in that holder."

"Good point. And he might hurt himself trying to knock it over." I put the rack down and picked up a smaller desktop-size organizing system. "I can use this for the diner, though. The mail and paperwork often end up on the floor, and there's no Benny there to enjoy them."

We returned to the front, walking down the only other aisle in the shop, equally crowded with merchandise. Still no one named Tony.

On the way to the cash register, Annie had picked up some flowered contact paper for relining the drawers in the inn's guest rooms and a package of chamois cloths for all-purpose cleaning. She wiggled the package.

"I thought this was a hardware store," she said, laughing, emphasizing the "hard" part of the word. "This feels more like software."

Annie was in a very good mood. I suspected it was in no small measure because she'd gotten her big question off her chest in the ice-cream shop. And it had cost her only the price of a couple of shakes. I, on the other hand, still hadn't quite let go of this new development and was left feeling a little foolish, having assumed it was only up to me and Chris to resolve whatever was between us. Or not.

The thought also crossed my mind that, given Annie's history, the infatuation with Chris wouldn't last very long. The next charming, good-looking guest to sign in to Annie's Inn might easily turn her head.

Still, it was nice to do something normal, like browse in a shop. So what if it didn't involve clothes and shoes. It was handy that we could claim to be real customers.

It was, after all, about the investigation. Time to decide whether we'd ask about Tony. With no help from a name tag or a photo, we needed assistance to identify KC's most recent boyfriend, the jerk, according to teenaged Milo.

Annie was on a roll today, definitely even more so now that she'd gotten the green light to flirt with Chris, if that's what she was planning. I let her take the lead with Riley, who'd appeared at the old-fashioned cash register to check us out. In my time in San Francisco, I'd become used to larger stores where clerks wandered the aisles with devices that let you pay on the spot, or point of service, as they called it in the trade magazines I read. Lucky for me, the Bear Claw was small enough that every transaction was point of service.

"Hi," Annie said, lifting her selections to the counter, which was lined with worn-out linoleum, as if it had been ripped from someone's old kitchen floor. "Is Tony around today?"

"No, he's out. Probably won't be back this week. Something I can help you with?" Riley asked.

"In fact—" Annie began.

This time I cut her off, putting my organizer close to her items. "Oh, look. He's Employee of the Week," I said, and pointed to a sheet on a bulletin board behind Riley. The printout showed a poor-quality photocopy of a man with a shirt and tie, reminding me of the headshots in our yearbooks, except with more facial hair. Under the photo were his full name—Tony Bellamy—and the words about his status this week.

Riley turned, her long ponytail swinging, and grimaced. "Oops. I was supposed to take that to the back room, our break room, but I haven't got to it yet."

"But isn't that an honor?" I asked.

Riley shrugged and handed me a slip of paper with my total. "To tell you the truth, this week it's because Tony had something sad happen to him, so we were making up cards and stuff to send him and we thought it would be nice to make him Employee of the Week, too. But things are— never mind. It's not supposed to be public anyway."

A reminder of a murder wasn't good for sales, I imagined.

"That's too bad," Annie said. "Can you tell us—"

Riley leaned in slightly and lowered her voice. "Really, I shouldn't have said anything. It's a private matter. Sorry."

"No problem," I said.

"Do you need bags?" she asked us.

"No—" I paused. "On second thought, yes, we would like bags. Separate ones, thanks," I told Riley, and managed to knock my desk organizer a couple of feet down the counter.

Riley leaned over to retrieve the organizer and then down to get the bags for us.

Like a pro, I whipped out my phone and caught an image of the Employee of the Week notice. Not as slick as "Bond, James Bond," but it was the best I could do. It was entirely possible the photo would be unusable or unneeded, or both, but it was worth the exercise.

If Riley heard or noticed my maneuver, she didn't say. But she did seem to be happy to be finished with us.

"Have a nice day," she said. She yanked the page off the bulletin board, stuffed it under the counter, and waved the next customer to the register.

"You, too," I said.

To her credit, Annie kept silent and walked out with me.

W HAT'S UP?" ANNIE ASKED WHEN WE WERE OUTSIDE.

"I didn't want to call attention to ourselves if Riley wasn't supposed to be talking about Tony and his"—I drew quotes in the air—"'sad' moment. Plus, I didn't want Spencer, Riley's boss, hearing we came down here looking for Tony right after we questioned him and Laurie in their home."

"We didn't come right here. We stopped for ice cream."

I took a breath. What might have passed for exasperation. "Really, Annie?"

When we reached my vehicle, she stood by the passenger door until I snapped the unlock button. "I guess I'll never get it right," she said sadly, climbing in.

I had a feeling she meant life in general.

I T WAS ABOUT TWO THIRTY BY THE TIME WE AP-proached our neighborhood. Annie suggested we stop at my house and enjoy a session of looking through Elkview's yearbooks, a pursuit I'd started last night.

"We might even get a clue about who wanted KC dead," she said. "We could take notes on who she hung out with, maybe, or who she competed with."

"Some other time," I said. "I think I've had enough activity for one day. I'm getting one of my classic headaches."

I smiled to take the edge off the refusal, but I could tell she was hurt.

I drove past my house and dropped her off at her inn. It was bright daylight—no telltale house or cabin lights—so it wasn't possible to determine how densely populated with guests the inn property was, but I was sure Annie would be busy enough to keep boredom at bay. And for all I knew, Chris might be waiting to take her to a movie.

Now I really was getting a headache.

# THIRTEEN

I PULLED INTO MY DRIVEWAY, HOPING BENNY WOULD be waiting at the front door when I opened it. I'd even given my accelerator pedal an extra tap, adding to the probability that he'd hear me arrive.

But I didn't see Benny until I entered my family room. My cat was resting in a most unlikely position, stretched out in an empty cardboard box in a corner. To me, he looked uncomfortable. The box was too small for a real stretch and he ended up with his tail hanging over one corner and his neck resting on the diagonally opposite corner. He looked up at me lazily, and I knew I had to be the grown-up and make sure he got some exercise.

I put my load of tote, purse, and Spencer's Hardware goods on the dining room table and located his feather wand. I'd recently bought a set of replacement toys for the tip, and I fastened a multicolor array of new feathers on it now. I coaxed Benny out of the box and down the hall to his tower in the guest bedroom and ran the new feather up and down his tower and back and forth across the floor.

"Keep them jumping, running, exercising," the ad for

the new feathers had read, and that's what I did while lying across the bed myself.

I looked through today's mail with my free hand and found the modern Portland diner postcard my mom had told me about. The photo on the oversize card was a long view, taken from one end of the room. What made it modern? First, there was no red vinyl anywhere. The floor was of a shiny brown wood, the same color as the seats of the stools. The booths and counter trim were a dull blue. The lights were globes that hung from the ceiling in what looked like wire baskets. Most stunning was the ultralong, sleek counter, with electrical outlets every few feet, but without a trace of food or drink. No cake pedestals, pie racks, condiments, drinking straw holders, or turned-over thick white mugs. It was possible that this photo was staged, but even so, an empty place of business wasn't my idea of good advertising.

If I wondered what the menu was like, I had my answer in my mom's review on the other side of the card.

*Not what I would call diner food! More international. French, etc. Sous vide, that kind of thing. Love, Mom & Dad*

Not only that, in a very small font, I read a recipe for transparent ravioli, made with edible film.

I could only hope Mom hadn't sent the same card to Victor. Just in case, I planned to check out the equipment involved in cooking under a vacuum and all the other molecular gastronomy techniques. I knew the tools were pricey, and I needed to be ready if Victor wanted to get even more creative than usual.

I appreciated Victor's passion for his work, augmented by his sister's, but I had to concern myself not only with our bottom line but with the preferences of our regular patrons. Many of our customers were truckers, driving major semis filled with goods up and down the George Parks Highway. We knew the men and one woman by first name and trucker handle, by color of cab, and by menu choice. Burgers or meatloaf with ketchup, sides of fries and slaw. I couldn't think of one who would welcome a deconstructed Nicoise salad with horseradish foam and a quail egg.

I noticed Benny had disappeared while I was musing about the Bear Claw, the biggest part of my life next to the current murder investigation. My cat had become tired of chasing the feathers, apparently, or bored with the unimaginative way I had been waving them around. I needed to add a bell or a rubber fish next time. He'd retreated to his tower cubby and gone to sleep. I trotted around changing the towels and blankets in Benny's various beds, careful not to disturb him.

Ordinarily, I'd call Chris to see how he'd made out tracking down the teens at the fair, but this evening I didn't dare, lest I catch him on a date with Annie.

Funny, I'd never worried or thought about that before. What made me think he'd gone dateless all this time? His dating life had never come up—until this afternoon over ice cream.

It almost came up again when Chris called me while I was pondering the state of his love life.

"Remember Roland Hortenson?" he asked.

"Sure. A local farmer. I ran into him at the fair."

"Guess where his farm is located?"

I wouldn't have had the slightest clue if it weren't that one of the agenda items was "property lines."

I'd taken a seat in the family room, where I'd collected one more of Benny's soft napping cloths for the laundry. At his question, I sat bolt upright. "Could it be," I asked Chris, "right next to KC's?"

"You got it." Chris was excited, as I was, that we had another piece of information to add to our good lead, the dispute over farmland. "I was talking to Trooper about the conference he's been commuting to this week. Wally is determined to get every single local event into the *Bugle*, even if someone just runs his tractor into his fence. That's my boss."

I recognized that Chris wanted me to know he hadn't been talking to Trooper out of turn about the case that was "ours." It was too bad that there had been some competition at times among the team, all of whom wanted to be in on whatever was happening. It had straightened itself out, and I hoped this new wrinkle of Annie J likes Chris D, as we would have said on Valentine's Day in fifth grade, wouldn't ruin that peace. I decided that for sure I was not going to be the one responsible for such a setback.

"But never mind that," Chris added. "What's important to our case is what Trooper found at the Recorder's Office—that Hortenson's farm abuts KC's. The file apparently had overlapping records that included deeds, liens, and the usual documents, but also a last will and testament of Hortenson's grandfather."

"And the grandfather's will conflicts with the official record KC's family would otherwise be going by?"

"Of course." Chris grunted. "Trooper will give us more details at dinner. We are having a diner dinner, right? There's a tongue twister."

Chris was in his enthusiastic journalist mode, eager to talk about a story.

"I'm guessing all this goes to the lawyers now to straighten out," I said.

"Yeah, but if one of the parties is now deceased, there's a whole different angle to the case."

"There sure is."

"I was thinking it would be nice to see what it all looks like in person. Have you ever been to KC's farm?"

"I haven't." I had to admit I'd accepted KC's produce by the week, but had never visited where it was grown.

"Feel like taking a ride?" he asked.

"Doesn't Trooper have all the documents?"

A stall if there ever was one. Before this afternoon, I wouldn't have questioned this trip for a minute, allowing no possibility that it was a date, or even a pseudo-date, on a mission for Trooper. But now that this newly formed, if loose, triangle of Annie-Chris-Charlie had been created, all bets were off.

"I like to put some dirt between the paper and my brain, if you know what I mean," Chris said.

I laughed. "Barely. But I'm in."

"I'll be there in fifteen."

"Make it twenty," I said, adding five to give myself a chance to change from formal house-call clothes to farm clothes, just in case Chris really meant to dig in the dirt.

*What about Annie?* rang through my head. Again, before, I wouldn't have given a second thought to whether or not she should know about this trip or be included in it. The trek was clearly connected to the investigation, not a date. How many times had Trooper's pseudo-deputies gone off in ones or twos without a problem? We simply all reported back in a timely fashion.

*And that's what I'll have to do this evening,* I told myself.

But it didn't feel right.

I CHECKED ON BENNY AND FOUND HIM SOUND ASLEEP. There was no chance that he'd miss me, especially since I'd added a bowl of his favorite tuna treat next to his normal meal.

I made sure I had a copy of the investigation's agenda with me, and of course threw some elk jerky, cheese sticks, chocolate marshmallow candies, and peanut butter crackers into my tote.

Food, especially snacks, was always on my trip list,

whether it was a half-hour errand or a couple of hours on the road. This pattern had been a source of discussion between Annie and me since our school days. Periodically, she claimed she could gain weight if she ate desserts over one weekend while I could eat three huge meals and snack all day and still be skinny. I knew she didn't mean it as an insult.

"You're like skin and bones," she'd said often, followed by, "and look at me."

What could I say?

Chris pulled up on time. I tossed him my keys as usual, and we took off north to the Carson farm. I knew, or assumed, the property had belonged to Kelly's family at least since we were in high school, but we were all about to find out what the law decided.

Chris was in work clothes, too. We were both in jeans and plaid shirts, like some upscale sporting goods ad, or maybe a reenactment of *American Gothic*. I couldn't help envying his shaved head while I struggled to keep my long hair off my neck in this too-summery weather. I did realize how fortunate I was to be living in Alaska, where "hot" could mean the rare eighty-degree day and not the closing in on one hundred degrees that my friends in the Los Angeles area complained about.

We made a gesture toward small talk—a quick summary of our days in the trenches of a murder investigation. We'd go into more detail tonight at the Bear Claw.

For now, I took the folder Chris handed me on the property that was at the center of a lawsuit. The top sheet was an aerial view of a piece of land bordered on the east by a road service area and on the west by more farmland. The area was divided into three sections and marked up according to owners' parcels. The plot was divided into three sections of twenty-three acres, nineteen acres, and fifteen acres.

Chris had figured out from the other documents in the folder the simplest way to describe the disagreement between the owners.

"The western section was owned by the Carsons, KC's family, as you'll see from other documents, going back to her grandfather. The eastern parcel is owned by Hortenson, a newer owner. Then there's that strip across the top in the photo, the one with the greenhouse on it. That fifteen-acre piece is what's in dispute."

"It's a great graphic," I said.

"It's definitely a good start for discussion later."

"I can't wait to see the actual property. I never have, even though I buy from both vendors for the diner. I don't usually deal with Hortenson until late in the fall, November and December, when I get potatoes and turnips from him. Although sometimes he comes around with excellent raspberries and rhubarb."

"So you just buy the produce. You don't watch it grow?"

I checked to see if Chris was serious. With great relief, I saw he was not. "I purchase it and I pay my staff to cook it. Isn't that enough?"

Chris nodded, and we both laughed.

WHEN WE ARRIVED AT THE PROPERTY THROUGH A county road, it wasn't as easy as we had expected to simply pull up and park near it. The signs were clear: we'd better not trespass.

Chris finally found a short road that led to a set of outbuildings, none of which looked like a residence. The largest could have been a hangar, a distinct possibility since the road was smooth and it was common for Alaskans on significant pieces of property to keep their own small planes. I thought I'd never look at a small plane or runway again without thinking of KC's mom and her face when she had mentioned the crash that took her older daughter.

The place where we'd parked seemed deserted at the moment. Several trailers or RVs were scattered around the main structure, but although there were farms adjacent, I saw no people or farming equipment.

Chris kept the motor running. "In case we need to bolt out of here fast," he said with a grin.

"Too bad there aren't notations on the ground like the ones on this diagram," I said, trying to identify fences, at least.

"Wouldn't that be nice. Oversized markers showing property lines."

I laughed. "Throw in numbers with the acreage noted. And, by the way, also write in which crops are growing where." I pointed to a section that held large blooming bright green flowers. "That's cabbage. The only one I can identify."

Chris chose to point in a different direction and took a guess. "Turnips? The leaves are all crowded together. I think I saw a photo of that once in the Gertie the Gardener column in the *Bugle*."

"Maybe turnips. Darned if I know. Carrots? Beets? Don't they all look alike before you pull them from the ground? Who writes that column, anyway?"

"I think it's Wally himself, but he won't admit it."

Neither of us was well-versed enough to figure out crop lines, let alone property lines. The greenhouse was too small and far from where we'd parked to be able to discern its use.

"We should have hired a farmhand to accompany us." Chris turned to look at me. "I'm sorry I brought you out here for nothing."

"It's not your fault that it was a bust," I said.

Seeming to come out of nowhere, a tractor was headed our way on the runway. I wasn't sure how fast they could travel, but didn't want to find out.

"Time to go," I said, and Chris threw the car into reverse. "Maybe the trip's not entirely a bust," he said. "Not if we stop for coffee on the way back. What do you say?"

"I say yes."

But not without a gulp and a slight twinge in the vicinity of my heart.

CHRIS HEADED NORTHEAST, A SURPRISE, SINCE WE were already at the northern end of Elkview when we were at KC's farm and points east were off the beaten track of the main highway.

"I know this little place," he said. "Just coffee and snacks, maybe a bear claw."

He turned to me, his expression expecting a laugh, I thought. "Get it? 'Bear' is trucker language for the police."

All I could manage was a smile. I pointed to the clock in my car. Four thirty. I was about to remind him that we were due back at the real Bear Claw at seven to meet Annie and Trooper, but Chris was ahead of me.

"Don't worry. We'll be back by morning."

I had the good sense to study his face before reacting. "Okay, then," I said, and put my feet up on the dashboard.

"That's the spirit." He gave me a look, amused and sympathetic at the same time. "Charlie, I'm not trying to make light of this. I know Kelly—KC—was a friend of yours. And I know her murder feels personal to you. But we'll have a better chance of solving this if we're focused but also as normal as possible, if that makes sense."

I straightened up, feet on the floor, and took a deep breath. "It does, and I know it. No one does her best work all tensed up."

I turned my head to enjoy the scenery, a lush green all the way, with not much traffic. Only once did we have to stop for a moose crossing, a mother and her calf.

I looked over at Chris, wondering what he was thinking about, other than not colliding with the great animal. It occurred to me that Chris and I might have spent more time together in my SUV than out of it. In the course of our duties as pseudo-deputies for Trooper, we'd made trips to the Anchorage airport, as well as back and forth to many of the dry cabins in the Mat-Su Borough. We'd eaten together along the way, but always during a mission, with a criminal investigation driving our timeline and our conversation.

I wondered if that would ever change, or to what extent I wanted it to.

My thoughts turned to KC. I hoped she'd found time to enjoy her surroundings. It couldn't have been easy to run a thirty-eight-plus-acre farm while raising a little boy through the teen years and to young manhood as a single parent. I wondered about Tony the hardware store accountant—whether he was a new guy, whether he'd been a help to her. I'd taken a brief look at the photo I shot of his Employee of the Week poster. It probably wouldn't hold up in a court of law, but it was serviceable if we needed it.

Most important, I wanted the mystery of KC's murder to be solved. Her family deserved that much.

And I was determined to help see that they got it.

Even before the promised shot of coffee I looked forward to, I felt a new spurt of energy.

# Fourteen

THE "LITTLE PLACE," AS CHRIS CALLED IT, WAS A FEW miles and one bridge past Talkeetna, and not as charming as he'd made it out to be from his promise of good coffee. But with a gas station out front, the place seemed to be a haven for truckers. The parking lot was lined with tankers, large delivery trucks, and serious RVs, the kind that had cozy sleeping accommodations at the back.

We entered the half-stone, half-wood structure, which resembled the myriad of lodges, rental cabins, and rest stops Chris and I had seen on all our trips. This building, however, had a lobby filled with the greatest number of vending machines I'd ever seen in one place.

On the healthy side, there were machines that held sliced apples, celery sticks, cherry tomatoes, and several flavors of yogurt, as well as cups of what might have been fresh melon and pineapple chunks. The machines with the most users were the ones that gave up bags of candy, popcorn, and a dozen varieties of chips. I was tempted to try the cappuccino chips, but Chris directed my attention to a door almost hidden among the food dispensers.

Here was another variation on this rest stop. A sign said we were about to set foot into The Black Eye Café.

"By the way, 'black eye' means you have a headlight out," Chris said.

"Good to know."

The so-called café comprised a long display case, a short counter for customer service, and several tables. Not your usual café, for more reasons than one. The first clue should have been the pretzel-shaped brass door handle.

"Pretzels," Chris said as he led me to a case with almost as many varieties of pretzels as there were of vending machine choices in the lobby. "You're going to think you're in Times Square." I shrugged, giving him pause. "You've never been to New York?"

I shook my head, slightly embarrassed by my pathetic travel history. Up and down the West Coast of the US was about it for me, other than a weekend in Hawaii for a good friend's destination wedding. I had a bridesmaid's dress at the back of my closet as a souvenir of that trip, along with a book of matches on which was printed "Wendy and Robert Forever." I wondered if their vows were as intact as my poufy teal dress.

Instead of criticizing my ignorance of Times Square, Chris bailed me out.

"I was stationed for a while at Fort Hamilton in Brooklyn. It was a relatively easy trip into Manhattan. Pretzel wagons on every street corner. And much tastier snacks than anything that came from the kitchen at the base."

"I'll put it on my list."

We stood in front of the pretzel array of different sizes, shapes, and degrees of crispness, ranging from the thin, brittle kind to those that appeared soft on the inside. And something for every taste. Chocolate, cheese, sea salt, cinnamon sugar, and—was that buffalo wing?

Chris had chosen a table for us, away from the door. On the table were napkins and three jars of mustard that looked homemade, with a small sign that read TODAY'S CHOICES and labels that included ingredients. It seemed I never really left the Bear Claw, as I considered adding unique flavors to our mustard offerings. I wondered what my mom would think of adding smoked mustard seeds or horseradish and five kinds of pepper to the mix.

I accepted Chris's idea of sharing a bag of mixed pretzel nuggets. My first two were delicious, so I kept digging into the bag, and dipping into the mustards. Chris did the same. We'd both squeezed dollops of all the mustard varieties onto our plates.

It was hard to think of the Black Eye as my competition, since it didn't serve meals and the decor was minimal. (I might even call it missing.) But I could picture some of my trucker friends from the Bear Claw dropping in for a coffee to go, a few items from the vending machines, and a pretzel to top it off.

I thought of three of my favorite truck driver patrons, who traveled together a lot of the time. I wouldn't have put it past them to carry off a few bags of peanuts or pork rinds from the vending machines before heading back to the highway. And a bag of pretzels could be handy as they took to the road, especially in areas where it was a long way between cafés or diners.

The Black Eye was busy, mostly with men, but no one stayed very long. There seemed to be more people standing around chatting in the combination parking lot and gas station than inside.

"I come here for the gourmet mustard and the stories," Chris said, dipping a nugget, heavy with salt, into a mustard that contained beer and leaned decidedly toward orange in color. "A lot of these guys are long-distance truckers, and they're always talking about either what they've seen on the road or what's going on in cities they pass through. You'll hear about the police finding suspicious bone fragments when they dug up property in Guitar, meaning in Nashville, or about a hit-and-run in the Dome, which is Houston. That kind of thing."

"You have quite a wide range of interests."

"One time, this trucker told me he thought he was about to run into two kids with white socks in the middle of his lane. He pulled over and it turned out to be a dark cow with white feet."

I shivered. "Okay, I get the point. Great stories."

"I'm not saying I use all the stories, or even believe all of them, but you never know when a little gem will be in the mix."

A husky man about our age came over to our table. With his jeans and plaid shirt, he fit right in with us as far as our wardrobes, except perhaps for a ball cap that had seen better days. I could see a mud-smudged New York Yankees logo on the cap. If he was from there, he was a long way from home. Maybe he came for the reminder of Times Square.

Chris introduced him as Nick.

"Hey, how's my favorite reporter?" Nick asked, nudging Chris's shoulder.

"Any scoops for me?" Chris asked. "A parking ticket in Wasilla, maybe?"

Nick shook his head. "Pretty boring lately. There was an alligator up by Cantwell, though," Nick said, and laughed.

"An alligator is a blown tire in the road," Chris said. "Not to keep showing off my extensive knowledge of truckers' jargon or anything."

Nick looked at me. I had a feeling he was about to tell an old story to a new audience.

"You know Murphy's Law of Alibis, don't you?" he asked.

"No," I said.

"Yeah, but remind me," Chris said.

"If you tell the boss you're running late because there was a blown-out tire in the road, the next day you'll find a blown-out tire in the road."

We found this funny, Nick most of all.

After a few more bits of talk, Nick signed off by tipping his cap. "Nice to see you, pal," he said, addressing Chris, then turning to me. "But I gotta say, much as I like it here, this is a heck of a place to bring a date."

Chris cleared his throat.

A moment of truth.

I held my breath.

"I'm running low on cash," Chris said.

Nick left, laughing. A man not afraid to express his opinion.

Chris gave me a questioning look, one I didn't know what to do with.

Finally, I tapped one of the bowls on the table. "This mustard is my favorite," I said.

THE RIDE HOME WAS MORE OF THE SAME IN TERMS OF random topics related to our investigation, mostly of the form of *What about this?* and *What about that?*

"We have a lot to work through," I said.

"Trooper said he'd have more from Doc Sherman this evening. Not sure what he means."

"I hope he's not too graphic."

"We can ask him not to be. It would be nice to have some forensics for the SUV and the miscellaneous other items, also."

I surprised myself by bringing up a new subject, something that had bothered me since Annie and I had left the Pattersons' today—and not the personal subject Annie had broached in the ice-cream shop.

I gave Chris a summary of what had led up to the nagging comment. "Laurie—KC's mom, you remember—mentioned a lawsuit following the plane crash that killed four people." I paused, then listed the victims, with lingering sadness for KC: "Laurie's other daughter, Diedre; Diedre's husband; and two other people, I believe. Another couple. Would you have files at the *Bugle* that go back that far? It would be about sixteen years ago, I think, if Milo was two."

"Wow. It would sure be interesting to read about that in the light of what's happened to KC. Wally is meticulous about our archives. They're in the basement of the building— the morgue, as we call it—and pretty well organized, so it shouldn't be a problem for us."

I wondered if that would be another field trip for Chris and me, but decided not to bring it up.

After all, this "date" wasn't over.


IT WAS ONLY A LITTLE AWKWARD WHEN CHRIS AND I pulled up to the diner together in my vehicle. An accident on the George Parks on the way home—not an alligator, as the truckers would call it—upset our plans. We didn't have time to drive to my house first so Chris could claim his pickup and drive to the Bear Claw separately.

There was a cacophony of explanations during which Chris and I talked around each other, citing the highway tie-up as the reason we were one, a little late, and two, together. Trooper backed up the story about the accident, since he'd run into it also.

I caught the expression on Annie's face, a grimace, in fact, which is what I dreaded. She simply said, "Oh."

I wondered if that would be the end of it from her, but I doubted it.

Once all that was behind us, my staff was ready to provide its usual excellent service, and we settled into our usual booth at the back of the diner, far enough away from where Nina had seated the other three groups needing dinner.

I smiled as I heard Nina engage the kitchen staff in diner theatrics for the amusement of the customers, who were not locals.

"Burn three, dry," she called out, hoping someone would ask what that meant.

As usual, a child asked her.

"Put three burgers on the grill, with no condiments," she said. Since the boy was probably only eight or nine years old, she explained further, "No mayo, relish, ketchup, dressing. Nothing like that."

I felt sure the boy would find a way to use the jargon at the dinner table when he got home and in school to educate his friends.

"Who wants to start?" Trooper asked, bringing our meeting to order. He didn't offer to begin himself, since he was busy with the fried clam strips Nina had placed in the middle of our table.

"Charlie and I visited the Pattersons," Annie said. "We met Spencer, KC's stepfather, and also Milo, the nephew she raised. He was not a happy young man, which you can understand."

We all nodded.

"Did the property dispute come up?" Trooper asked.

"Only in passing, and then Laurie was called away, so we didn't find out any more about it," I said.

"Well, here's what I have." Trooper opened a folder and distributed copies of photos of the property, the same image Chris and I had used when we were physically on site, except better quality. Trooper, or Sadie, his loyal one-woman clerical staff, had spent some time enlarging the images and mounting them on thicker stock.

He used what served as a map to point out the three different sections belonging to the Carsons, the Hortensons, and the "to be determined."

Without explicitly talking about it beforehand, neither Chris nor I brought up the fact that we'd just come from the site. Not quite directly from there, I mused. There was that pleasant stop at the Black Eye, which might have been a date. Maybe trucker Nick knew better than we did whether it was or not.

It didn't seem necessary to reveal any of those details.

Trooper launched into the information he had, pointing to the strip of property that ran east to west, the ownership of which was now in dispute.

"It started when KC's grandfather, Timothy Carson, paid Joseph Quinley, the owner of the property on the east side, a leasing fee so he could expand his crop inventory. The deal went smoothly for several years until Quinley died. Apparently, the old man had no family and no formal arrangements for his assets."

"How sad," Annie said.

We all nodded and gave Annie's remembrance of Mr. Quinley a few seconds of silence before Trooper proceeded. Nina had been on her way to our table with a carafe of coffee for refills. She stopped short and turned back to the kitchen, looking confused by the quiet and solemnity that hadn't been brought on by a meal delivery. I had confidence that she'd be back soon.

Trooper cleared his throat and continued. "At some point—the exact date is somewhere in those papers; you can read them at your leisure—KC's father, Timothy Carson Junior, decided to build a greenhouse on that strip."

"He probably wanted to plant corn," Annie said. "Corn needs warmer soil, so it doesn't grow outside in Alaska. I read that once, although it didn't say, how do you take the temperature of soil?"

No one answered, but I had a question of my own, one with a different slant. "How could he build on that property if he didn't own the land? He certainly wasn't paying a leasing fee to a dead man."

"You'd think it would be that simple, wouldn't you?" Trooper noted. "It's easiest if you have property deeds or mortgage notes, deeds of trust, satisfaction of mortgage letters that are recorded. Simple in theory, but as you'll see, even though some of those have been filed, there are conflicting details."

Chris had been scribbling on his old-fashioned stenographer's pad. He tapped his pen repeatedly. "So the short version is that no one bothered to dig far enough to determine legal ownership of that strip."

Trooper nodded. "Looks like it was simple expediency. Quinley was deceased. He obviously hadn't been paying taxes or a mortgage, if he had one. Now someone—Carson, as it happened—was paying the borough, getting building permits and so on. As long as the paperwork was completed, it didn't matter who was the signatory."

"Then Hortenson appears," I said, "and all of a sudden, it matters."

"Sloppy paperwork," Chris said. No one contradicted him.

"Then Hortenson sees the original Quinley deed."

"Maybe Carson claims squatter's rights," Annie said.

"The greenhouse had been there more than seven years, so Carson could claim squatter's rights to the property. I'm not saying he did that, or that his daughter KC has done that, but she could. It's too much for me, frankly."

"And me, too," I said, remembering why I'd left law school after only a year of juggling logic as I knew it with sometimes illegal arguments.

"Maybe it was something in the attic," Annie said. "That's always where old things are discovered, and they turn it into novels."

"Or their memoirs," Chris said. It seemed he and Annie had gone off to another world together, one where stories are born.

Annie was on a roll. "Or, like, a deed was buried in the dirt in the greenhouse."

"Then, of course, Tim Junior died suddenly, and that added to the mystery of who owned what when," Chris said.

"And let's not forget that in the course of the time frame

we're talking about, Alaska went from a territory to our forty-ninth state," I noted. "There had to be a lot of changes, big and little, in laws of all kinds."

"That's another story," Trooper said. "Remember, there was even a plan to split up the state so only the so-called developed area along the highways would be admitted and the rest, three hundred thousand square miles, would still be a territory." He shook his head. "I see you've heard this before."

We nodded, and Chris made a promise. "Someday I'm going to write a feature on the partitioning project so people will know the complicated history of our state."

I was never so happy to see food arrive. Not because I was hungry, but because untangling these legal and historical issues was giving me a headache. Nevertheless, I knew it was important to keep a timeline in mind, starting with KC's grandfather and including all the milestones up to this current legal battle.

"We all agree we're going to leave the details of the property dispute to the lawyers to figure out, right?" Trooper asked.

"Except shouldn't we interview Hortenson?" I asked, even though I didn't look forward to worsening my legalities-induced headache. "He certainly had a motive to move KC out of the picture." In other words, murder her.

"My guess is his lawyers have told him not to talk to anyone about the case," Chris said. "Especially no one associated with the justice system." He pointed his fork at Trooper, then to all of us.

Everyone agreed, including me, once I thought about it. Now I was even more annoyed with myself that I hadn't talked to Hortenson when I ran into him at the fair's entrance yesterday morning. At the time, I'd had no idea that his was the property next to KC's. The one that was involved in the dispute. My questions would have been innocent and maybe more likely to produce answers.

True to form, Trooper declared a break when the food

arrived: fish chowder all around, to start with. Trooper took us back to a conversation about the big deal it was to admit a new state that wasn't connected to the others, separated by a whole other country, not to mention about eighty-five percent undeveloped, as it was called.

"Someday I'm going to go clamming in Ninilchik," Annie said.

Those who didn't know Annie would wonder how that connected to the territorial state of Alaska. Or why she chose to envision an Alaska Native village three hundred miles from where we were sitting for her fishing trip. But that was Annie for you, and the Census Designated Place might have appeared in the news, or been mentioned by a guest at Annie's Inn, or won Annie lots of points in Scrabble, now that proper nouns were allowed.

Whatever her reason, it was clear that the formal meeting, with its agenda of issues related to the murder of Kelly Carson, was now on break.

# Fifteen

After our clam strips appetizer, fish chowder, four-vegetable quiche, and fresh bread, the vote was unanimous that we take a twenty-minute walk. We'd return to touch on the rest of the agenda and set the tasks for tomorrow, and top off the evening with dessert.

Nina had promised a cherry cobbler. I wondered if the tart North Star variety of cherries was part of the last delivery from KC's farm. Although she needed product to sell at the fair, she'd never shortchange her regular customers, like me.

I cheated by walking for only six minutes and taking a seat on a bench in a small park across from the diner. The area was quiet except for the occasional jogger or barking dog, or both together.

I had my personal agenda to tend to: connect with my mom and Benny; confirm the temporary help I'd need for Wednesday, when my staff would be at the fair; and answer emails from vendors and creditors. I could also get a start on scrolling through the photos on my phone from the fair.

All in fourteen minutes. Oops, minus the six it would take to get back to the Bear Claw. Eight minutes.

It was already nine thirty in Portland, Oregon, so Mom was first. Not that I ever remembered her turning in earlier than midnight, and then it was to read her crime novels.

"They relax me," she'd say.

Now and then, I'd read a few pages at her recommendation, and didn't feel relaxed at all. I had enough stress with the crime I was involved in now, in real life. I didn't need more as I'd tried to sleep the last couple of nights.

Finally, Mom realized she hadn't raised a crime fiction reader, or hardly a fiction reader at all. However, I did like the interesting book she'd given me on the many appearances of cats in literature, going back to Shakespeare. My favorite was a quote by Mark Twain: "If man could be crossed with the cat, it would improve the man, but it would deteriorate the cat." I sensed approval from Benny the last time I read it aloud when he was nearby.

This evening, Mom didn't wait very long before asking, "Where's my cat?" She laughed at her own slipup. "I mean your cat, of course, sweetie."

"Our cat," I said, tapping the FaceTime app. Mom was wearing a Portland T-shirt that I knew she'd pass on to me once she got home. Behind her was a typical hotel room with an ugly brown paisley bedspread. "I'm still at the diner, or rather, close by in that tiny park just down the street. Benny is at home."

"I wouldn't mind seeing him." Code for "put Benny on the line, please."

I put Mom on hold and called up the Benny app, hoping he'd be in the family room in front of the camera.

"Sorry, Mom," I said, coming up empty, which seemed to be a perfect metaphor for my life lately.

"No worries, sweetheart. Did I tell you we were going to the Oregon Zoo? We walked so much, Dad is zonked out right now. You might hear the snores."

"Say hi tomorrow."

"I will. I had to travel all these miles to learn about our own elephant. Maggie the elephant was a one-year-old in the nineteen eighties when she was bought by the Alaska Zoo in Anchorage. But eventually, it was too small for her and she was flown—can you imagine?—to a wildlife sanctuary in Northern California."

"Fascinating, Mom."

"Uh-huh," she said, missing my sarcasm. "There's more to her story. I'll send you a Maggie postcard. Did you get the one with the modern diner?"

"Yes, I'm keeping it away from Victor."

"I don't blame you. We're a diner, not some ritzy brunch place like the one in Union Square in New York City."

"Aha, someone has been reading travel brochures. Is that your next stop?" I asked, skipping over the part where even in retirement she referred to the Bear Claw as at least partly hers. I hoped she always would.

She laughed. "Possibly. And yes, I have been looking at the top ten brunch places in the Big Apple." She paused. "I'd better not call it that or they'll know I'm a tourist."

"Maybe I'll join you."

What was I thinking? The sentiment was out of my mouth before I knew it.

"Oh, sweetie, wouldn't that be wonderful. Let's plan it as soon as we're home. I have lots of other literature, too."

"Meanwhile, I'd better stay on the Bear Claw menu and our vendors, and our progressive chef."

"Yes, do. I think you were too young to remember the time I added cinnamon crunch banana bread to the menu and absolutely no one ordered it. I ended up taking it home, and not even your father would try it."

I didn't remember, but I laughed anyway.

I realized I'd used up much of my break time on the first item on my list. We signed off without discussing KC's murder, which was fine with me—a relief, in fact. I renewed my plan to install Bennycam Two in the guest room where his condo was. The fewer places he could hide from me, the better.

I left a quick message with the temp agency to confirm that the diner would be fully staffed by them on Wednesday, with at least one person per shift who'd had previous Bear Claw experience. At the moment, I had no idea where I, its owner and manager, might be that day. Possibly wrapped in my Bear Claw apron myself, flipping pancakes.

One of my regular Bear Claw patrons rode by on the bicycle path in front of me, ringing the bell on her handlebar and waving. I waved back, wishing I were on a bike, too. Why did everyone else seem to be living a carefree, murder-free life? Then I chided myself. I should be grateful to be able to play a part—eventually, I hoped—in bringing a killer to justice.

But now, I needed to set out on that six-minute walk back to the business of homicide, and I needed to do it in four minutes.

I stood to leave the little park.

"Not yet, Miss Cooke."

I felt a light but firm push on my shoulder from someone behind me, letting me know I'd better sit again. A quick look around told me no one other than the two of us had chosen to make use of the park at this moment. There was no noise from a dog walker or a jogging pair. I thought of only one plus: it was still daylight. Three cheers for Alaska summers.

Roland Hortenson planted his feet in front of me, his hands in his pockets. As threatening a stance as one in an old Western movie just before the pistols came out. It didn't help that he had on a black ten-gallon hat—much more dramatic than Trooper's domed headgear. I thought I caught a sour whiff of old sweat, but it might have come from fertilizer.

"Roland." Though I tried to remain calm, I heard a

croak from my throat. "What can I do for you?" *Other than fall over dead,* I was thinking, *while the credits roll.*

"No, what can I do for you? I hear you were on my property this afternoon."

I swallowed hard. "I don't believe so."

"Your Subaru Outback sure was." He rattled off my license plate.

Roland took his hands out of his pockets. Empty, giving me a little more confidence that I would live to make it back to my diner.

"My map must have failed me," I said. "I thought I was on a county road."

"My question is why were you out there? Looking to buy up some land?"

I wished I had a watch I could check. I looked at my phone instead, happy I hadn't yet stowed it in my tote. I tapped my screen. "You know, Roland, I'm on a short break from a meeting. Trooper Graham and a few others are waiting to start up again, back at the Bear Claw, so I'd better get moving."

He took a couple of steps back, out of my way. "You have a good evening, now, Charlie. We'll talk another time."

Back to "Charlie" from "Miss Cooke." A good sign or a bad one? Was he truly meaning to talk another time? In the dark, maybe? When an Alaska State Trooper didn't know where I was? I didn't stop to figure it all out, but held my breath and hurried past him.

I wasn't sure I'd let out the breath until I was able to see into the Bear Claw's windows, clear through to Trooper's light blue hat hanging on the hook behind him.

I WAS THE LAST TO RETURN TO THE BOOTH. THE OTHER three team members had rosy complexions from the heat of the day and slightly rapid breathing, indicating they'd taken the twenty-minute-walk rule to heart.

Me? My rapid heartbeat was due not to aerobic walking but to my encounter with Roland Hortenson.

My biggest quandary now was whether to lay it all out to my teammates. No harm had come to me other than the stress brought about by my own fear. I didn't want to worry anyone. On the other hand, what if Roland went after Annie or Chris next? Shouldn't I warn them? If he knew my vehicle was near his property, did he also know Chris was the driver?

"Dessert," Nina called, and came bearing a large baking dish, overflowing with cherry cobbler. She gave me a look, then didn't hold back. "Charlie, you look like you ran hard the whole twenty minutes. More, since you're the last one here."

I made an attempt at a laugh. "Guess I'm not as young as I used to be." I was disappointed that the young college student didn't contradict me.

"I took the list with me," Trooper said, "and I see that this session will be pretty short, since there's not much to report."

We moved quickly through a couple of agenda items. There were no forensics yet from the Jessups' SUV.

"I tried to apologize to them for keeping it so long," Trooper said, "but since Sue Ann thinks it's bad luck now, I wouldn't be surprised if they put it up for sale anyway."

Chris perked up. "Hey," he said. "Like I said before, I'd be happy to take it off their hands. I can handle a little bad luck, as long as the thing runs."

Everyone at the table had seen Chris's battered old pickup and knew he was serious, especially when he jotted something down in his notebook, underlined it several times, and added a few exclamation points.

"That smartwatch?" Trooper asked. "Any fingerprints were wiped out when the vehicle ran over it. And who knows how long it was stuck in the tire. Is there some data from the numbers you checked?"

This was Chris's agenda item, and he shook his head. "It seems there are watches where you can send your data into the cloud to keep track of it, but"—he shook his head, almost forlornly—"not this one."

"Same strikeout with the gum, et cetera, that you picked up at the scene, Charlie," Trooper said. "I'm afraid nothing turned up there, either."

Now there were four of us forlorn. Is this what police work was always like? I felt sorry for the full-timers at the job.

I had a feeling we were about to break up, and I hadn't mentioned the threat I'd felt from Roland Hortenson. That's what it was, I reminded myself, a feeling. He hadn't thrown a punch or brandished a weapon or even issued a threat, like "Stay off my property." He'd just asked why I was where I was.

What if I woke up in the morning and learned that Annie had been hurt in some way and that it might have been by Roland? The Outback's windows were tinted. Roland could have thought Annie was driving, or that she was the passenger while I was driving. It was no use trying to keep score, how many pros and how many cons for talking about Roland's confrontation.

I had to admit another key aspect of revealing Roland's ominous presence was that it also revealed how Chris and I had taken an exploratory trip to his property. And we'd done so without prior approval, either formally from Trooper or personally from Annie.

"Before we go, just a reminder," Chris said, "that we should find Milo and ask him a few questions. It sounds as though he didn't have much to say to Charlie and Annie when they met him."

"He did not," Annie said. "And he went off really quickly when his friend came by."

"One person I talked to said he had manned the cabbage booth earlier in the day, but she didn't know exactly what time," I said.

"And there was the altercation, as the firefighter called it, between KC and a guy on a motorbike," Chris said.

"We should find out if Milo knew about that," I said.

"Also, I'm wondering if Milo ever got that personalized leather key holder that Annie learned about. Was it with KC's things, Trooper?"

"All good questions," Trooper said. "I'll be back with answers."

I wished he'd sounded more convincing.

"Who's going back to find Milo?" I asked, looking at Trooper for the answer. There I was, playing the good girl, asking for permission or guidance before running off, though with a willing companion in Chris. I felt like a schoolgirl with the excuse, *He started it. He called and made me go with him to Hortenson's property.*

"Let's try Chris this time, to talk to Milo," Trooper said. "Man to man, so to speak. No offense, ladies."

"None taken," said almost simultaneously.

"I wonder if Milo has a lawyer by now?" I said.

"It wouldn't surprise me, but let's hope not," Chris said. "I'll let you know."

"I still have to go through my cell phone photos," I said. "I can do that tomorrow, plus be available if anything comes up."

"Same here," Annie said.

We were almost all up and out of the booth when Annie raised her arm, waving her hand. Needing to be heard.

"Wait, wait," she said. "We haven't assigned this last one on Charlie's list. She read off her sheet. "'Other possible interviews: Roland, teens.'"

"I covered the teens who worked the booths and also the farms themselves, remember?" Chris said. "I can give you a list and contact information, but they weren't paying attention to the adults in either setting. It was a bust." He sighed. "One of my many."

"Right," Trooper said. "And Roland?"

Silence.

"Hortenson, anyone?" Trooper asked again.

This time I raised my arm. "I have a small thing," I said.

# Sixteen

I MANAGED TO DESCRIBE MY ENCOUNTER WITH RO-
land Hortenson without sounding scared to death. But not
without drawing some criticism from Trooper, whose first
comment was, "A small thing?"

"Poor choice of words," I said. "I meant 'no harm
done.'"

If anything, I wished I'd had a chance to warn Chris that
I was going to expose our adventure. In spite of his surprise
at my announcement—two of them, if you counted our going to Hortenson's property as well Hortenson's approaching me on the park bench—Chris stepped up and admitted
his part in suggesting the trip. As if he'd had to twist my arm.

"Don't blame yourselves. I guess it's my fault," Trooper
said, oh so sarcastically. "I neglected to brief you on the
rules." He took a long breath, as if to keep himself from
exploding, which I knew he wouldn't do. Not in the Bear
Claw. Not with even a few diners in the booths up front.

"The incident, if I'd even call it that, was over before it
started," I said. "I told Hortenson I needed to get back here,
and that was that." I left out the part where I'd invoked a

meeting that included Trooper, and that Hortenson had alerted me that we'd talk again. "I just thought you should know."

"You're right about that. I'll be putting a car in front of your house."

"But he didn't actually threaten me."

"You do remember the number of incidents Hortenson has been involved in?" Trooper said.

"Vaguely," Chris said.

"The complaint briefs you wrote up for your newspaper aren't vague," Trooper said. "Hortenson brooks no quarter with trespassers. We're just lucky he fires off warning shots before taking aim at them. Most of the time."

"I don't know about this," Annie said.

"No reason to," Trooper said. "You've never stomped on his field."

"We didn't stomp—"

Chris nudged me, and I knew enough not to express any thought that might sound defensive.

As much as I thought I knew Trooper, my "uncle" growing up, I wasn't always prepared for his reaction to my helping with his investigations. Or Chris's and Annie's helping also, for that matter. On the one hand, he'd deputized us. On the other, he was overly protective of our safety.

"Who makes it into the complaint briefs?" Annie asked, seeming upset she'd been left out of yet another chapter in the current investigation.

"Depends," Trooper said. "Only once did Hortenson nick a guy's arm, and he insisted he only meant to scare him off."

"How do you think Hortenson found out we were on his property?" Chris asked. "I'll bet there's a camera somewhere on site, though there sure didn't seem to be."

"We weren't actually on the property," I said, and immediately regretted the splitting of hairs that represented.

"That's not the point, is it?" Annie said, uncharacteristically humorless.

I couldn't help feeling Annie also had two points of disgruntlement, only one of which involved the trip itself, the other being that Chris and I had made it together, without including her. I hoped I could make it up to her somehow. I had more confidence that Trooper could be made to forget the transgression.

"You two are also getting cars on your places," Trooper told Annie and Chris. "We are not taking any chances here."

Trooper was busy with his phone as he talked, presumably leaving messages for his volunteer crew. In the last few months, Trooper had become adept at cell phone use, threatening to abandon his pager.

Chris grimaced. "I doubt Hortenson is going to come after me."

Trooper continued on his own path. "Did anything come of this little excursion to the farmland, by the way?" he asked.

I shook my head. I figured he wouldn't care about the great pretzels and many-flavored mustards of the Black Eye Café.

"It was just interesting to put some real land between us and all the documents associated with the property issue," Chris said.

"Well, I hope you enjoyed it. There are reasons we have rules, and I'm still counting how many you broke today."

I cringed at Trooper's scolding, sarcastic tone. I thought of questioning his accusation of broken rules, then changed my mind. The less said when Trooper was on the edge the better.

Trooper was soft-spoken by nature, but there was never any doubt of the power of his words. Tonight I felt his goal was to issue a reprimand but also to make it clear that our safety was uppermost in his mind. He accomplished all of that.

Trooper donned his hat, and Chris walked him to the door of the diner. I wondered if Chris was reporting on the feature article he was doing unrelated to KC's case, trying to get out of having a bodyguard outside his door, or apologizing for himself and me. Neither man was smiling, that was for sure.

Out the window, I noticed Trooper stepping into a patrol car driven by the trooper friend he'd reunited with at the conference and hoped this would mean his evening would have a more pleasant ending.

Only then did I see that my staff was huddled behind a partition, taking it all in, all the reprimands that seemed to predominate the serious part of the meeting.

"Shoo," I told them, and managed to laugh.

My next conundrum was the need to drop Chris off at my house to claim his pickup. With apologies to Benny, I realized the cat was already out of the bag, in that Annie now knew and was finding subtle ways of expressing her displeasure that Chris and I had taken a case-related jaunt without inviting her. Maybe that was better than a non-case-related jaunt, to her newly crushing mind? Could I make it up to her by asking her to drive Chris to his vehicle? Did it matter at all?

I went for it. "Can you drop Chris off at my place?" I asked her. "I need to do a few things around here." I thrust my thumb toward the kitchen, to that helpless staff who needed me to check on them.

"Sure," she said, stone-faced.

I dug my keys out of my tote and gave them to her. "He might have left something of his in my car," I said. Meaning, "See, no secrets."

When Chris was back from seeing Trooper off and Annie had returned my keys, the two left in Annie's car.

But before she went, Annie hung back a minute, with something to say to me.

"Charlie, I need to talk to you. I'll call you when I get home. Will you be here?"

*Uh-oh.* "Probably," I said, "but I'll have my cell on either way."

"Good." It was the most perfunctory "good" I'd ever heard Annie utter.

In some ways, she sounded more threatening than Roland Hortenson.

IT WAS A TOUGH DECISION, BUT I DECIDED I'D RATHER be home than at the Bear Claw when Annie called. Depending on how that call went, I could always wake Benny up afterward, or during, if I needed comfort or advice. Sometimes listening to his purr was all I needed.

I checked with the staff and verified that the diner was covered for the next couple of hours. I'd be back later and stay until the graveyard shift moved in. I was full enough from the five-course Bear Claw dinner, but I looked forward to alone time in the diner kitchen before Tammy and Bert arrived at one a.m. I wanted to test a recipe for mustard.

On the way home, I ran through various scenarios in my mind. What could Annie want to talk about that she couldn't tell me ahead of time? Or at least have dropped a hint? If she was expecting a tour bus she hadn't planned on and needed more bear claws or some special omelet filling for tomorrow, she'd have told me. If she was ill—I hated that possibility—she wouldn't have sounded so harsh, as if I'd done something wrong. Which, of course, I had.

Worst case, my BFF was completely torn up, more than Trooper had been and for a different reason, and blamed me for trying to seduce Chris away from her. In that case, she'd never want to speak to me again after tonight's phone call.

I tried to remember the last time Annie and I'd had a fight, or even a serious disagreement. If we ever did, it would most certainly have been my fault. I wasn't called a hothead in high school for nothing. Usually my temper was brought about by a trivial matter, like losing a close game or doing battle with my parents concerning school-night curfews. Annie would always be able to talk me down, with calming words or a silly joke. Or simply her normally convoluted grammar.

If the two of us ever had a spat, it would also have had to do with an insignificant issue. A borrowed sweater, a broken trinket, or a misunderstanding regarding a meeting time.

Neither then, nor in all the years since, was the discord over a guy. I was sure of that.

I pulled into my driveway next to a volunteer's bland-colored sedan, with two men I knew from similar stake-outs, but only as Buzz and Fergie, in the front seat. Trooper had acted quickly.

It was still warm enough outside for the guys to keep their windows down, and I took the opportunity to push through a hefty bag of leftovers from tonight's dinner.

Buzz, the younger of the two, held his hand out to Fergie. "I told you, man. Five bucks, please."

"He bet me you'd come bearing food," Fergie said, a bit sheepishly, as if he'd offended me, doubting my generosity. He shrugged and pulled out his wallet. "I'm sure it's worth more than a fiver."

I smiled. "In that case, I'd better bring down some plates and cutlery."

The pair were like an old married couple or, as Trooper referred to them, the old-time comic strip characters Mutt (Buzz, the tall thin one) and Jeff (Fergie, the short stocky one). They'd come in for breakfast at the Bear Claw often enough on nights like this, when they'd pulled all-night duty. Fergie was the complainer when they did, threatening to retire the next time he had to leave his wife alone in front of the TV.

The men handed me late mail. I shuffled through all the catalogues and flyers as I trotted up my front steps. Another postcard from my parents, this one with a recipe for bananas foster on the front. I'd take it to Victor in the morning.

I was pleased to have Benny waiting and welcoming when I unlocked the door. I talked to him all the while I was gathering supplies for Buzz and Fergie, then closed the door behind me when I went down to deliver them. No need to tempt Benny outside with a random bird cawing in one of my trees.

"I'm coming right back," I told my cat.

By the time I got back up the steps, my cell phone was ringing in my pocket. I took a deep breath and hit ACCEPT while I walked to my rocker. As I had hoped, Benny was right behind me. It might have been because I'd opened the cabinet that held his treats on the way and grabbed a few for him.

Benny climbed onto my lap, where I'd tossed a couple of his crunchy shellfish nuggets.

I was ready.

"Hi, Annie."

I was aware that if I didn't lighten up on my stroking of Benny's fur while he ate, he was going to disembark and head for his own condo in the guest room. It was enough for me that my mom had trained him to let her be this involved while he was eating.

I heard a deep, heavy breath from Annie. "I'm going to say this, Charlie, and I don't want a discussion, okay? Because if we start to discuss, you'll win. You always win. You were a debater; I wasn't. And I want to win this one. Do you understand?"

"Okay."

"Okay, you understand, or okay, you'll let me win?"

"Both."

"Okay."

That this comic repartee didn't have us both doubled over with laughter was not a good sign.

"Can I start with an apology?" I asked.

"No."

"Okay."

"Here's what I want. I want to host the next meeting."

Maybe the tension made me denser than usual, but I had to admit I didn't understand.

"I don't know what you mean." I paused. "Is it okay for me to tell you that?"

"See what I mean? I'm not as good as you are. I don't know how to say things the way you do."

"That's not true, Annie. You—"

"Tomorrow evening. Our meeting with Trooper and Chris. I want to have the meeting here at the inn. In my dining room. There, I said it."

I pictured Annie in her favorite easy chair in her bedroom, her feet up on the footstool with the cover embroidered by her grandmother. Or maybe in the dining room itself, furnished with antiques and always inviting, but seldom used.

Annie's inn comprised a grand Victorian at the center of the property and several cabins to either side. She'd always said she wanted to focus on the bedrooms and suites themselves, not on the dining room or the food.

When she remodeled the kitchen after her parents handed it down to her, she trimmed it to accommodate a coffee bar—not what I would call full-service. She offered coffee, tea, toast, and juice to her guests in the mornings. For a full breakfast they came to the Bear Claw, a great boost for us. For other meals, when the groups or individuals were not on day trips, it was the Bear Claw again—we even provided snack packs for day-trippers—or the various eating establishments in nearby Talkeetna or along Elkview's Main Street.

In her own quarters, she had a kitchenette with a two-burner stove, a small sink, a mini-fridge, and a small oven that she never used.

"Charlie? Don't be thinking of an argument. I bought a toaster oven."

I wanted to ask some questions. When was the last time she had cooked a regular meal for more than herself? When was the last time she had shopped for groceries?

More important, how to broach this without insulting her facility or her skills?

The answer? I couldn't.

"That sounds great, Annie," I said.

Ordinarily, which this wasn't, Annie and I would chat for a while after we'd finished with the principal message or some agenda. There was always gossip to share. Annie read the *Bugle*, the newspaper Chris wrote for, from cover to cover, and I counted on her to tell me the latest. Did the unidentified tagger's graffiti in the public pool house result in closing the facility all summer? Did that new mosquito spray really work? What were the new hours of the post office and old Lucas's souvenir shop on Main?

Annie was a gold mine of local information.

The state fair had its own column in the *Bugle* in August, and Annie had already told me that finding KC's body on the edge of the grounds had received only the briefest of mentions. Just as well, for the sake of her mom and others who loved her.

Tonight's phone call was different. Annie had said goodbye as soon as I'd agreed to her plan. There was no briefing, no chatting about whether her volunteer patrol had arrived, who they were, if she'd chatted with them. I didn't know what she planned to do tomorrow, other than figure out a way to have guests for dinner. I hadn't had the chance to ask if I could help, but that was most likely a good thing.

I'm not sure I could have asked without upsetting her. She would probably have taken it as an affront.

This was not the Annie I was used to.

Benny, however, was as I'd hoped, remaining on my lap even after he'd consumed his treats. Apparently, he knew he had more work to do to ease my distress. We stayed in my rocker, my tension easing away as I continued to smooth down his fur and give him a few gentle scratches between his ears, waiting for his purring box to be activated.

By the time I needed to head back to the Bear Claw, Benny had found his way to his condo bed. I refilled his feeder, checked on his water and litter box, and prepared to depart.

It was never easy to tell volunteer patrol guys that you had to leave again.

"I'll be back shortly," I told Buzz and Fergie. "Anything special you need from the diner?"

They laughed and patted their stomachs. "We're coming with you," Fergie said.

"I'll be fine. You know I do this all the time. I go back between the dinner rush and the graveyard shift."

"But it's not all the time that Trooper sends us to watch out for you," Fergie said.

"I'll call when I get there," I said.

I couldn't very well complain to these nice guys, giving up their own evenings and nights, that I longed to have some time alone in my kitchen.

"We're supposed to stay here in case—you know," Buzz said.

I gathered Buzz didn't want to use examples of what might go wrong that might frighten me.

"At least text when you get there," Fergie said.

I nodded vigorously, surprised that old Fergie was now into texting.

"I know what we'll do," Buzz said. "We'll shuttle back and forth."

I didn't remind them again that this was my routine most nights, when they were guarding someone else, or helping the firefighters, and had no idea where I was.

But as the image of Roland Hortenson in his black Stetson came to mind, I had to acknowledge this was different from most other nights, and I was glad two guys had my back.

# SEVENTEEN

THOUGH I TRIED TO MAKE LIGHT OF THE VOLUNTEERS' advice, I did follow their instructions. I locked myself into the Bear Claw and texted Fergie that I was secure.

I loved my diner at night. Naturally, I also loved and needed it to be busy as often as possible, but the nighttime environment was serene, as if the bright red booths and shiny stools were resting. When I dimmed the lights in the main section to the right point, I could imagine being in a noir film. At times like that, I was probably channeling my mom, who also loved the late-night or early-morning hours and would compare the look to the cover of a midcentury paperback or movie.

I regretted that tonight I felt it necessary to keep watch on the parking lot for an appearance by Roland Hortenson. I tried not to let that ruin my time alone on my property. The best way to ensure that was to don my apron and proceed to my kitchen.

Unlike Annie, who could go a very long time without setting foot near a stove, I needed a cooking fix and had my plan all ready.

With the kitchen lights turned up all the way, I wrapped myself in a white apron emblazoned with the words BEAR CLAW embroidered on the bib and set to work on a recipe for an interesting mustard. I smiled as I made my case in my head: I couldn't let a tiny rest stop eatery outdo me.

It was tempting to bake soft pretzels also, but I preferred to keep the bread or pastry emphasis on our signature bear claws. We already had a tasty mustard sauce for salmon, so I chose one that would complement hot dogs, ever a popular diner choice, especially for families with children.

Thanks to Victor, who was always trying new recipes and creating his own, I had all the ingredients I needed for brown mustard, including both brown and yellow seeds. I guessed it was partly because it had been only a month ago that the Bear Claw had celebrated National Hot Dog Day.

Vinegar and honey were staples, so it was no time before I had a tangy mustard. I parceled the batch into small mason jars and looked forward to sharing the project with my staff. I hadn't gone to culinary school for nothing, I told myself.

Too bad I was still stuffed from dinner and would have to wait until tomorrow to test the mustard on a hot dog. Too bad I couldn't offer the new condiment to Annie. *Not yet,* I thought, with the hope that this phase of our friendship would be short-lived.

That done, I spotted a flat of strawberries on the back counter. I remembered that Victor and Rachel had gone to a pick-your-own party at a farm near Talkeetna. I thought they wouldn't mind if I scooped some out and turned them into a strawberry crisp. I made a note to visit the farms in that neighborhood before the season was over. I hadn't allowed myself the luxury of wandering through berry patches in some time.

As I pulled the oats, sugars, cinnamon, and other staples from the shelves, I was only too aware of my stalling tactics. Sure, I loved having free rein in my kitchen, winging it with whatever ingredients were in stock, but I also knew I had a job to do as part of Trooper's investigating team, a job I was avoiding.

A good guess would be to blame my procrastination on the awareness that I'd spent two whole days as a so-called investigator and come up with so little that I might as well have stayed in the kitchen and developed surefire new recipes.

My discoveries had turned into more dead ends, like the watch-in-the-tire non-clue and several others. None were leads that would take us to KC's killer.

If my mom were here, she'd have some proverb handy, something about how long it took to build Rome, or a few wise words about patience. And Benny, if he were present, would agree with her.

I had no such disappointments when dealing with food. If you followed the directions, you were guaranteed success. The strawberry crisp sitting in the requisite preheated oven, for example, was already smelling delicious and was sure to please many people. I was eager to try out a new tip, one where instead of baking the topping and berries together, I'd put the crumble ingredients on a baking sheet and bake for a few minutes without the berries. That way, the topping wouldn't get soaked by the berry juice. The result: a crispier crisp.

I could also have deviated into creative territory, if I'd chosen to, adding other berries, or a pinch of another spice in the batter, and still ended up with a tasty dish.

I steeled myself and resisted the urge to whip up a pan of shortcake to be served with the rest of the strawberries and whipped cream. I took a seat instead and pulled out my cell phone. First, I desperately needed to check my emails—not—and read notifications—another not—before getting to work on my photos from the fair.

When a car pulled up close to the side window at eleven thirty, I went on alert and watched as the passengers exited the vehicle. I checked out a group of three women who seemed to be enjoying themselves, chatting and laughing. At the same time, I noticed Buzz and Fergie in the parking lot and heard them start their car and drive off. Apparently, they thought the women, who were here to eat, I assumed, were good enough guards for me.

I unlocked the door and welcomed the three, for more reasons than one.

"We're so glad you're still open," said the first woman, tall, with red hair to her shoulders. "We're starving."

"What smells so good?" said the second woman, shorter, dressed as the others in casual clothes and walking shoes.

Before I had a chance to describe and offer the strawberry crisp, the third woman chimed in.

"We've been to the fair," she said. "We were there till it closed and then couldn't believe it was still light out, so we walked around town for a while."

"And now we're here," said the redhead, reminding me of Annie and her penchant for self-evident statements.

There followed a list of surprises about Alaska from the women, who were on vacation from a town in Ohio. They took turns noting features, like the majesty of our mountains and glaciers and the size and swarming nature of our mosquitoes.

At this point, I would ordinarily launch into my collection of interesting facts about Denali National Park, just a few miles up the road, how Denali is the highest peak in North America, and the third-highest peak in the world. I was afraid if I got started, I'd inadvertently mention how lawmakers in Ohio—the birth state of President McKinley, and the home state of the women who were now the only customers in my diner—tried to block the name change from Mount McKinley back to Denali.

"We're between summer school and fall term," the short woman explained.

"We're starving," the redhead said again, surely a hint to her companions to let me take their orders.

I was overjoyed that the choices were the same: hot dogs all around, and a willingness on the part of two of them to experiment with a new mustard. Strawberry crisp right out of the oven was declared a no-brainer.

I walked around the counter to fill the orders, once again acutely aware that my less than ninety minutes with kitchenware, appliances, and ingredients on hand had generated greater successes than two days as an investigator.

Not unlike teenagers I'd known and served, the women took out their phones as they visited. I overheard some of their banter.

"Oops, I did it again, honey," said the third woman, who'd been quiet until now. "I keep forgetting how much later it is there. This constant light confuses me."

I felt sorry for whoever in Ohio had been awakened at about four in the morning.

"I'm glad I got a shot of that ginormous carrot," the redhead said, moving on to her state fair photos.

"Here you are, Gina, at the quilt display. I thought sure you were going to buy that wooden ladder to display your quilts."

"And find a way to get it home?" the woman named Gina said. "I don't think so. Besides, I can get one at home." She paused and moved her phone closer to her eyes. "Hey, look at this guy. Is that a knife he's carrying?"

I stopped in my tracks. If the counter hadn't been in front of me, I'd have dropped the tray of dishes I'd cleared away from the booth.

"Let's see," the redhead said, followed by a similar request by the shorter woman.

"It does look like a knife in that young guy's hand." Gina used her fingers, presumably enlarging the image.

I made my way over to them as nonchalantly as I could, planning to ask if they needed coffee refills, hoping to get a look at the photo.

Gina spoke up before I made a fool of myself. "No,

look." She laughed. "Silly. It's one of those long sandwiches they were making at that food truck, like a sub, only skinnier. It's wrapped in foil, and he's holding it by his side for some strange reason."

Gina laughed again, as did the others.

As for me, I knew it was time for me to look through my own photos.

THE WOMEN FROM OHIO LEFT SATISFIED, EVEN BUYING Bear Claw logo aprons.

I wiped down the table but left the dishes for Tammy and Bert, who'd arrive at one a.m. I figured they needed at least one chore, and they wouldn't have to do any prep for tomorrow's dinner.

My apron stock was running low, as were the T-shirts. I could order more, but first I wanted to find an artist, perhaps Tammy, who could work on a new logo for us to replace the cartoon bear currently representing my diner on mugs and fabric souvenirs. I hadn't come up with the right way to present the idea to my mom, who'd overseen the original design.

I'd considered using an image of Benny, but since he was an indoor cat, and stayed in my home, no one who came to the Bear Claw had seen him.

Finally, with a non-logo mug of coffee, I settled in a booth and opened the camera app on my phone. What did it say about me that I couldn't help wishing that sub sandwich had been a knife, and the wielder of it a clearly identifiable killer?

As usual, I found many useless videos, since my thumb was bigger than the allotted space for choosing which mode to use for the camera. I hadn't really meant to capture the crowd of little kids hovering around the ten-foot clown passing out lollipops or the set of trees sculpted into the form of an elephant, complete with bright white tusks made of a material, organic or otherwise, unidentifiable from a distance.

I had to remind myself that I was supposed to be focusing on the backgrounds of the photos. The foreground was an excuse to snap the picture in case I was being stalked. It seemed ages ago that I'd strolled through the fairgrounds, making my way through blaring music and enticing aromas, clicking my camera relentlessly, acquiring images of paintings, baked goods, woodworking, canning. Even a free-standing beehive on a table, with an array of honey and other bee products.

This was another dead end, I was sure, as I scrolled up and down and side to side deleting inadvertent duplicates, using my thumb and index finger to enlarge a photo if it seemed promising, hoping to reveal the face of a roaming killer.

I was about to give up when I noticed a figure that looked familiar, not so much in features but in stance. I enlarged the image, but the person's face was turned just enough to avoid my lens. Definitely male, husky, standing with his hands in his pockets. I scrolled past and saw a duplicate, this one with the familiar arrow indicating that a video lurked beneath it.

At last, an unplanned video about twenty seconds long that might be useful. I played it over and over, muting the sounds from the crowd so I could concentrate on the visual. The man was young, I thought, and wearing a sleeveless black T-shirt. At the halfway point, he removed his cap and wiped his bald head. The same shaved-head style Chris sported, and a stance that looked like he was ready to do battle.

I lost count of how often I reran the video, but eventually I zeroed in on why the man's shape and stance and even T-shirt looked familiar.

Judd Waters. Shark. Milo's friend.

He was standing in front of Donna Madsen, who was

subbing for KC in her booth. He appeared to be alone. And unarmed. I made a mental note to ask Trooper about the knife used to murder KC and whether it was small enough to fit in a pocket.

My head was swimming with possibilities. *So what?* was my first question. There was no law against attending the fair and observing the cabbage booth. *Why KC's booth in particular?* was my second question. Did this mean that Judd was expecting KC to be staffing the booth?

I'd taken the photo on Sunday, after I'd walked around to other vendors. KC had been murdered on the previous Friday evening. If Judd was Milo's good friend, he would have known of KC's murder and wouldn't have been watching for her. A horrible third question was: *Did Judd plan to murder all of KC's employees?* I erased that thought from my mind. It scared me how quickly I'd gone from carousel music to a very dark place.

I pulled the map of the fairgrounds with the vendors and rides marked from my tote to see what was nearby. What other booth or vendor might Judd have been looking at? None, it turned out. Steph at sweet corn was not that close, nor was Aly's coffee and pastry booth. The fair organizers were generous in working out space, not crowding vendors together.

I also checked for an image of Milo in the Judd video. He was nowhere in the immediate vicinity. Each time, I watched for Milo in vain, and observed only Judd as he faced KC's booth, then turned slightly at the last second.

But I'd spent very little time with Milo at his grandmother's home this morning, and I couldn't be sure I'd recognize him in a quick frame or two. I'd seen Judd for even less time, however, and was now beginning to doubt it was Judd I had identified. I scoured Sunday's album on my phone for a clearer image, but he was nowhere to be seen.

So much for my breakthrough. If I hadn't been so attached to my cell phone, literally and emotionally, I might have smashed it on the tile floor.

I needed a break. I stood and stretched, then helped myself to a small piece of strawberry crisp, careful to leave enough for Tammy and Bert. "When frustrated, eat" had been a long-standing tactic of mine, possibly the result of growing up in a diner.

The next task would be to see what photos Annie and Chris had shot. It was too late to call either of them. Not that I would have hesitated to call Annie if we were on speaking terms—regular speaking terms, that is.

I'd have to wait till morning.

I took a seat and picked up a stack of cooking magazines to look through, but not for the first time, the side doorbell rang and woke me from an unplanned nap. Although Tammy and Bert had keys, they always rang the bell when they looked through the windows or door and saw that I was asleep.

"Sorry to interrupt a nice dream," was their usual remark at times like this.

I greeted them and reviewed the tasks for tomorrow, also pointing out the new mustard and the last of the strawberry crisp, which was theirs to polish off.

"You okay to drive home?" Tammy asked. "I can take you."

"I look that bad, do I?"

"No, no," Tammy rushed to assure me. She still sometimes treated me like a boss, one who might fire her if offended.

I convinced them I was fine and that I had Buzz and Fergie waiting at the other end if I needed help getting up the steps. Bert thought that was funny, while Tammy was already scooping crisp onto two plates.

I scanned the parking lot as I left the diner, locking Tammy and Bert inside.

All clear.

\* \* \*

A STRANGE FEELING NAGGED AT ME ALL THE WAY home, so strongly that I frequently checked my mirrors to be sure no one was following me.

Again, all was clear.

I turned into my driveway, waved to the friendly guard dogs in the unmarked sedan, and entered my house.

I immediately checked on Benny and breathed easy when I found him asleep on the cushy middle level of his condo. So what if I couldn't chat with him; he was okay, and that's what mattered. I knew if I sat up in bed reading for a while, he'd come in to visit eventually.

As I started to get ready for bed, the nagging feeling I'd had while driving home became more and more distinct. Not necessarily dark or ominous now, but an inkling that there was something on the video I was missing.

I pulled my phone from my tote and returned to the rocker in my family room. I replayed the video, this time at a slower rate. I almost missed the mark again, except that I was able to pause the recording quickly, just a split second before it ended.

I didn't know why I hadn't factored in this simple fact: I was the one taking the video.

My stomach clenched.

So at the end, when Judd turned, he was looking at me.

# Eighteen

It took me a minute to adjust to the new input to my brain: Judd Waters was at the Alaska State Fair, in front of KC's booth, on the same day and at the same time that I was. I couldn't bring myself yet to study Judd's expression as he looked at me.

I tried briefly to remember whether I'd noticed it at the time—a guy standing in the middle of the road essentially staring me down as I snapped a photo. Wasn't this the reason I was wandering the fairgrounds with my phone out? To determine if anyone looked suspicious, worth thinking about as a suspect?

I knew from the Pattersons that he had a juvie record at the very least. But Laurie thought of him as a nice young man, very polite. How many who commit crimes as juveniles become polite young men, as compared to the number who go on to commit murder? Did I want to know?

Until I knew more, protecting myself might be a good start.

I went to my window and saw that Buzz and Fergie were still out front in Fergie's car. From a distance, Buzz looked like he was sleeping, so his was the number I dialed. Suddenly I felt I needed two fully awake bodyguards.

"Hey, Charlie. Everything okay?" Buzz asked.

"Nothing urgent, but would you mind coming up here?"

The passenger door flew open before I could end the call. Fergie, on the driver's side of the car, stepped out also. Fergie stayed in that position as Buzz bounded up the steps to my porch and into my house.

"I'm probably overreacting," I said, concerned that I'd worried the guys for nothing.

"But now that I'm here . . ." Buzz said. His gaze traveled the area as he spoke.

"Would you mind just having a look around?"

He indicated that I should take a seat and headed for the back hallway, talking to Fergie on his phone at the same time. I caught snatches of the update he was passing on to his partner, including the words "stand by."

"Benny's in the guest room," I called out to Buzz. Benny didn't know Buzz well, but they'd interacted a couple of times, and Benny had approved. I'd always thought it might have been that Benny smelled his friend Trooper on his men. One day I'd check out the research on how cats' sense of smell compared to that of dogs. Better, I was sure.

It took all my resolve to stay put. If I hadn't already looked in on Benny, I'd have been rushing past Buzz.

I did get up and look out my window for Fergie. He was walking slowly around his car and mine, turning this way and that as he cruised, as if practicing a crazy waltz, his phone in his hand. I supposed he had learned the tactics in surveillance school.

After what seemed like ages, Buzz came back to the family room.

"All's well, Charlie. Except the lock on your back door is pretty flimsy. Do you mind if I mess up your doorframe a little?"

I gave him a quizzical look. "You can change it now?"

He nodded. "The advantage—or perils, depending on how you look at it—of using Fergie's old car tonight. He carries more supplies and tools in his trunk than a full-fledged hardware store. He'll be able to install a new lock in no time. You might have a few wood chips to clean up, though."

"A small price," I said. "Plus whatever he charges."

Buzz smiled. "I'll go out and switch places with him."

About thirty minutes later, I had a new lock on my back door, all my windows secure, and two guys outside my house with nothing to do but watch for trouble while they kept awake with specially prepared containers of snacks.

The noise from the amateur, but capable, locksmith woke Benny, who kept me company.

"What shall I do about all this, Benny?" I asked him, as I settled under the covers.

His answer was to curl up on my stomach, which I took to mean that we should both go to sleep.

I WOKE EARLY ON TUESDAY AND, ONCE AWAKE, FELT all the anxiety and confusion about the last couple of days come roaring back. KC's murder investigation; Roland Hortenson and Judd Waters possibly threatening me in some way; Annie alienated from me.

Tuesday's chore for all of the team was to go through photos we'd taken at the fair. We hadn't been specific about when we'd discuss the results. Tonight at the regular seven p.m. meeting, along with other agenda items? Or was there another plan? It bothered me terribly that I couldn't just call or text Annie without fear that I'd use the wrong word or phrase and set her off.

My parents were due home this weekend. If Annie and I weren't reconciled before then, Mom would have advice. I didn't want to bother her with this tiff while she was enjoying Portland with her friends. I was surprised to receive a separate postcard from my dad, who seldom wrote, and which emphasized the special nature of the trip. He had gone kayaking, he wrote, something I don't remember him ever taking advantage of in our home state, where there were miles of kayaking streams and rivers around Anchorage alone.

I took breakfast out to Buzz and Fergie and encouraged them to go home.

My plan was to head to the Bear Claw for my own breakfast and send Tammy and Bert home. I could cover until the regular staff arrived around nine a.m.

That was one end of the schedule taken care of.

The other end was this evening, and it was more difficult to arrange. It occurred to me that if Trooper's team was going to Annie's for our dinner meeting, I'd have to make other plans for the diner. Usually when I hired temporary workers, as I had for tomorrow, the day Victor and company were off to the fair, my practice was to have my staff and the temps overlap a bit for dinner while I checked everything out. I couldn't do that if I was dining at Annie's Inn. I smiled as I thought of "dining" there. Food snob that I was.

Back to the drawing board to figure out a way to meet and work with the temp people and still go to Annie's. I was almost ready to beg Annie for a pass on her idea, to put it off until the following evening. But that was a scarier idea than leaving the diner with no staff at all.

I'd been promised by the company, one I'd dealt with successfully in the past, that at least one of the temps for each shift would be familiar with the Bear Claw, but there was no guarantee it would happen. Temp workers were flexible, available to go here and there, but sometimes there when you wanted them here.

I might just have to abandon my obsessive management protocols and leave the diner in the hands of the company I trusted.

For now, I got in my car, and only then did Buzz and Fergie drive away.

When my phone rang, just in time to echo throughout my car, I jumped and banged my knees on the bottom of my steering wheel.

"Did I wake you?" Chris's voice at top volume.

I wanted to say, *Yes, you did. Now hang up.* Not a pleasant way to start the day. Not today.

"Charlie?"

"I'm here. I'm in my car on the way to the diner. What's up?"

"First, I can't find Milo. I tried KC's number. His home, that is. I left a couple of messages. I guess I could try his grandmother."

I hoped Laurie was in better shape than she was when Annie and I had left her yesterday morning. "It's early. Maybe no one else is up," I said.

In other words, *Why did you feel it necessary to call me when I've hardly finished one cup of coffee?* This last thought came about as I gazed at my travel mug, sitting in the vehicle's well.

He cleared his throat. I had a bad feeling about what was coming next.

"Do you want to go to the morgue?"

My turn for a throat-clearing, mingled with a cover-up laugh.

"Sounds like fun," I said.

"I'm serious. I mean the *Bugle* morgue. To look at old newspapers."

I knew that, but didn't admit it. "Now?" I looked at the clock on my dash. "It's not even eight o'clock."

"Early in the morning is the best time. You'd be surprised how busy it can be when the office is officially open at ten."

"Yes, I would be surprised."

"So? What do you say?"

I had no idea. Besides nursing my sore knees, I was checking the area around my house and behind me on the driveway.

"Let me think." I immediately regretted uttering out loud what was in my head.

"We don't even have to use your car. It's so close, I'll drive myself and meet you there. You'll have to wait for me, however, since the building will be locked."

"Shall we get Annie?"

"She called me last night and told me she's having the meeting at the inn?" I noted the question mark in his voice.

He sounded incredulous, and why not? Chris hadn't known Annie as long as I had, but he'd known her long enough to know that this was an unusual arrangement. As for me, whenever I'd been in Annie's tiny kitchen, it had been to cook, either because she was under the weather or just for fun, for me.

"Anyway," Chris continued, "I think Annie's going to be busy, so how about it? The morgue?"

*Think fast,* I told myself.

I could take advantage of the fact that Annie had never said anything specific about not being invited to Hortenson's farm yesterday. She'd pouted when Chris and I had returned from it together, and she had sent out a lot of other signals that she was annoyed. She'd also been very put out when she'd told me she'd be hosting the next meeting.

But she'd never said *Don't go to the morgue without me* or *Never go on a trip with just you and Chris.*

Therefore, how could I be sure that she would mind? I could understandably assume she'd be only too glad to be able to stay home and get ready for her dinner party. After all, it was her idea that she host the dinner meeting.

That was my argument, and I was sticking with it.

"Okay," I told Chris, "but I'll need a few minutes to talk to my staff."

Having agreed to the morgue visit, I called the diner and laid out my change in plans.

First, I wouldn't be staying for breakfast this morning. Could they please bundle up some bear claw bits and fruit for three and have them ready when I made a brief stop there in a few minutes? The third serving was necessary in case old Wally, Chris's boss, came into the building and questioned my presence. Second, there would be no dinner meeting at the Bear Claw this evening with Trooper's team. Third, it would be up to them to take care of briefing and vetting the temp help who had been hired to replace them tomorrow, their fair day.

And finally, they should be ready in case there was a dinner emergency this evening.

Of course, I had confidence that Annie could host dinner for four.

Whether she could deliver something edible to the table was another question entirely.

# Nineteen

Taking separate vehicles turned out to be handy in that I didn't have to decide immediately whether to tell Chris about the video I'd come across on my phone. The one I was probably making too much of anyway. A young guy was standing at the fair, not bothering anyone. What if he'd been staring at someone standing behind me? Or what if he, like many people, simply didn't like having his picture taken, even if he was just being captured in a candid of the fair? I didn't especially want my likeness recorded, either, but I didn't think I'd twist my face into a menacing scowl over it.

I was embarrassed to think how I'd awakened Buzz to come up and search my house and had put Fergie to work changing a lock. Not in his job description, let alone among the duties required of a civilian volunteer. All over a perceived death stare.

By the time Chris and I parked our vehicles next to each other in the *Bugle* parking lot, I'd decided not to think about the video again until it was time for all of the team to report on their individual photographic results.

I tried to remember if I'd felt this much angst before I was deputized. Life seemed simpler when all I had to do was keep a twenty-four-hour diner running.

I'D BEEN TO THE *BUGLE* BUILDING BEFORE, BUT THIS was my first time heading for its morgue.

Chris used his key to enter through a side door. Knowing the dedication Chris had to his profession, working at all hours during the week and bleeding into the weekend, I wasn't surprised to find a few reporters at their desks this early in the morning.

They were not running around with green eyeshades and pencils behind their ears as in old movies, and not producing a cacophony of noise, from clacking typewriters to shouts across the room. These reporters were keyboarding solo, the only sound the creaks of ergonomic chairs. They seemed so focused, I was sure most weren't aware we'd entered the large newsroom.

Only one middle-aged man, in an olive green T-shirt, looked up and saluted to us. Chris saluted back, something I hadn't seen before, leaving me to figure that the guy was a vet, like Chris.

We walked past a relic called a watercooler, I noted, and stepped onto the corrugated metal floor of an ancient elevator. Chris pulled the collapsible gate closed, and the cage made its way slowly down the shaft.

Fitting equipment for a morgue, I thought, and had to keep reminding myself this was not a real morgue, as in a coroner's lair, but the place where newspaper history was buried.

Or kept alive, as Chris told me once. The back files were used to give depth and perspective to a current story.

"This is what newspapers had to rely on for background before there was an Internet," he'd said. "The name probably comes from the way these issues provided information for use in writing obits in the old days."

Unlike the more formal decor upstairs, with its walls of professionally framed photos and articles, the morgue, ironically, was more fun.

The first thing I saw was a bulletin board with so many notes and photos, it was almost impossible to read one without pushing aside two others. The short ones that did stand out would have made good bumper stickers.

NEWS NEVER SLEEPS

WE'RE ALWAYS WRITE

WE HAVE ISSUES

And so on, leading me to believe that these particular journalists enjoyed their work.

But what dominated the room were the floor-to-ceiling shelves holding newspapers bound into books, all as large as the newspaper pages themselves.

Each shelf was the height of one book laid flat. They were of many different colors, all clearly marked on the spine with the year only. Older volumes were labeled with what seemed to be crayon, newer ones with stenciled lettering that included the designation *The Elkview Bugle*. Understandably, the older ones were tattered, the edges of the heavy and awkward books coming apart, the fragile pages torn. Threadbare, like an old, well-used, well-worn T-shirt.

We continued our walk around the aisles. Tall as I was, I needed to strain my neck to see the top shelf where we'd stopped, with a binder marked "32–33."

"Would that really be 1932 to 1933?" I asked Chris.

"It would."

"Before we were a state?"

He laughed. "There were still newspapers. Let's look at an even older one."

He pulled a huge, unwieldy book from the shelf and plopped it on one of the tables that butted against one another in the center of the room. A cloud of dust that would match a day at the rodeo rose up. When we'd caught our breath, Chris opened the book to a random page, revealing a 1912 issue of *The Alaska Daily Empire*, with a front-page story on the funeral of then vice president James Sherman.

I wasn't sure what my reaction was supposed to be, other than another sneeze, but Chris seemed proud of his morgue and its newsworthy treasures. I murmured something that I hoped would indicate I was duly impressed.

I smiled to see that sometimes in the 1960s, there were two volumes per year. "A lot more going on, I guess." Chris nodded his agreement.

"Most of the old newspapers have been digitized," Chris said. "It will probably take another fifty years or so for the *Bugle* to reach that stature."

"Or until you win your Pulitzer," I said.

Chris grinned, as he did every time the Pulitzer came up. "Well, while we wait for that to happen, let's get the year we came here for."

Interesting as it might be to open more old binders, I agreed with Chris about getting to work.

We'd done the calculation several times, figuring that if Milo was two years old at the time of the crash, we were looking at a sixteen-year-old article. Since there seemed to be only one binder per year in that era, we split up the tasks.

Chris would look through the sixteen-year-old book and I'd take one on either side, in case Milo was a year younger or older than we'd been led to believe.

Although Chris was the host for this particular meeting, I helped with the heavy lifting and lugged my volumes to an empty table.

I opened one of my volumes and thought I'd hit pay dirt right away, since the news item was about a three-year-old male. Too bad the story was of a young brown bear caught roaming a residential neighborhood.

It was hard not to read irrelevant articles, like some of

those in the *Bugle*'s special Anchorage Briefs column. A winner had been declared in the greased pole contest. A late-night talk show host had been offered honorary Alaska citizenship by the governor. Alaska's statewide population increased by nearly eight percent. And, the most poignant, an Outsider, as we referred to those from the lower forty-eight, had tried to take an elk home to Minnesota in the bed of a truck. That act was a violation of federal law.

"But enough of that," I muttered. "So what if all this is more interesting at the moment than actual research that might turn up nothing?" Which is exactly what page after page that I read through yielded. I found nothing related to the plane crash that killed KC's sister and brother-in-law.

Now and then, Chris and I would exchange observations.

"Here's an ad for a tough nylon chest gun holster," I told him.

"Don't forget to read the decks," Chris told me. "Sometimes the headline doesn't tell you enough."

I felt pretty proud of myself for remembering what he'd taught me about the deck, the smaller headline that came between the major headline and the story.

Now and then one of us would throw up our hands and take a lap around the morgue to stretch our legs and rest our eyes from squinting at the small print and dusty pages of newsprint. With no window available, I'd look at the posters and other paraphernalia people had left in the room.

My favorite cartoon was one that showed a man in pajamas coming down the stairs, watching a thief load up a bag of items. The man is saying, "What a relief. I thought it was a reporter."

Thus, I was laughing when Chris called out, "Here it is." I hurried to his seat, looked over his shoulder, and read the opening sentence of the article he pointed to. "Do we care at the moment that the rate of fatal airplane crashes in Alaska is higher than the national average?" I asked. "Or that quote 'contributing conditions include fast-changing weather, the enormous size of the state, and more landings and takeoffs occurring in harbors or on rugged terrain' unquote?"

"Read on. They always started with some universal hook back then. Now we start with more personal or dramatic intros. Like, 'Little Timmy was playing with his blocks near his crib when . . . ' instead of 'A fire broke out on Eighty-third Street at three forty-two yesterday afternoon.'"

"Got it."

I read on, as instructed.

A small plane with the pilot and three passengers crashed in a rugged area near the Puntilla Lake checkpoint on the Iditarod route, killing all four on board, officials said.

The names of the pilot and the passengers are being withheld until families can be notified.

The cause of the crash has not been determined, but possible mechanical failure and unfavorable weather conditions are tentatively being considered.

"Way to cover all bases," Chris said. "What else could it be? Hijackers?"

The image of the plane was frightening to see. The front part was buried in trees, many of them toppled, while the blue and white tail stuck straight up, like some sculpture mounted on a twisted propeller. Identifying letters and numbers were obscured by broken branches.

In a creepy twist, right below the notice and photo of the crash was a tour company's ad for "an up close and personal experience of the Iditarod race." The company offered six packages, tailored to different levels of personal contact with the dogs and the mushers. Some tours included a mushers' banquet and a scenic flight over the route.

I gulped.

Chris apparently noticed the placement of the ad also. "Unfortunate juxtaposition," he said as we both took a moment to consider the realities.

"There's not a lot of information in the notice," I said. "But it gives us the starting point. That photo is disturbing."

"Sure is," Chris said. "I'm following up with later issues to see if any other names pop up and if the cause becomes more clear after an investigation. Given the circumstances, you know there must have been one."

That was that for the volume I was perusing, plus others that held older issues. I placed the volumes on my seat, slid the chair a few feet across the room—not difficult since there was no carpeting—then lifted the books into their slots on the shelf.

"Smart," said Chris, who could only have seen me out of the corner of his eye as he continued looking through his volume.

While Chris was searching for a part two of the crash story, which was a one-volume, one-person job, I walked off to a corner of the room. I sat on a tattered folding chair beneath a photo of Joseph Pulitzer standing against a backdrop of newsprint and placed a call to my diner.

"Hey, boss, the Bear Claw is going to be in good hands tomorrow while we're on all the thrill rides the fair has to offer." Victor's voice, with his usual enthusiasm.

"Good to hear."

"The new guy called to check in and we were chatting and he taught me a new callout. Want to hear it?"

"I can hardly wait."

"Get me one houseboat," he said, imitating a callout from the Bear Claw's booths to its kitchen. "Do you know what that is?"

"I do not."

My chief chef, as he insisted on being called, had a hard time containing himself.

"A banana split."

I heard a chorus of laughter in the background, which I was sure was not the first time the kitchen crew had heard Victor's performance. I did my best to show my own appreciation. It was the least I could do.

Before I could get a serious report on what was going on at the Bear Claw, Chris waved at me from his place at the table, and I told Victor I'd see him soon. What kind of manager would switch as quickly from hearing about her business to jogging toward news about a plane crash that happened sixteen years ago? I told myself I'd had worse managers.

This time Chris gestured for me to sit down while he stood over my shoulder and we read together.

> The experienced pilot, George Roberts, was flying his single-engine light aircraft from near Talkeetna to Puntilla Lake, a checkpoint on the Iditarod trail, with his wife, Diedre Carson Roberts, and another couple, Marilyn and Brian Meadows, as passengers. All aboard were killed. Each couple leaves behind a young child.

"Wow," was my eloquent response. Although I'd known about this incident for years, a chill traveled through my body, as if I had needed formal newspaper confirmation of the tragedy and the names of the victims to grasp its severity.

"So the pilot, George Roberts, was Milo's father, and Diedre was his mother, KC's sister, right?"

I rubbed my arms against an imaginary cold breeze.

"Right. As KC told us—not that she talked about them that much—they were wonderful parents. They never went anywhere without Milo."

"Until they did."

"Until they did," I said.

Chris put his hands on my shoulders. "I know," he said.

"It's hard." He waited. "Turn to the page I've marked, from a couple of months later."

An update appeared.

The estate of George and Diedre Roberts is being sued for negligence after a small plane, piloted by George Roberts, crashed near Puntilla Lake. The family of two of the victims, Brian and Marilyn Meadows, maintain that the pilot, George Roberts, should never have taken off, given the prevailing weather conditions.

I stopped reading. "The lawsuit KC's mother referred to." Chris nodded.

It seemed KC's life hadn't been an easy one. I thought again of the cheerful woman who had brought me cabbages and how I wished again that I'd paid more attention. Sat down with her for a cup of coffee.

"Interesting, huh?" Chris said. "You have to figure that by the time of this article, mechanical failure had been ruled out as the cause of the crash. So the Meadowses went after the pilot. There's one final mention, as far as I can tell, a little later, about the result of the suit." Chris turned flimsy old newspaper pages to a later issue.

The contentious lawsuit between the family of deceased pilot George Roberts and that of his passengers, Marilyn and Brian Meadows, was dismissed when a judge ruled that the pilot made a reasonable decision to take off for a landing strip less than one hundred miles away.

"I'll make copies so we can read the details," Chris said, "but it basically says weather in the area is so wildly variable and turns around at a moment's notice, yada yada, that it would have been impossible for the pilot to have anticipated what transpired."

"A victory of sorts for KC," I said. "I mean, she still lost her sister, and not that long after losing her father. But I'm sure it was a disappointment to the Meadows family."

"I scanned the article pretty quickly, but it seems KC played a big role in getting the charges dropped, essentially defending her brother-in-law," Chris said. "Not that she got any money, but neither did the Meadows family."

"I can ask my attorney friend, Willow Yazzie, if she has time to look over the documents. Just to give us an idea if this an unusual ruling in any way."

"It's always a tough call, and it usually takes a lot longer than this to settle a case." Chris pointed to the dates of the issues. "It didn't take long to rule out mechanical failure. But bottom line is, if you weren't in the plane at that spot at that time, how do you know exactly what the visibility was?"

"Aren't there numbers available for that? Data about clouds and precipitation? Even about visibility itself?"

"Sure. There have always been a lot of sources for data on weather conditions, and it's even better now, with weather cameras everywhere. But still, as I say, unless you're behind the wheel . . ." He threw up his hands, as he often did to make a point. "Especially in Alaska, weather really matters. You know what they say: 'If you don't like the weather here, wait a minute, it'll change.'"

I was pretty sure that was Mark Twain speaking about New England, but I didn't want to break Chris's rhythm. Neither did I want to pass up an opportunity to learn more about my non-dating partner.

"I wonder if those small planes have to file flight plans," I said. "If someone knows they're up there and where they are."

"That could go either way," Chris said, waving his hand in an either-way gesture, though my question hadn't really been directed at him. It was more of a musing. "Most of the time, they don't, but they'll probably tell someone where they're going and what route they're taking. In fact, it's often a barter situation as far as payment. Some guy will want to be dropped off to ski or climb and not want to be bothered with a charter company. The payment in those cases is complicated, taxwise, so instead, he'll offer the pilot a load of firewood in exchange, or a box of salmon, or—"

"Wait. Do you have a pilot's license, Chris?"

He nodded, sheepish, as if he'd kept an embarrassing secret from me. "Got it in the army, which is also the last time I flew on a regular basis. Well, almost."

"How come?" Now I was embarrassed. "Sorry. I didn't mean to—"

"No problem. I still do a little flightseeing work with floatplanes and bush planes, helping out a friend who's a one-man company. The full-time job kinda cuts into my flight time." He pointed to the ceiling to indicate upstairs, where his job was. "My dream is to have enough to buy my own plane someday. Until then, I get my hours in to keep my license active and help out a friend."

"So your license is active?"

"Oh, sure. Why? You want to go somewhere?" He smiled.

"Maybe," I said, smiling back.

We both laughed as though we'd just shared the wildest joke.

# TWENTY

CHRIS AND I HAD WORKED SO STEADILY IN THE *BUGLE*'S morgue, we hadn't opened the bag of breakfast snacks I'd brought, courtesy of my diner. We stopped for a break, taking a bear claw nugget each. I remembered a tourist one time who'd taken more than his share of the nuggets on the counter at the diner and suggested we call them "bear paws." My mom would have jumped on that, the way she latched on to any bear- or bear-claw-related pun.

Whatever we called them, Chris and I decided we needed something more substantial.

"How about a real lunch?" he said.

"I know a place," I said.

He laughed.

Chris had been correct about the newsroom filling up later in the day. It was almost eleven, according to the large clock above the main entrance, when we exited the creaky old elevator on the news floor. While the room wasn't mobbed, there was a significant group of people at the information desk or on a bench waiting their turn for service.

I was reminded of all the times I'd been on that side of the counter myself, chiefly on an errand for my mom. When I was a teenager, she'd send me to the newspaper office to place an ad or to check on a subscription, before all of that could be done remotely. I noticed a large table off to the side where people sat around reading newspapers. Since Elkview's library was open only a few hours a day on weekdays, and usually with only one librarian on duty at any time, I figured the *Bugle* was picking up the slack as a reading room.

While I'd been reminiscing, Chris had been planning the rest of our day.

"Maybe we should go out to the Carson farm after lunch and see if we can catch up with Milo," he said.

*Uh-oh.* I was feeling treasonous already, having spent most of the morning with Chris in the *Bugle* morgue. Now I'd agreed to have lunch with him. Was I really planning to go all out and take another Annie-less investigative trip to track down Milo?

It appeared so.

"Okay," I said softly, so none of the patrons would hear. Or so I myself wouldn't hear. "But in that case, I need to stop at home first to check on Benny."

Before we left the building, we dropped off the extra bear claw nuggets and containers of fruit in the small snack corner of the reporters' area, where it appeared the same crew we'd seen earlier was plugging away to bring the news of the day to Elkview's citizens.

Rather than take two cars out to the Carson farm, we stopped first at my house to execute our now-routine vehicle switch, leaving Chris's pickup in my driveway.

Chris understood why I couldn't possibly make this stop without visiting Benny. He volunteered to ensure my quality time with my cat by staying in his truck to make some phone calls and write up notes for the feature article on the fair that he'd promised his boss.

We'd agreed it would be better not to try to contact Milo first but to use the advantage we'd gain by surprising him.

But first, Benny. I decided to walk around to the back of my house and test the new lock, installed last night by Fergie, my personal locksmith. This would put me closer to the guest room, where Benny's condo tower stood.

After a brief struggle with the new security equipment, I managed to get the door unlocked.

I opened it to a hissy fit. Being thrown by Benny.

Alarmed, I looked down at my beautiful cat. His back was arched, his fur standing on end, his tail high. His green eyes were wide open. A frightened Benny, or a battle-ready Benny? It was hard to tell, since my own nervous system was also on shaky ground.

I tossed my keys aside and squatted. Once he'd calmed somewhat, I lifted him.

"It's okay," I said over and over. "I didn't mean to scare you."

I carried him over my shoulder to the nearby guest room and sat with him for a few minutes to calm us both, and to surreptitiously run my hands over his body, checking for blood or bumps.

All seemed well, and I settled on the fact that Benny's distress stemmed from his not being used to the sound of the new lock or to me or anyone else entering by my back door. I seldom used it, other than on the rare times I left the house for a session in my small garden.

Cats are more adaptable than humans, I decided, and I needn't make too much of this one upsetting moment in Benny's day. I gave him one more rubdown, waiting for the pleasant purr, then let him spill off my lap and follow me into the kitchen, where his favorite cabinet stored his treats. A few small, crunchy chicken bits brought down his raised hackles.

Were cats' memories shorter than ours? It seemed so, because it took no time for him to start pouncing playfully around, chasing a plush rodent-on-a-stick. I made sure his

Olympic-style movements paid off often with a successful landing on the mouse.

All this drama cut into the agreed-upon break time. With Chris waiting in his car, I now had no time to chat with Benny about the rest of my day. I'd hoped to talk about my falling-out with Annie. Was I foolish to go to lunch with Chris, and then also to Milo's without her? Why was I taking on activities that could exacerbate the problem between Annie and me? I questioned my motives and lack of sensitivity to my friend's vulnerable state.

I waited until Benny had curled himself into a nap in a spot of sunlight in the family room.

"I'll be back," I told him. "Be ready to offer counsel."

HOW ABOUT ALY'S FOR LUNCH?" I ASKED CHRIS.

Another question for Benny. Who was this diner owner, embarking on a day without a single meal at her own establishment? Was she avoiding someone, or just avoiding her duty? Or did she not want to be seen at the Bear Claw with Chris in the middle of the day?

In the back of my mind was the question, *What if Annie walks in?* I channeled Benny, reminding myself that Annie could just as easily walk into Aly's, and in fact, that would look more like a date with Chris than if I were with him in my own diner, ostensibly at work.

"Aly's. Good idea," Chris said. "Maybe she'll be there and have more to say about KC and their days at the fair."

Chris settled in the driver's seat of my car, smiling as always at my cool dashboard with its display of the outside temperature, currently a pleasant sixty-one degrees. At my fingertips were more music and news channels than one person needed unless they were on a cross-country trip. Plus, there was a bookmark function that allowed immediate access to my favorite songs, and I'd recently added a dual USB port.

Chris glanced at his ancient pickup, wrinkled his forehead in a frown, and waved goodbye.

ALY'S CAFÉ WAS IN DOWNTOWN ELKVIEW. I'D TALKED briefly to Aly at the fair on Sunday, and I wondered if she'd be there at the fair booth or in her own establishment. She and I had a tacit agreement that she would never serve bear claws unless she bought them from me, and I would never have pizza on my menu under any conditions.

"Remember the last time you and I were here together?" Chris asked.

I leaned my elbow on the table and put my hand to my forehead. "Do I have to?"

He laughed. I forced a smile. There was nothing funny about our last working lunch at Aly's. We'd been interrupted by none other than Ryan Jamison, my ex, on business from his law firm in San Francisco. Chris had covered for me, more or less pretending to be a new boyfriend and picking up on my cue that we were in a hurry and needed to take our pizza to go. As far as I knew, or cared, Ryan was safely back in California now and we could enjoy our pizza in the comfort of the brightly lit café instead of in the front seat of my SUV.

Chris went to the counter to place our usual order—pizza with mushrooms and extra cheese—while I snagged our favorite table, which wasn't too difficult, since we'd arrived a little before the lunch rush. Aly was nowhere in sight, but that didn't mean she wasn't back in the kitchen.

Chris returned, excited, and bent to speak to me in a low voice.

"New girl up there," he said, referring to the young woman at the counter, not one I recognized. "I asked if Aly was around. She's not, but I sniffed something out."

I leaned in. "Which is?"

He stepped around and took his seat across from me.

"You need to talk to her. I purposely didn't order our coffees so you'd have her to yourself."

"I'm not getting this," I told him.

"She told me Aly's at the fair today. So I went on a fishing expedition. 'I'll bet she feels awful about what happened,' I said. 'She does,' she says."

Now he was talking in Annie-ese. I did my best to follow. Chris was repeating a brief conversation between him and Counter Girl.

"What's new about that?" I asked him.

"She misunderstood me. Thought I knew more than I do and went on about how, yes, it's awful when you have a fight with someone and then that someone dies before you can make up."

*Aha.* "Wouldn't it be great to know what the fight was about?"

"But if I pushed for specifics—" Chris began.

"It would seem weird. But if I—"

"Exactly."

Anyone overhearing us would have thought we had a code. And in a way we did.

Hard as I tried, I couldn't get one nightmarish wish out of my mind—that neither Annie nor I would be murdered soon, lest the other one be left with a memory of our breakup forever after. I resolved to do my best to straighten things out between us, whatever it took.

I plotted my strategy for when Emmie delivered our order. Unlike Counter Girl, Emmie was someone I'd known for a while. A business major in college, she often shared her career goals with me. Our running chats were usually about whether I'd recommend culinary school after she got her degree. Of course I would, but today I was hoping to steer our conversation toward KC. My goal was to learn more about the alleged fight between Aly and KC from an employee other than Counter Girl, who'd mentioned it to Chris.

I hoped I could pull it off.

Chris was easy to talk to, to kill time with. One question, such as, "Who was the guy who saluted you back in the newsroom? Another vet, I assume?" would get him started on enough stories to fill a book. But then, that was his business. Stories.

He was telling me about Jersey Jerry, the guy in the military T-shirt, and how he was the third brother in a big East Coast family to serve, after Jersey Joe and Jersey Jim. In the middle of a sentence about each brother's war wounds, Chris rose abruptly, which I took to mean Emmie was approaching with our pizza and it was "batter up" for me.

"I'd better get our coffees," Chris said, loud enough for many besides me to hear.

Emmie gave him a quizzical look as he brushed past her.

"How's it working out taking two classes this summer?" I asked before she could query me about my tablemate's strange behavior.

"Oh, you know, crazy busy. That statistics class especially is a bear. I should have waited till fall for that one, but I want to finish the degree before I'm, you know, old."

I may have been too sensitive, but she seemed to look at me more closely when she said "old."

"I know Aly really appreciates all you do here," I said. "She doesn't know what she'd do without you."

Emmie brightened, making me squirm, as if my little white lie were sending me a message. But, I reasoned, Aly would have fired Emmie if she weren't a valuable employee. Still, the aroma of the hot pizza, usually so enticing, was causing my stomach to gurgle in an unpleasant manner. I hoped Emmie would just accept the compliment and not try to verify it with her boss.

*Too late*. I couldn't worry about that now. I had work to do.

"Aly is still trying to work out her feelings over KC and that last interaction, so it's nice that she can count on you," I added.

Emmie went silent, and I thought I'd blown it with the wrong choice of word. I'd played in my head with "argument" or "conflict" or "squabble." Lacking specifics, I'd gone with "interaction" as more general.

Emmie added extra napkins to our table and shook her head, in sympathy for her boss, I imagined, as well as for our murdered friend. "Yeah, I'm glad I can ease her mind a little. He isn't worth it, you know? It was like high school, arguing over some stupid guy."

"I agree, totally," I said. Was this the new me, picking up college-speak? "Buddy's not worth it, right?"

Emmie frowned. "I never heard that nickname for him. We always called him Tony." She looked around. "I'm surprised he's not here now, looking for his usual free lunch."

*Tony.* As in Tony Bellamy, employee at KC's stepfather's hardware store. I'd forgotten that I had a photo of him, though an ice-cream shake combined with a potential romantic triangle had distracted me from checking out its quality. I'd do so and share it at the team meeting.

At this point my mom, the crime fiction reader, would say, "The plot thickens."

# TWENTY-ONE

CHRIS AND I WAITED UNTIL WE'D FINISHED OUR PIZZA and coffee at Aly's and were on the road in my car before we congratulated ourselves.

"But what's going to happen when Aly comes back and Emmie thanks her for the nice words?" I asked, still nervous about my lie.

"Hopefully, we won't be here," Chris said.

We went back and forth over our tactics and over the significance of what we'd learned. Had we picked up what might be a significant clue in the search for motives for KC's murder? Or had we made too much of a casual disagreement between friends?

"Do we really think Aly, generally someone we would consider a sweet woman, is capable of murder? And over a guy?" I asked.

Chris shook his head, more a questioning shake than a negative shake. "I don't know her as well as you do, but isn't jealousy one of the top motives for murder? Especially where love or lust is involved?"

"I guess so. And besides, this does look like a crime of

passion, like it happened in the spur of the moment. It doesn't look like a planned homicide."

"It's doubtful the killer brought the knife to the fair."

"Probably picked it off the nearest booth, which would be KC's. But even if we knew how many knives she had at the start of the day, it wouldn't tell us much," I said.

"We'd need to find out how many knives were at the fair in total, and whether they were present and accounted for the next day."

"Impossible." I mentally scratched that question from my list of things to ask Trooper.

I remembered the gist of my conversation with Aly at her fair booth. She had never mentioned having had an argument with KC, nor anything about having a boyfriend in common, so to speak. But that was understandable. I hadn't asked, and she had no obligation to share that with me. It wasn't as if she were under oath or we'd been besties in school.

Without further discussion about the next activity for the day, Chris and I appeared to be headed to the Carson farm. I didn't remember explicitly agreeing to this trip, but neither was I against it. *In for a penny,* I thought, and besides, we'd already spent the day investigating without Annie.

This time we'd be sure to park on the Carson side.

As we approached the farm, I found myself looking around for cameras or another clue as to how Hortenson found us. If there was any surveillance equipment in the area, it was strapped to a utility pole, the only structures in sight. I did see the same lonely tractor on the edge of the country road and had the wild idea that the equipment was actually a robot with a bevy of cameras attached, looking in all directions.

I took out the map I'd printed out delineating the Carson, Hortenson, and in-dispute sections and directed Chris past the rows of beans to the western portion of the property. We entered a circular driveway that took us to a modest two-story white house.

It was hard to tell at first glance if the residence was occupied. A newish pickup was parked outside, facing a two-car garage. I wondered if it was Milo's. I thought of the leather key holder Annie had learned about at the fair, the one that had been personalized for KC to present to Milo for his eighteenth birthday. According to the artisans who had crafted it, the key holder was destined to accompany a vehicle—if not a new one, then at least one that was new to Milo.

Had KC been able to deliver the presents? Trooper would know.

I looked forward to asking Trooper to give us more details about KC's body, other than the terrible drawing in the file, the one that depicted where the fatal wound had landed. I wondered anew how the professionals managed to stay sane when they faced crime and its ugly ramifications on a regular basis.

I was glad for Chris's choice of a Vera Lynn tribute on the radio. "There'll be love and laughter and peace ever after" coming through my vehicle's speakers distracted from my shivers and provided a much-needed spark of hope.

We parked in the driveway and approached the front door, still not seeing or hearing signs of life.

Chris stepped up and rang the bell. We waited maybe half a minute, then he rang it again. A little longer, and we looked at each other and shrugged.

We were a few yards down the path, having given up, when the door opened.

"Hey?" Milo's voice.

A surprise. Milo knew who I was, if not Chris, and he still opened the door. Could be a good sign.

"I'm not sure you remember me—" I said, as we headed back toward the entrance.

"Course I do. Or I wouldn't have opened the door. My grandma said you'd be looking for me." Milo said this while walking into his house, his back to us. I assumed we were to follow, as well as close the door behind us, which we did.

Okay, maybe not the best sign. Not exactly a welcoming tone or a hospitable intro to his home, but at least we were in. I reminded myself that, mourner or not, Milo was a teenager.

A minute too late, I froze. What if Judd was inside? What if this was a trap?

So far, the only bad thing Judd had done for sure was stare at me, I reminded myself. And possibly steal the Jessups' SUV. And possibly kill KC, although I couldn't figure out what motive he'd have to do so. Unlike for Aly. But I couldn't go there. Come to think of it, KC had tried to get between Judd and Milo. Did that rise to the level of motive? Something to think about.

Milo was dressed in black, as he had been yesterday, and as Judd had been dressed both times I'd seen him. Today, Milo's shirt had a large Celtic cross on the front. He seemed to have lost weight in the last twenty-four hours.

Where to start?

Milo took care of that, it turned out.

"It's my fault," he said. "You don't have to tell me. I'm responsible."

It never crossed my mind that we should take Milo literally. His was a heartbreaking attempt at a confession. I tried to imagine the situation from the point of view of an eighteen-year-old. Legally an adult, but still a teenager. Although I felt that Chris and I were among the least threatening visitors a kid could have, I saw what we represented to him. After all, we'd been sent by the Alaska State Troopers. And we'd already questioned his grandmother. At that moment, I couldn't have had more sympathy for him.

Chris held it together better and responded. "I'm sure you feel that way, Milo," he said, in a voice softer than I'd ever heard from him. "And it's a crappy situation. But even if you'd been there, you couldn't have done anything."

We were sitting on various pieces of a sectional in a

nicely appointed living room, the one Milo grew up in. He sat in the section nearest an end table.

Which he now banged his fist on as he continued to assume blame for his adopted mother's murder.

"I should have stayed with her in the booth. Instead, I had to go hang out with my friends." He said this as if hanging out with his friends was a felony.

"I know it doesn't seem possible now, but one day you'll only remember the good stuff," Chris said.

All the platitudes that came to my mind made my tongue thick, and I couldn't get anything meaningful from my lips.

"We'd like to know a little more about your mom," Chris said. "Your adoptive mom, KC. It will help us as we work with the police to figure out who did this to her."

"Why don't you tell us something nice about her, Milo?" I said, finally getting my wits back. Slightly. "I'm sure you have lots of stories."

Milo almost smiled, which was a relief.

"When I was a kid, I really, really wanted a puppy, and my mom kept saying no, no, they were too much trouble. Then it was my birthday. Like this week." Milo choked up and let tears well up. I was glad he didn't feel embarrassed about his sobs, but I certainly didn't know what to do about them. Chris knew. He put his hand on Milo's shoulder and gave it a shake, or a pat, or some gesture I couldn't identify, but definitely a guy gesture, and Milo continued. "I was turning eight, and Mom surprised me with a trip to a rescue kennel and I got to pick out Balto." Milo turned and pointed to a brown and white dog lying in the shade on a brick-lined patio outside the sliding doors.

"Cool," Chris said. "The sled dog. The Siberian husky who led the dog team that transported the diphtheria medicine to Nome in . . ."

"Nineteen twenty-five," I said, as Chris trailed off and I picked up the story, learned by heart in my docent days. "And in blizzard conditions."

"And he saved the town," Milo said, joining in the narrative. "I'd been learning about the epidemic in school, and how the serum was in Anchorage, like, seven hundred miles away from the sick people, and they had this relay with dog sleds. And that's when I got my dog, so"—Milo shrugged—"it was a no-brainer."

"Did you ever see the statue of Balto in New York City?" Chris asked.

Milo's eyes widened. "Oh, yeah. Would you believe Mom took me there and that one of the first things we did was see the statue? They were putting this coat of hot wax over the statue to protect it. This guy was doing it the day we were there, and there were so many of us kids there, laughing and clapping as the guy was spraying the wax. Did you know Balto—the real Balto—was at the dedication?"

At this pause, Milo choked up again, for Balto and for the woman who seemed to have showered him with love.

I was sure Chris knew the whole Balto story, as I did, but, unlike me, had most likely seen the statue himself, well-traveled as he was. Neither of us mentioned any other details, however, leaving Milo in charge of the scene.

Before long, Milo was telling us more about the hero dog and how the trek was followed by people around the globe and how a group of New York City artists felt his indomitable spirit, as noted on the plaque below his statue, should be commemorated in Central Park.

I looked out at Milo's dog. The Elkview canine had no fewer than four bowls for food and water, two outside on the patio, and two inside the doors. For all I knew there were another four or more scattered around the house.

"How old is he?" I asked, still turned to a view of the dog.

"He was just a pup that no one wanted. We think he was about a month old when we got him. And that was ten years ago. So he's getting up there, but he still runs around a lot. I'd bring him in so you could pet him—he's very friendly—but I don't usually wake him up."

"He looks very content, Milo. He's lucky to have you," Chris said.

I realized it was necessary to bond this way with Milo, and I was super grateful to Chris for getting this topic started. But I was also eager to extract helpful information from KC's son, information that might put her killer away.

"Were you involved in your mom's business a lot?" I asked him, plunging right in.

Milo shrugged, rocked his head from side to side. "A little. I mean, until this summer, I still had schoolwork. I know about the fight, if that's what you're getting at, about the property I'm supposed to own now."

"Have you gotten any legal documents? I know you just turned eighteen, but has anything formal taken place? Papers to sign?" Chris asked. "Transfer of title, notifications?"

"Not yet. Supposedly I have a lawyer taking care of it. That's what Grandma says. I guess Mr. Hortenson is holding things up." Milo stood abruptly. "But you know what? I don't even care." He began arduous pacing in front of us. "He can have it all. Every bit of it."

The mellowness of the Milo who had been talking about his dog was gone.

Neither Chris nor I told him he'd eventually change his mind and he shouldn't make any irreversible decisions in the meantime. I wanted to ask him about his new-to-him car and leather key holder, but that no longer seemed appropriate. Nothing did, except leaving the young man alone.

Chris and I stood, putting all three of us at the same eye level. I handed him a card. "I have very flexible hours, Milo. Chris here does, also. So if you ever need anything, please let us know."

"You fish?" Chris asked.

Another flicker of a smile. Milo nodded. "Uh-huh."

"I have my friend's boat for the next week or so. If you feel like going out, give me a call." Chris handed his card over. "Maybe check out the creeks around Anchorage? Rainbow trout? Dolly Varden, right?"

"Right," Milo said.

While Milo and Chris embarked on a chat about types of trout, I looked around the house, trying not to be too obvious. I focused on the very large kitchen straight ahead, through an open doorway. I remembered KC loved to cook and imagined she'd enjoyed the farm-to-table life she had.

Now the sprawling counter was loaded with food—casseroles, baking dishes, sacks of groceries—no doubt from generous, sympathetic friends and neighbors. I wondered if Roland Hortenson had found it in his heart to offer condolences to his young neighbor.

"Would you like me to sort through the food in the kitchen?" I asked Milo. "I can divide it into meals, take care of the fridge items, et cetera." *And wash the dishes overflowing in the sink,* I added to myself.

Milo nodded. He looked relieved, as though an enormous burden had been lifted from his shoulders. "That would be really great. Thanks."

"Are you hungry? I could put together a snack, or a meal? A cup of coffee?"

Milo put his hand on his stomach and shook his head. "Grandma made me eat a lot before I left there this morning. But it would be great if you cleared up the food in our kitchen."

It was just Milo's kitchen now, but he'd figure that out eventually.

"Happy to do it," I said.

I set to work at what I do best, which was not dealing with teenage boys whose mothers had just been murdered.

I found the cabinet with plastic and glass containers and divided the many casseroles into portions good for one meal. Milo would have his choice of beef and kidney beans, chicken with cheese or rice, and two different lasagnas, for starters. There were also cold cuts and a multitude of cookies and snacks, all vying to be the most prevalent aroma filling the kitchen.

I was glad I'd already had lunch, or I'd have been tempted to taste test a few of the interesting dishes. I made sure the portions were large enough for a growing boy. I refrigerated some perishables, froze others, and discarded food I thought had passed its prime. To finish off, I whipped up a batch of corn muffins and put them in the oven.

By the time Chris and Milo had considered every creek in the Anchorage area and which fish was okay to catch in which creek, I'd wrapped up the food organization and washed all the dishes. I felt much better. Finally, I'd done something to make Milo's life a little easier.

"The oven timer will go off in about fifteen minutes," I told Milo. "Just remove the pan, and you'll have a dozen corn muffins." I looked at him and decided I needed to take an even more active role in the muffins. "Hand me your phone," I said, brazen as I was. I tapped fifteen minutes into the timer app. "You're all set."

My reward was a tentative smile and a one-arm-around-the-shoulder almost hug, for which I was very grateful.

We started for the door. Though I badly wanted a cup of coffee, I couldn't bring myself to ask for one, and I certainly hadn't felt free to make one for myself, since neither Milo nor Chris wanted one.

I did, however, get up the nerve for one more question.

Columbo-style, as my mom would say, I turned as we headed out. "I hope you don't get too lonely out here. Does your friend Judd keep you company a lot?" I asked. I could tell my voice had jumped an octave, but I counted on the fact that Milo wouldn't notice.

"Shark? Yeah, but he's pretty busy now. He's thinking of moving back to the Los Angeles area, where he grew up. I'm okay, though."

*Interesting,* I thought, but did not say.

In the car, I did ask Chris about his offer to take Milo fishing. "You have your friend's boat this week?"

I thought I detected a wink. "I can come up with one should the need arise."

"Smooth."

# TWENTY-TWO

ONCE WE WERE ON THE ROAD, LEAVING WHAT WAS now Milo's house and farm, I let out a breath I felt I'd been holding for a long time. My jaw was sore, and I thought my shoulders would never recover from the tension. My mom always told me I had the "Taylor shoulders," that my tendency to store my stress in my shoulders came from her side of the family tree.

"Everyone holds their tension in a different part of the body," she'd tell me while massaging me as a kid before a test or a recital or a big game. "You need to exercise that part when you know something stressful is coming around."

Evelyn Taylor Cooke was a wise woman. It occurred to me to let her know I appreciated that, since I may have neglected to do so while I was growing up.

The reason for my aching shoulders today stemmed from my fear of alienating a young man in pain, and not only because he was one of our best sources of intel for his mother's murder. Unlike his curt behavior yesterday when Annie and I had showed up at his grandmother's, today he had seemed beaten and exhausted. I was glad Chris could bond with him as he had, even if Milo never took him up on his offer to fish in one of the southern creeks.

While Chris drove us back to town, I levered the passenger seat of my car back to a comfortable recline and tried to take in the beauty of the pines on both sides of the road. I cracked open my window to take advantage of a cool breeze.

At some point, I realized I'd turned my phone off so we wouldn't be interrupted at Milo's. Nothing like a happy ring tone to rattle a session that was uncomfortable to begin with. I switched it back on now and found a long list of messages, both texts and emails. Most of the business texts had Victor copied, so I didn't have to worry about vendors reporting raises in prices, advertising specials, or substitutions in deliveries.

But also on the lists were texts, voicemails, and emails from Annie.

*Uh-oh.* Was she disinviting me to the seven o'clock meeting at her place? *Here it comes,* I thought. Annie somehow figured out that Chris and I had been working at the *Bugle*'s morgue and then had lunch together. Tracking down Milo had been Chris's assignment to begin with, but I'd probably have to defend my accompanying him.

"I have to answer Annie's message," I told Chris.

"No problem. See if we can pick up anything for her."

I nodded. "Good idea."

I clicked on the earliest voicemail from her, ready to hear her lash out.

Not yet. The first messages were simply of the please-call-me type. The later ones were more insistent, with a surprisingly urgent tone. The last one, sent just before I switched my phone back on, was downright panicky, finally getting to the point.

Charlie I can't do this without you. Cook I mean.
Come quick.

Clear enough. I checked the clock on my dashboard. Nearly five o'clock, and we were about fifteen minutes out of town.

"We might have to stop at the Bear Claw," I told Chris. "I think we have a dinner emergency."

Out of respect for Annie, we tried not to laugh. It wouldn't do to share a chuckle about our friend's distress.

I thought of asking Annie to let us move the meeting back to the diner, its usual locale, which would have been easier all around. I passed up that idea, not wanting to test the new but tenuous thread that had us BFFs again. After all, who but a best friend could be called upon to salvage a dinner meeting? Also, from the wording of the texts, I gathered she still wanted to host. She just didn't want to cook. Or, more likely, she had gotten in over her head with a recipe she couldn't handle.

I needed to find out the details, and I needed to hear her voice. I'd be able to tell if there was residual antagonism.

I clicked on Annie's number and heard the shortest first ring ever.

"Charlie. We need to talk."

"Okay."

I waited.

"This is it, Charlie," she said. "I don't want to do this anymore. I hate to cook. And now Trooper left me a message saying he's bringing another person. And that person would be staying here."

"Don't you have a room ready?"

"Oh, sure, I have lots of cabins, on both sides of the house. But it will be a new person," she said, as if she hadn't already said it. "And who knows what they'd expect for a meal. It wouldn't be so bad if it was just us, but I don't want to be embarrassed in front of someone new. I don't know why I thought it would be easy if I just found a simple recipe, like for salmon and rice. Victor makes it a lot, and it looks so simple."

I sailed over the salmon and rice and landed on what mattered to me. "Another person? Did he say who?"

"But then I didn't have all the ingredients, and I had to go buy some butter and dill. I didn't even know where the dill was in the store. And then—"

"Don't worry about anything. I'll help you." I cleared my throat in an effort to sound calm. I hoped Trooper wasn't bringing in his deputy, Josh Peters, who made it clear he didn't want civilians like me and my friends interfering with his job. "Who's the extra person, Annie? Did Trooper tell you?"

"He's from another borough, someone transferring in to Mat-Su."

A transfer to our borough. He couldn't be more unpleasant than Deputy Josh. Did this mean Trooper was retiring? It wasn't the first time I'd wondered. He was around when I was a little kid, and of course he'd seemed ancient to me then, at least as old as my parents. Now that I thought of it, my parents were past their sixties. My mom hadn't exactly taken "early" retirement.

From all appearances, Trooper was in excellent shape except for the occasional weariness, but that was to be expected, given his workload. I hoped that's all it was.

I tuned in again to Annie. I figured I hadn't missed much, and I was right.

"Are you listening, Charlie? I forgot about dessert, so I had to go back, and I bought some flour, but I didn't have the right size baking dish for this cake recipe I found." She was nearly breathless now, as if she'd returned from running all those errands again, chasing down those pesky ingredients one more time. "So I went back again and bought a frozen pie."

"Calm down, Annie. You do enough for us. You're a great interviewer. You don't need to host this meeting also."

I didn't remind Annie that these dinners had been my idea in the first place. Over the last few months, I'd managed to turn what could have been simple reporting sessions over coffee and cookies into a major dinner party. Because I never seemed to have time for a purely social get-together? Once this investigation was over, I told myself, I was going to gather friends for a regular five-course meal at my home.

"But I want to," Annie wailed. "I want to cook for my friends. I mean, don't you do it all the time? Why can't I even make a simple casserole or warm up a frozen pie or find the dill?"

I heard the panic in Annie's voice, even more intense than what had been captured on my phone's voicemail system.

I needed to help her focus.

"Maybe when this investigation is over, when we've helped Trooper solve this case, we can work together on a meal. When we're not in a hurry like this evening."

"Really?" she said. "That would be so good."

"It will be fun," I said, trying to picture such a session. "For now, tell me how I can help. What have you started? Is anything cooking right now?"

"Some recipe I had for a fish casserole. I don't even know where it came from. I thought I could bake it early, and then heat it up so I'd have time to make dessert. Which, don't ask me what happened there."

"You told me. I'm sorry it's been such a rough day."

"And I can't fit two pans in my tiny oven." I heard another half sob. "What was I thinking?"

I could have answered that question, but wisely did not.

"No problem, Annie. Here are some options. I could try to salvage—"

"I already tossed the casserole. Part of it was burnt, and the other part was still raw."

*That bad.* "I can stop at the Bear Claw and pick up dinners from the freezer. I know we have chicken tenders marinated in buttermilk, with the usual breadcrumbs and seasoning. I can add coleslaw, fries, and a new mustard I've been testing. We probably also have mooseloaf with mashed potatoes, a pulled pork with barbecue sauce, cornbread."

Another deep breath, but this one of the "relieved" variety.

"Oh, wow," she said. "That slaw you made for the last tour group?"

"Same recipe," I said. "Do any of those meals sound okay? I can call and find out quickly what else we have." I chose not to confess that I'd already put my staff on notice that this crisis might develop. Thus the wide variety of special selections. "Or I can stop and shop, then cook something of your choice from scratch. Which would you prefer?"

"I don't know. What's easiest? I can't think right now."

I understood why Annie was in no mood to make decisions. The first ones of the day hadn't worked out for her. Who could blame her?

"I'll stop at the diner and see what's freshest and so on, and I'll be at your place long before the meeting." In other words, she'd be able to say she put it together.

"Thank you, Charlie. I—"

"No problem. Grab a piece of chocolate and sit for a while with Yulie."

It was wonderful to hear Annie laugh. It had been little more than twenty-four hours, but I'd missed my friend and was glad to have her back.


CHRIS HAD HEARD MY SIDE OF THE CONVERSATION and figured it out perfectly, except for the part about the extra person.

"What's this about the new person coming tonight?" he asked. "Is Trooper adding someone to the team?"

I shrugged. "All I know is that he's from another borough. A trainee, maybe?"

"I wonder what this means?"

"It's hard not to take it as a rebuke," I said.

"Nah," said the military man. "Probably just a regroup-ing. I'll drop you off at your house, claim my pickup, and drive to Annie's later," he said.

I nodded. I was glad he'd thought of the best strategy for the evening. He'd be approaching the inn on his own, in his own beat-up truck.

I clicked on the Bear Claw number, and Nina picked up right away. "You know that emergency I asked you to be on the alert for?" I asked her.

"It's here?" Nina sounded almost gleeful.

"It's here. Right on time. What do we have for dinner, for five people? Plus a little extra, just in case."

In case Trooper brings a whole contingent, I thought.

Nina was ready. I listened as she rattled off the meals I was aware of. I was glad they hadn't all been scooped up by an early dinner crowd.

"Let's do five smallish servings of everything, so we'll all be able to taste each of the dishes. We can make it a buffet, with leftovers. What do we have for dessert?"

"Two pies. A French silk and a Dutch apple. Plus odds and ends of lemon tarts and cookies."

"That's all?"

"I guess I could see if—"

"I'm kidding, Nina."

"Oh, right." She chortled, sounding so much like Victor. "I'll have it all packed in about twenty minutes."

We clicked off and I sat back, relaxed. At least two prob-lems were solved. There would be food, and I had my friend back.

Chris looked over at me. "How does it feel to rule an empire like that?"

I smiled. "It has its moments."

"It sounds like we're expecting an army."

"You can't be too prepared."

"Speaking of which, we haven't talked about an agenda for tonight."

"Forget what I said about being prepared. I guess we'll have to wing it on the agenda," I said.

That was just like me. Food before content when it came to a meeting.

So much for my relaxed state.

# TWENTY-THREE

CHRIS PULLED INTO MY DRIVEWAY. IT SEEMED WE'D been driving forever. And in a way, we had been. First thing in the morning, we had been off to the *Elkview Bugle*'s morgue, made a stop at my house on the way to Aly's for lunch, and then rode into farmland to see Milo.

With miles to go.

I'd planned to scoot around to the driver's side of my SUV and head for the Bear Claw, but I found it impossible to pull up to my house without dropping in to visit with Benny, if only for a few minutes. For once, he'd hear a more normal tone to my voice. After all, we'd made some progress with Milo, and my friend and I were speaking again. I only hoped Annie and I would last beyond tonight's meeting.

I'd been tempted to get a new toy for Benny, but my mom was watching carefully from wherever she was, right now Portland, Oregon, reminding me not to spoil him. This time, she had an ulterior motive for the advice.

"You can pick up something for Midway instead," she'd said.

*Aha.* "For a puppy?"

"They need toys, too," Mom had said.

My parents had come back from San Diego a few weeks ago with a chihuahua they'd named Midway, after the USS *Midway* aircraft carrier, commissioned in 1945. My dad confessed he'd been waiting for Benny to come and live with me so he could have the dog he'd always wanted. I hoped he hadn't been waiting since he was in grammar school to have this wish granted. Though he'd envisioned a bigger breed, he confessed it was Midway who'd stolen his heart at the rescue kennel.

I finally succumbed and did some research on dog toys, eventually ordering a few. Easy enough, especially after the tense moment when my parents and I discussed the wisdom of leaving Midway with me while they were gone.

"I know you'd love to have him," Mom said. "But I don't think it would be good for Eggs Benedict. He's too old for a change like that."

"You're probably right." I feigned resignation while heaving a sigh of relief.

"The Russells are going to take him. Midway loves their new terrier, so it will be like a long playdate for them."

How different it was for cats. The times I'd seen cats engaged in so-called play together, it looked more like fighting, featuring biting, kicking, pouncing, and other signs of attack mode. I couldn't imagine Benny in such a situation.

Someday I was going to ask my friend and one-time English major Willow Yazzie to explain what Shakespeare meant by "The cat will mew, and dog will have his day." If the Bard meant that dogs had it over cats in any way, I was through with classical literature forever.

As different as dogs and cats were from one another, it turned out their toys were not so different, except dogs' were larger in general, according to the specs in the ad.

As I climbed the steps to my porch, I saw that my order had been delivered. The pet company package was sitting next to my front door. I expected a selection of chew toys, including my favorite, one in the shape of a turkey drumstick, fake bone and all. The package was outside because I'd been locking my doors recently. I was sure Chloe, our mail person, wondered why. I hoped she didn't think I didn't trust her to put my deliveries in my foyer as usual.

I unlocked the door and carried the package inside to my family room. I was sorry the outer wrapping was the white poly mailer that was commonly used lately, instead of a box with crinkly paper inside, the kind Benny enjoyed playing with.

For the first time in a while, my cat was awake and came to greet me. Lately I'd been missing his few waking hours, and I'd even called our vet to be sure Benny's extended sleeping time didn't signal ill health.

"He's just getting a little old," the doctor had said. I guessed he threw in the words "a little" because he knew I wouldn't listen otherwise.

When I first took over Benny's care from my mom, the doctor had sent me home with a stack of literature on cats' natural cycle of hunting, feasting, and sleeping. It was hard to believe that after all his years as an indoor cat, Benny was still answering the call of his ancestors, his large, feline counterparts who lived in the wild and roamed the woods for their food. I'd read that cats had been domesticated as long ago as twelve thousand years.

I sat on the rocker with Benny on my lap, listening to his purr. At times like this, it didn't seem like he'd ever had a wildcat grandparent, as far back as we could go.

At the last minute, I called the Bear Claw and asked Nina if she had time to do me a favor.

"You want me to deliver?" she asked. My inimitable and smart business major waitress.

"Am I too late? Are you heading out the door for home?"

"Sort of, but everything's ready. I can drop it off. Your place or Annie's?"

"My house."

"Is Benny awake?"

"He sure is."

"I have some extra salmon flakes for him."

Did everyone know the way to my heart?

I thanked her profusely, and she thanked me right back.

"We're still off tomorrow, right?" Reminding me of the staff's day at the fair.

I laughed. "I don't want to see you until noon on Thursday."

"Noon? Yeah! I'll spread the word."

I hoped theirs was a carefree, crime-free day.

Mine, too.

It was time for me to think about leaving. One task was to reorder my tote so I could clear out cough drop wrappers and other detritus that seemed to come from nowhere. I took care of this while sitting on my rocker, glancing now and then at Benny. He seemed to be enjoying the smaller pieces of paper that each toy had been wrapped in. I'd stashed the chewy fake turkey leg for Midway out of sight, lest Benny think it was for him.

Benny had been knocking the toys and the poly bag about when I noticed thick black handwritten markings on one side of the bag. In my hurry to open the package, I hadn't seen the markings.

I moved Benny aside gently, pushing the toys closer to him by way of a hint while I dealt with the wrappings.

I flattened the bag and saw the words:

I'LL BE BACK.

A shiver ran through me. I used my arms and feet, weak as they were, to push the chair back on its rockers, putting some distance between me and the note.

Unwittingly, Benny helped by returning to the array of pieces on the floor, some toys, some paper, and the scary bag. He sat in the middle of the pile, his tail swishing, and looked around. Then he stood and walked over the scraps, occasionally trying to push his head underneath one or clutch a piece with all fours, then roll over and wrestle with it.

All this activity hid the message, if that's what it was, and gave me a moment to think. What if US postal worker Chloe, who delivered the package, had used it to write a note, a reminder of some kind? I imagined her writing the note, taking a photo of it, and texting it to a friend or colleague. But why wouldn't she just write the text directly? Or a better explanation was that Chloe was telling me she had another delivery for me and would be back later. But was it out of character for her to use a line from an action flick to inform me?

How should I know?

I was clinging to nonthreatening ideas. Such as: someone in the chain of custody from the pet toy company to my porch had an entirely different purpose in scribbling a memo from the one that set my nervous system tingling. The one that KC's killer was stalking me, warning me from looking into her murder.

I blew out a breath. Would I ever be able to enjoy more than a few hours without a threat, perceived or real? Or a night without civilian volunteers outside my door?

Not tonight, apparently, when Buzz and Fergie would be showing up.

Visions danced in my head as a result of seeing the scrawled note. They were not of sugar plums, but of someone capable of stabbing a woman in the back and leaving her to die.

Thus, my jumping from the chair, frightening Benny, when my doorbell rang. Benny ran to the closet that was closest to the front entrance, perhaps to hide, perhaps to be ready to pounce if he didn't like the looks, or the smell, of the person on the other side of the door.

On a better day, I would have assumed my cat had run

to the coat closet to play with the assortment of his toys scattered on its floor on a regular basis. But this was not a better day, and even though the letters forming I'LL BE BACK, like a line from a movie, had been nearly shredded by Benny, in my mind they still carried weight.

I was more than a little embarrassed and relieved when I heard a knock, followed by Nina's voice.

"Hey, Charlie. You in there?"

In spite of my agitated state, I had the fleeting thought that Nina was picking up her brother's speech patterns. Not a good idea for a student on a path to being a professional businesswoman.

"Coming," I called, as if I'd been busy at the back of the house, instead of frozen with fright a few feet from the doorbell.

I opened the door to my treasured employee, empty-handed except for a small container, which concerned me for a minute. But what was one more minute of concern in a day full of them?

"Everything's in my car," she said, thrusting her thumb toward my driveway. She was already out of her Bear Claw waitress clothes and in her short denim on-the-town skirt, a look she could pull off well with her petite figure. "I figure I'll just move it all directly into your car, except for Benny's salmon."

"Good thinking."

And out he came on cue, sniffing at Nina's fingers, now down at his level as she squatted to greet him and open the container.

I took advantage of this sweet domestic scene to pull myself together.

I still had a long evening ahead of me.

Since coming home, I'd had no time to work on the agenda for the meeting with the team. It wasn't explicitly my responsibility, except that I'd generated the list to begin with and felt I should maintain it. But now the food was here and I thought I should proceed quickly to Annie's and relieve her burden.

I spent a few more minutes with Benny, certain he held no residual fright from my overreaction to what was probably a harmless scribble. Would a real killer resort to such a hackneyed phrase?

*No,* I convinced myself, and left for Annie's.

THE AROMA IN MY CAR WAS RESTORATIVE—MEATS, starches, vegetables, and sweets all mixed together, a feast for my nose. Nina and the others had zipped the various dishes into insulated delivery bags, prompting me to consider again a take-out service for the Bear Claw. We already had snack packs, of course, but those were designed for the travelers passing through Elkview. Annie's tour bus guests were great consumers of those goodies.

But there was no reason we couldn't promote meals for Elkview and neighboring residents, for special occasions or for busy people who didn't want to spend a lot of time in a restaurant. I let my mind entertain the idea, something to occupy me instead of that other thing. As I drove on roads I knew so well, I busied myself mentally designing a logo for the carrier, with maybe a catchy slogan, also. Like "Bear Claw Hug" or "Grin and Bear Claw It."

Clearly it needed more thought, and saner input.

Annie was sitting on the porch as I drove up. She was dressed in light pants and a shirt, apparently having chucked her cooking apron. I guessed she couldn't wait to get out of her kitchen and away from reminders of her day's failures.

Our meeting would be in the main house of the inn, the old Victorian that Annie had restored just enough to make it inviting to the twenty-first century traveler, but not so much that it lost its old-world charm. She'd had it painted a pale blue with white and gold trim. The domed turret was reminiscent of Russian architecture, as were the arches on the windows and the decorative trim throughout. The neat path that led to the porch was lined with lovely flowers.

All of which firmed up my resolve to do something about the exterior of my own house, if only to hire a landscaper.

Annie bounded down the steps as quickly as she could.

"I can smell the food from here," she said, though I doubted it.

Together we transferred the carriers to the inn's kitchen and unzipped them, Annie exclaiming at each new dish as it was unloaded. She might have been taking inventory or reading from our menu as she rattled off, "Chicken. Mousse. Pork. Potatoes. Muffins." There was a special reverent tone to her voice as she lifted the chocolate silk pie from its container.

She exhaled a deep breath. "Charlie, this is so wonderful. How can I ever—"

I waved away her words and packed up the carriers. "Let me just take these bags back to my car so they're not cluttering up this nice table you've set."

Thus making it less obvious that all this arrived by delivery service.

I knew Annie would never lie about how the food came to be here, and neither would I. There was no need to discuss it. Chris knew, of course, and I could only hope Trooper or the new guy wouldn't ask.

Annie had decided that she would take over the heating or cooling or whatever needed to be done before the seven o'clock gathering. She suggested I go to her office, off the lobby; edit the agenda; and print new copies. Just what I needed.

I settled in the alcove and opened my laptop. It seemed like ages since I'd looked at the agenda I'd printed for the last two meetings. I went down the list, making adjustments, adding what little new information we'd uncovered, and deleting bullets we'd taken care of, one way or another.

- The SUV. *It has been on the agenda from day one. Off tonight?*

- The property lines. *Still in dispute, but was it motive? Trooper: Hortenson alibi?*

- 9 p.m. argument at the fair. *Timeline? Check Aly's version versus the one from Lee in security.*

- Photos. *Compare phones: Annie's, Chris's, Charlie's.*

- Plane crash. *Not on original list, but now we have info on the case against Milo's parents' estate. (Follow-up with Willow.)*

- Tony Bellamy. *Also not on original list, but the boyfriend Aly and KC might have shared. Show photo from hardware store bulletin board.*

Was it a good or a bad sign that this list was shorter than the ones from the last meetings?

Good, I decided, in that we'd settled some items.

Bad, in that we didn't have anything concrete in their place.

I felt I knew what Chris and Annie would have to say tonight—very little, as far as leads or new theories. It was up to Trooper to bail us out with new information. Or maybe the new guy.

# TWENTY-FOUR

THE NEW GUY, ALASKA STATE TROOPER WAYNE TYSON, turned out to be about as non-Deputy-Josh-Peters as you could get. Josh looked boyish, but acted and sounded like a bully. Wayne looked a bit weathered, but had a sincerity and pleasantness to his voice that had you trusting him immediately. He was younger than Trooper, and definitely wider and shorter, closer to Annie's width and height.

My first impression might have been colored by his way of complimenting each of us.

Like me, for example.

"Thanks for organizing this for us, Charlie," he'd said, picking up a copy of the agenda even before we'd assembled at the table. "It's just what I need to get me up to speed." He'd laughed. "I promise not to rhyme every time." And he'd laughed again.

He'd walked around the dining area, admiring the prints Annie had chosen—watercolor scenes of our state, from a local artist. He'd commended Chris on the series of articles he'd written on right-of-way permits for the construction of industrial roads through the northwestern census areas.

"I didn't know anyone read those pieces," Chris whispered to me later.

Trooper played down the presence of another member of law enforcement at our meeting, and we all knew enough not to ask the questions that were burning on our tongues.

All our trooper would tell us, by way of introduction, was that Trooper Tyson was from the North Slope, the northernmost borough in the United States, home to Utqiaġvik, the northernmost city. He was joining us as a temporary assignment, staying in Annie's Inn for now.

Only then did I remember the evening Trooper had come back from his conference with his supposed old buddy from up north. I nodded my head, telling myself, yes, that guy's name had indeed been Wayne. And there was the time Wayne picked Trooper up after one of our team meetings.

Had those been Wayne's first interviews, scoping out Elkview as Elkview scoped him out? And how come no one had reported seeing an Alaska State Trooper wandering around town? He must have been trying to keep a very low profile, maybe not even wearing his distinctive blue and gold uniform.

At the top of my list was the question: how temporary was this assignment? I was reasonably sure my quandary was echoed in the minds of Annie and Chris.

I was full of more questions. Was Trooper retiring? Where was the charming Deputy Josh? Reassigned? On sick leave? How active was the new guy—"Call me Wayne"—going to be in the Kelly Carson murder investigation? Our investigation.

*Uh-oh*. Was he replacing all of us?

I thought for a minute. Would that be so awful? Wasn't it the goal that KC's murder be solved, no matter who completed the mission and brought the killer to justice?

It wasn't as though I had nothing to do. I'd let a lot of

diner projects slide and looked forward to spending more time in my kitchen there.

Then there were the hints that my involvement in KC's murder case was attracting the wrong kind of attention. I wondered if Annie and Chris were aware of similar warnings, if that's what they were. I couldn't ask them until I was ready to expose my own. Which were inconsequential, I realized. A farmer keeping watch over his property, a young man protecting his privacy, and some scribbling on a package.

We stopped snacking on the chips and dips and the shrimp cocktail Annie had put out and took our seats, bringing us closer to some answers to the Wayne question, I hoped.

Annie had arranged us at her large oak table in the guests' dining room. She'd outdone herself with the place settings, using her blue and white toile-patterned plates and mugs. Our team was flanked by a state trooper at each end of the oval table.

While we passed platters, small bowls, large bowls, and more platters, the small talk went well.

Question from Annie: "How do you like the weather here, Wayne?"

"It's a balmy fifty-eight degrees here right now. I just checked and it's forty-one degrees in Utqiaġvik. Does that answer your question?" Another broad smile, as if he couldn't be happier that he was sitting around the table, taking our questions.

Question from Chris: "What's the main industry up there?"

"You know, the name means 'the place where snowy owls are hunted.' That's the main industry." He paused as we all absorbed his humor. "I'm kidding. There's a little of everything there, business-wise, including tourism. The natives were concerned that tourism would fall if we returned to the original 'Utqiaġvik,' from 'Barrow,' as it had been called. The vote was close—a three-vote margin."

Question from me, speaking of tourism: "Is there really a monument to the comedian Will Rogers up there? I may have indicated as much during my 'Fun Facts about Alaska' days as a docent in high school."

I couldn't believe I still fretted over having possibly doled out misinformation when I was a teenager. But I wasn't as savvy about the North Slope Borough as I was about my own Matanuska-Susitna, and neither was I adept at covering my tracks if I didn't know an answer to a question. It didn't help my level of guilt that the travelers had paid for the tour, and thus for the information.

This was how much I trusted our new trooper—it was the first time I'd had the courage to seek out the truth.

"Not to worry. You were partly correct. There's a dual monument to the pilot Wiley Post and Will Rogers, who died together when their plane crashed just outside of town. The local airport is also named after them."

"Whew," I said. "Not exactly a fun fact, but interesting to a tourist."

Then the word came down from Trooper. "Thanks for this feast, Annie. And now, it's time to get to business."

Annie pointed to me. "The feast was—"

"I'll clear some of these dishes away," I said. "Then we can work from the agenda when you're ready."

*So far, so good,* I thought. It was going to be harder to pull off the "Who Really Cooked All This?" theme when it came to dessert, but we had a long way to go before having to address that.

Or, maybe not, since progress on the first three items was hardly going to generate a lot of discussion. They were hardly worth the paper they were printed on, as far as progress to report, but Trooper forged ahead with them anyway.

"Before we get to item number one," Trooper said,

"there's sort of an item number zero. A few things that got wrapped up by crime scene reports." He rifled through some pages. "First is that KC's van was open in the back, probably meaning that she wasn't finished packing up for the night." He rifled some more. "The rest is just a bunch of no's. No fingerprints, no other evidence."

"A seasoned killer?" Chris asked.

Trooper shrugged. "Could be. Or just a neat guy. Or gal."

*Nice going, Trooper. Showing off for Wayne?*

"Now for the real item one," Trooper said. "The SUV. It's been harder than it should be to unseal a juvie record. So I'm no closer to determining who stole the Jessups' SUV—assuming it was Judd Waters, as we suspect. And he's all we have left."

I tried hard not to shiver in fear when Judd's name was out there in the open. I could hardly wait for the item on sharing our cell phone photos from the fair, wondering if Judd had stared at either Annie or Chris as he had at me.

"Maybe I can help," Wayne said. "Up in North Slope, they might be having a slower day than the people down here. Besides"—he cleared his throat—"I know people."

"Have at it," Trooper said. "I'll text you some info." I had the fleeting thought that Trooper's new facility with his cell phone had something to do with Wayne.

Trooper paused to check the agenda. "Next up? I'm not that much farther along with farmer Hortenson and his alibi for Friday evening, and there's a big plot of farmland at stake. Upwards of fifteen acres. That's a lot of cabbages." He paused for a smile. "Hortenson claims he was at his booth at the fair until past closing time. Took him a while to check out, he says. But the kids he hired to help that day can't back it up. One says Hortenson left early; another says he has no idea. And Hortenson's booth wasn't that close to KC's, so that's no help. I don't know why he'd lie, though, when he knows we'd check with them."

"He might be counting on the fact that teenagers aren't the most reliable when it comes to details like the exact time something happened," Chris offered.

I hoped I was wrong, that Chris wasn't looking at me and thinking about the fun facts I might have played a little loose with back in high school.

"True," Annie said, though as far as I knew she didn't know teens very well, and she certainly hadn't been one to play loose with anything back in high school.

"What we have now is that, with Kelly Carson deceased, it's Milo Carson who's the other party in the lawsuit," Trooper said. "Him against Hortenson. Their lawyers, anyway."

"Does that mean Milo is at risk?" I asked.

Annie raised her hand, reverting to grade school, it seemed, but without waiting to be called on. "Well, but if the killer knew Milo was next in line for the property, and even Laurie, his grandmother, if the Carsons win the lawsuit, that is, the killer would have waited for the verdict, and killed the whole family."

She seemed surprised when we all gave her strange looks, except for Wayne, who spoke up.

"Good point, Annie," Wayne said. "Why not wait for the verdict, and either bask in his victory if he won or kill everyone in his way if he lost?' Now we all gave Wayne strange looks. How did someone not familiar with Annie-speak learn it so quickly? "Do we know when the verdict will come down?" he asked.

I waited for him to say he "knew people," but not this time.

"No clue yet, but it shouldn't take too long. The arguments have been made," Trooper said.

"It's almost a Solomon case, where they should just split it down the middle and give each party half," I said. If anyone thought it odd that a former law student would use the Bible as a decision-making tool, no one voiced it. In my defense, Solomon was a wise king, which didn't mean he had no training in law.

Next up was the argument or fight at the fair between KC and an unknown person. I smiled thinking how my crime-fiction-fan mother would have referred to him or her as "the unsub," short for "unknown subject."

Chris suggested we go back to all three of the principals who had weighed in on the incident: KC's mother, Laurie; KC's friend, but rival for a boyfriend, Aly; and security staff member Lee Hadley.

"Two of them are still at the fair," Annie said, a hint of delight in her voice.

"And if we're going to backtrack like that, we should seek out this Tony with whom both Aly and KC were involved. Allegedly," I said.

"So we're going back to the fair?" Annie asked.

"We'll split up the work," Trooper said. "Charlie, you take KC's mother. Annie, go to the fair and find Aly."

"Okay," Annie said, trying not to grin too broadly.

I was happy to dodge another fair visit and looked forward to checking on KC's mother again.

"Chris, I think you can contact Lee Hadley by phone. It's not as though we have to look her in the eyes and gauge her reaction. And any two of you, find Tony. Wayne, if you have the time between conference duties, stay on that juvie record for Waters. Nickname Shark, by the way, in case it matters."

I saw Trooper's strategy. Tony was the unknown, meaning possibly a dangerous unsub. Therefore, send two.

"Is anyone keeping an eye on Roland Hortenson and Judd Waters, even if he didn't steal the SUV?" I asked, feeling my throat constricting as I mentioned Judd.

"I have people on both of them," Trooper said. "Just a light surveillance, no wiretaps."

He laughed.

I didn't.

But he couldn't have known how relieved that made me feel.

"Who's ready for dessert?" I asked.

AFTER A QUICK STRETCH AND CHECK-IN WITH FRIENDS and family on our cell phones, we reassembled to dig into the pies and cookies from the Bear Claw. There was never a question about making time to enjoy Nina's desserts, no matter how many agenda items were left on our list. Tonight was no exception.

Wayne's vote came in early. He waved a forkful of pie meaningfully at Trooper and said, "If this is what your meal breaks are like, Cody, don't you ever complain to me about your job again."

Trooper, or Cody to his other old friends, had a few words to say about strategy with respect to the missions we'd each be embarking on. Nothing we didn't know already, but it didn't hurt to hear it again. *Don't come on strong. Don't tell them what you already know; ask them to start from the beginning.*

"And blame it on me if you have trouble," he added. "Say your boss at the station is a stickler for details and insists on having everything down in triplicate and you're sorry you didn't finish the job when you interviewed them earlier."

"How is this not the truth?" Wayne asked. "The part about your boss being a stickler and so on?"

Trooper laughed again, breaking his record for number of times laughing in one evening. I figured either he really was looking to retire or Wayne was the friend who brought this out in him. Or both.

At last we came to the agenda item I was most interested in pursuing—the photos on everyone's phone. Although the activity had lost a bit of its urgency once Trooper said his men were keeping track of Judd and Hortenson. The three of us fairgoers had agreed early on that we'd print out all our photos, making copies for everyone in the group, not editing, eliminating only those that were too out of focus to be useful.

Not knowing beforehand that the extra person at Annie's dinner would be someone involved, or to be involved, in our investigation, we had made only four copies of our photos. Not to worry, however, because Annie was on it, offering to share her set with Wayne before we even noticed. The gentleman trooper moved his chair around from the end of the oval to the middle, where Annie sat.

*Nice going, Annie.*

To keep track, we'd written our names on the paper the photos were printed on, at the bottom of the white frames. It was hardly necessary. Chris's were ready for an article in the *Elkview Bugle*, properly composed and covering a few of each category—the rodeo arena, the ribbon winners, the midway with carnival rides and games, signs for the Borealis big-name concert series, and, his favorite, the Diaper Derby. Annie had focused on food and crafts, spending a lot of time, it seemed, at the knitting booth. Somehow, I knew what I could expect for Christmas this year.

My own set of photos was mostly trained on the produce booths, and none stood out like the one with Judd "Shark" Waters posing as the poster boy for the cover of a thriller. Without giving myself away, I focused on observing the others' reactions to the photo that had me riled up. I saw no special reaction, and I began to see mine as over-the-top, distracting me from considering other options.

I studied the photos of Aly's booth, looking for knives. Of course there were knives. Her booth was more like a small kitchen, with a few of every tool she might need, from cutting up pastries and fruit to opening containers of milk and other ingredients. There were photos to back that up, but Aly wielding a knife wasn't exactly a deal breaker for her innocence.

I was deflated that nothing more came of the photos we'd put together, but trudged on to join Chris in a report of our trip to the morgue and a few details of the plane crash that had killed Milo's parents. The discussion centered on whether a member of the Meadows family, who had lost a lawsuit due largely to KC's efforts, had returned to seek revenge.

"After all these years?" Annie asked.

Chris and I tag-teamed on the old saw "Revenge is a dish best served cold."

"The idea is that revenge is more satisfying when the perpetrator has had time to prepare vengeance that's well thought out," I explained.

"And the victim has feared it for a long time, which is a kind of revenge already, and eventually maybe he decides it's never going to happen," Chris added.

"It's unexpected, therefore."

"So, *bam*." Chris clapped his hands to dramatize the scene. "And much worse, if you will."

Annie's eyes were wide. "I always wondered what that meant. The 'served cold' part," she said. "Now I see."

One of Annie's endearing traits was that she never minded admitting when she didn't know something, even if everyone else seemed to. Which made it all the more surprising and out of character that she had wanted so desperately to look good for tonight's dinner.

I was happy she was back to her old self, eager to participate and enjoying the company.

"It's a long shot," Trooper said. "But we can't rule it out. Maybe somebody can look into where they are today. The Meadows family, that is."

"I can do that," Wayne said. "Just point me to the year of the crash and the names of the parties."

"Done," Chris said. "Charlie and I can take on Tony."

I hoped he was right. It certainly felt nice to hear him say it.

The meeting broke up amid bundled leftovers and promises to report any news to the team ASAP. I also promised
to update the agenda yet again and text or email the new
version to them.

I was the last to leave. As I headed for the door, and it
was just Annie and me, except for Yulie sniffing around the
table, Annie gave me a hug.

"You can have the meetings again," she said. "I don't
want them anymore."

I thought, technically, that I'd had this meeting, vis-à-vis
the food, but I didn't dare take a chance on spoiling the
moment.

"Okay," I said.

"Plus," she said, "you can have Chris."

I gulped. "Annie, I was telling you the truth when I said
that Chris and I—"

She waved her arms. "You know what I mean. I'm not
interested in him anymore. I mean, as, you know."

*That was fast.* Another sentiment better left unsaid.

It hit me pretty quickly. "Trooper Wayne?" I asked, with
sort of a wink.

"Uh-huh. He loves Yulie, and Yulie loves him. Did you
notice?"

I shook my head. "I wasn't paying attention, but I'm very
glad to hear it."

I was also very glad to hear that Annie was leaning toward a nice guy like Wayne. Too often, Annie fell for the
handsomest guy in the room. Not that Wayne was hard on
the eyes, but that wasn't the first thing you noticed about him.

She reached over to a credenza against the wall. "This
is for you," she said, handing me a small gift bag with tissue pouring out the top.

"What's this?"

"Oh, just a little thing I picked up at the fair. I was going
to wait until Christmas, but, since I was such a, you know,
over this." She shrugged.

I opened the bag, pulled out tissue, and lifted out a knitted ornament in the shape and colors of my own tabby, formally known as Eggs Benedict.

I let out a small gasp. "I love it, Annie. Thank you. And I'm not going to wait till Christmas to hang it."

Another hug, this one longer, and I left.

Thus ended the longest falling-out period between me and my BFF.

# TWENTY-FIVE

I SAW THAT BUZZ AND FERGIE WERE WAITING IN MY driveway when I arrived home from the meeting at Annie's, leftovers and lovely present from Annie intact. The presence of Trooper's volunteers didn't mesh with his announcement that he had only light surveillance in operation for Roland Hortenson and Judd Waters. It turned out to be handy to have the men here, however, in that I could distribute some of the leftovers from our meeting. I warned them that the dinner portions would need to be heated when they got home.

"But the desserts are okay to eat now, right?" Fergie, my sometime locksmith, asked.

I assured them that was true and pointed to the labels for the pies and cookies. I laughed when I saw Fergie open the glove compartment and pull out two packages of plastic utensils. The men unwrapped the three-piece sets that places like the Bear Claw keep near the cash register for doggy bags. I watched with amusement as the men extracted the forks, spoons, and knives, and carefully laid the flimsy paper napkins on their laps as if they were of the finest linen.

For once, I was glad to find Benny asleep when I entered

my house. I wanted to update the agenda items while the meeting was fresh in my mind. I took out my laptop, opened the file with the agenda, and proceeded to edit:

- The SUV. *On the agenda from day one. Trooper WAYNE is now on it!*

- The property lines. *Still waiting for Judge's ruling.*

- 9 p.m. argument at the fair. *Timeline? CHARLIE on Laurie; ANNIE on Aly at the fair; CHRIS on Lee in security (by phone).*

- Photos. *Nothing!*

- Plane crash. *Revenge re: losing lawsuit? WAYNE to check on current status of Meadows family. (Follow-up with Willow not materializing, though admittedly I've tried to call only once. Out of the country?)*

- Tony Bellamy. *New item. CHRIS and CHARLIE to interview boyfriend Aly and KC might have been involved with.*

I felt relieved that I didn't have to worry about annoying or upsetting Annie if I was paired with Chris. I thought I'd covered everything and sent the file off to the others, then realized I'd neglected to get Wayne's email address or phone number. I could have asked Trooper to forward the file, but instead added a note in my email to Annie.

*Annie, please share with Wayne! I don't have his contact info.* I added the emoticon for a wink to my message.

My cell phone rang almost immediately after I sent the files. If I didn't know better, I'd have thought Chris had been waiting for his copy.

"I knew you'd still be up," he said.

"Too full to sleep," I said.

"Same here. Thanks, by the way." I was happy neither of us felt the need to ask or explain that the thanks were for the Bear Claw meal. "How about we go to Spencer and Laurie's together tomorrow?" he asked. "It won't look like a complete duplication to them since it was Annie who was with you yesterday, right?"

This time I hoped to get whatever information Spencer had been trying to articulate the first time I was there, when Laurie had persisted in interrupting him. And this time, I didn't have to worry about Annie's reaction to the pairing. Not that it was a pairing, exactly.

"Right, Charlie?" Chris asked the question louder.

I jerked myself out of my mental drifting. "Right," I answered. "Will you get Lee Hadley's specs first? I'm sure Annie will head for the fair as soon as she can, and we'll have all three versions of what I'm calling 'the fight timeline' to work out."

"I'll call Lee's number first thing. I think she told us or wrote down all she knew, but it will be good to have it recorded, so to speak."

"I'll need to stop in at the Bear Claw since my entire staff will be at the fair."

"Very generous of you."

"They absolutely deserve it."

"We don't want to hit the Pattersons too early anyway," he said.

"The hardware store opens at ten. Hopefully we can catch Tony there for a two-pronged operation."

Chris laughed. "Since when do you talk military?"

"I must have read it in a book."

I FIGURED THE AROMA OF THE LEFTOVERS WOKE Benny. I suspected the culprit was the shrimp. Because as soon as I opened packages and began reorganizing food for my fridge and freezer, Benny was at the kitchen door with a questioning meow.

I rinsed off the shrimp from Annie's to get rid of extra salt or residual sauce, neither of which was cat friendly. While I did so, Benny wound around my ankles, stopping every once in a while to plant an impatient but loving head-butt on my calves. Clearly, Benny was grateful and felt the treat was worth leaving his cushy tower for.

After he was done snacking and I was done putting the leftovers away, I retreated to my rocker to go through my mail. Benny laid claim to my lap as I flipped quickly through the envelopes, more or less holding my breath until I was sure there was nothing suspicious. No warning of impending doom. Lots of flyers and bills, which were strangely comforting compared to anything more threatening. In between flyers was another card from my parents.

I switched to text messages in my phone and found one with a selfie of Willow, the Eiffel Tower in the background. The "sad" message was that she was sorry she hadn't been able to help me with the property dispute material because she was delivering a paper on family and children's rights, in Paris. She'd see what she could do, however, once her presentation was over.

I had hoped she might help us with the documents for the property dispute, but it hardly mattered now; it was in the hands of a judge or judges, and we'd know soon enough.

When I finally made the effort to leave my chair again, I'd place the Portland card in a row with several others from my parents, on the dining room table. And if I ever got back to my crafty self of years ago, I might do something with them for a "Travels in Retirement" album that I envisioned.

Today's card from Mom was of Portland's Tilikum Crossing bridge. The small print on the back called it the Bridge of the People, the largest car-free bridge in the United States. Mom hadn't written a message, but simply circled "car-free" and added several exclamation points, a smiley face, and a heart. Strangely, the card made me think of Midway, currently a guest of the Russells, my parents' friends and sometime traveling companions. I hoped Benny wouldn't sense that I was thinking of the well-being of a long-haired chihuahua and become jealous.

As long as Benny was happily purring on my lap, satisfied with my intermittent rubbing of his jawbone and behind his ears, I stayed on my rocker. Every few minutes, I entertained a different question.

What had Spencer been trying to tell Annie and me about Tony Bellamy, who was his employee as well as the boyfriend of both KC and Aly?

Why was Judd staring at me at the fair, when he hardly knew me? I had only the vaguest recollection of him delivering produce to the Bear Claw. At least, it might have been Judd, one time when KC was away and Milo was ill.

Why was Roland Hortenson so upset that I might be investigating issues he was party to?

And on and on through my list of questionable alibis and alleged fights.

It was all more than enough to give me a headache. If Benny couldn't answer these questions—I'd tried to divine his answers by paying attention to his body language, but all I got were swishes of his tail—he could and did at least keep me from screaming in frustration. He almost, but not quite, kept me from grabbing another cookie also, but sugar won, this time in the form of one of Nina's oversize gingersnaps.

That was apparently it for Benny.

He left me for his comfy, uncomplaining tower.

Without my cat to brainstorm with, I called Annie. She was a night owl and due for a phone call anyway, to say what a great hostess she'd been.

"The table looked beautiful," I said. "I'd forgotten about that lovely toile set from your grandmother."

She chuckled. "You'd say that no matter what, but I'll take it."

"I love my present," I said. "I'm trying to decide the best place to show it off. What are your plans for tomorrow?"

"Early to the fair, of course. I haven't seen Aly in a while, so it will be natural for us to stop by."

"Us?" For only a very few seconds, I thought she was referring to me.

"Wayne doesn't have to be in Petersville until midafternoon, so it works out." She paused, and I sensed a smile in her tone. "Oh, it's not a date or anything, Charlie, but I'll be glad to have the protection of an Alaska State Trooper in case things go south, you know."

"You can't be too safe," I said.


I DIDN'T USUALLY CALL MY STAFF AT HOME, BUT I RE-gretted not having made time to drop in on them and lend a hand during the dinner rush. I'd been busy with a dinner rush across town. I decided Victor wouldn't mind a quick call.

He answered right away.

"Hey, boss. How'd it go at Annie's?"

Of course Victor would have caller ID and would sound upbeat, even at ten thirty at night.

I gave him a brief report, with lots of accolades, and apologized for not stopping in this evening. I got the usual "No prob, boss."

"Any problems I should know about before you take off for Fair Day tomorrow?"

"No, but I was going to ask you if you came in—do you want us to ask questions? At the fair, I mean. You know, like investigation questions?"

Did I? Not without training, I decided, even if informal as mine was. On the other hand, Victor knew most of the delivery people better than I did, especially the younger ones. He was also present in the kitchen for most of our meetings with Trooper, and the diner had thin walls. In fact, no complete walls, but a completely open through-window.

"First, I want you to enjoy the day," I said. "I can't imagine you're going there to hang around the produce booths."

He laughed. "A lot of my pals from the diner will be at the booths, so I'll be stopping by some of them for sure. You know, make them envious of us for our extra day off."

"Play it by ear, then."

"Sure. Be glad to."

"Here's something, though—Annie will be there, probably in the morning. She'll have a friend with her." On the spot, I decided not to say the friend was a trooper, in case Wayne was not planning to wear his uniform. "I'll let her know that you'll all be there, too. I'll text you all the numbers, in case there's a reason to connect."

"Sounds good. Either for bad news or good news, right, boss?"

"Right, Victor."

# TWENTY-SIX

WHEN I PULLED UP TO THE BEAR CLAW EARLY ON Wednesday morning, it felt like I was the one who'd been on a trip to Portland. Or somewhere. I hadn't been to the diner for twenty-four hours. And I wasn't going to stay very long today.

I arrived in time to say goodbye to Tammy and Bert, who responded well to the teasing label I gave them when they first started working at the Bear Claw: "the academic graveyard shift." In response to a request I'd made some time ago, Tammy handed me several versions of a new logo for our aprons, mugs, and other Bear Claw items. I was seeking an alternative to the cartoon bear we now displayed. When I'd complained to my mom about the logo, she'd referred me to the bear image on the state troopers' cars, next to the phrase GUARDIANS OF THE 49TH.

"If a bear's good enough for our troopers . . ." she'd said, trailing off.

That bear was angry, frowning, which might be an appropriate message for a law enforcement vehicle, but not for a diner.

"Look through them at your leisure," Tammy said now. "I had fun coming up with these. I feel like I know bear anatomy now, should I ever need the info."

"Let's hope not," Bert said.

I thanked her and tucked the folder into my tote.

The youngsters, as I thought of all college students, took off. They planned to change clothes and then join the rest of the staff at the fair. They laughed when I suggested they might want to take a nap first.

I was handed over to Alexandra, the freelance short-order cook from the temp agency, whom I'd never met, and her partner of the day, Drake, who'd been to the Bear Claw several other times to fill in for one of my regulars. The agency had come through as promised with a newbie and a veteran for this shift. Now I could relax.

Partly because I wanted to be sure they knew the lay of the land behind the counter, and partly because it had been a while since I'd been at the chopping block, I put on an apron.

"I haven't had breakfast," I told them, without offering that I'd had upwards of six courses at dinner last night. "I'll just whip up an omelet for myself. Make yourselves at home however you'd like. There won't be much of a crowd for an hour or so."

The non-crowd at the moment consisted of one regular, a long-distance trucker who had three meals a day at the Bear Claw whenever he was in town. We all loved Manny and were always happy when his blue cab and trailer pulled up. He wasn't above helping us clear out leftovers to take back to his cabin.

"We can get your breakfast," Alexandra said to me. "Drake knows his way around here, he says, but I'd like to see what's what, and the best way to do that"—she twirled her long, thin body around one full circle, surprising me—"is to make a meal, even if it is only breakfast." She motioned to a stool in front of the through-window. "Take a seat, and you can supervise from there or just relax and be waited on."

"I believe I will," I said, taking a seat on a stool, because how could I brush off such eagerness?

I pulled out the drawings Tammy had submitted and wondered why she wasn't majoring in art instead of business. It didn't take me long to settle on a sketch with a cluster of four bears in various stages of sitting and standing, each looking in a different direction. Fortunately, she hadn't mimicked the common pose, with the bear standing up, looking like a toddler about to take his first steps, feet far apart, arms curved to waist level, and of course a silly grin while he's coming at you.

So that I wouldn't give in to the desire to supervise Alexandra, I picked up a copy of this morning's edition of the *Bugle*, which an early-bird diner had left behind, and flipped through it while waiting to be served my omelet. I always enjoyed looking for Chris's byline, marveling that he kept himself so busy writing about statewide events as well as local color.

This morning I read that there were more black bears than normal this season, clustering around Anchorage. Accompanying Chris's article was an aerial view of the landscape, and for the first time, I wondered if it was Chris flying over the terrain, researching the topic. I hadn't thought about it before I learned he had a pilot's license, but it wouldn't be unusual for the *Bugle* to have its own plane or use old Wally's for such assignments.

Chris had done his homework, noting that Alaska was home to about one hundred thousand black bears, who fed on moose calves in spring and salmon in summer.

"Interesting article?"

Chris!

His surprise appearance was nearly the cause of a major coffee spill or me falling off my stool, or both.

"You okay?" Drake asked. My sometime helper looked

like he owned a gym. I felt comfortable knowing he could have picked me up and placed me back on the stool if he needed to.

I nodded while Chris apologized, though he'd been as startled as I was when my arm nearly knocked him over.

"There goes my complimentary letter to the editor about this black bear article," I said, recovering my equilibrium. "Did you fly over Anchorage to get these photos?"

"I did. One of the perks of my job, instead of a good salary. Sorry again to scare you. I drove by your house. No car, so where else could you be?"

How did I feel about being so predictable? One of these days I was going to slip out and go to a movie. Not even tell anyone. *Go to a movie.* I realized I'd have to find one I liked first. When it came down to it, I'd probably choose to stay home with Benny and stream an old one instead.

My newspaper had fallen, and Chris swooped down to retrieve it. I reached to reassemble it, but he folded it neatly and put it at the end of the counter.

"Hi, new people," he said, waving to them via the through-window.

I made introductions and insisted Chris select from the breakfast menu to give Alexandra more practice. Drake busied himself doing the dishes and clearing out the fridge of anything that didn't smell right.

"I talked to Lee Hadley this morning," Chris said. "I figured she'd be up early if she had to report to the fair. She checked with the guy who does the log, and it matched her own estimate when we talked to her. Twenty-one forty-two hours. Nine p.m. It's all very military. A backup guy does the log, otherwise you'd have an officer having to sign a log before they rushed off to an urgent call. This way the log-in time is accurate, too."

"So what we have to do is match that against what Aly tells Annie today," I said.

"And what Laurie says when we visit."

An inviting aroma preceded Alexandra, who appeared at the counter in front of us. "Here comes our visiting waitress with muffins for us," I said.

"Not exactly," she said, as Drake's laughter spilled out from the kitchen.

Alexandra carried a muffin tin to the table, each of its twelve cups filled with ingredients for an omelet, baked in the oven. A first for me.

Chris laughed. "A muffin shaped omelet. What do you know?"

"I want that recipe," I said, even before I took a bite.


FORTY-EIGHT HOURS OF REST, IF THEY'D MANAGED IT, had done nothing to improve the looks and mood of Spencer and Laurie Patterson. I couldn't have felt more guilty barging in again. No Milo this time, and therefore no Judd, I surmised. I didn't know how I'd feel about seeing him in person. At least I wasn't alone.

I found the room to be uncomfortably cold, compared to the environment Monday and in spite of the mild temperature outside. I wondered if Laurie and Spencer noticed. I doubted it.

"Do you mind going over the timeline once more, Laurie?" Chris asked.

"It's our boss," I said. "He insists—"

Spencer waved his hand, not letting me finish, which was very nice of him, sparing me the embarrassment, because the white lie I was about to launch into was the most hackneyed excuse, used by TV cops on a regular basis.

"Obviously there's something you're missing, or questioning," he said. "Or you wouldn't be back. So can you please just tell us what it is so we can be done with this?" He let out a heavy sigh.

Laurie moved closer to him on the couch. "It's okay, Spence," she said. "I'm okay." She turned to Chris and me.

"But I don't know how many times I can tell you. Do you think I'm lying?"

She sounded more exhausted than annoyed. In other words, much better than I would do in her shoes.

"Of course not," I said. "But this is an incredibly stressful period, and sometimes it takes a while to remember details."

Not that I'd ever been through such stress, but it seemed better than saying *We're trying to square up all the versions about who was at KC's booth and when.*

In a couple of minutes, Laurie verified her initial statement about the last hours she'd spent with her daughter, matching Lee Hadley's report. She choked up recalling herself abandoning—her choice of word—the booth about an hour before the security office got a call, and then leaving for the night before her daughter packed up in preparation for driving home. Which, of course, she never did.

At that moment, I knew I was never going to bring up that topic with Laurie Patterson again. Let Trooper send a real cop if he needed more.

"We appreciate your being willing to repeat that for us," Chris said. "But there is one more thing—a new thing, if you don't mind."

I saw that Chris was making no such promise. I thought I caught a quick smile from Laurie on "new thing."

"Okay."

"We'd like to talk to Tony Bellamy. To complete the picture of Kelly's circle, if you will. Is he at work today? At your store, Spencer?" Chris asked.

"No, he is not," Laurie answered for her husband.

"And he won't be," Spencer said. "There have been some issues with money and—"

"They don't need to hear this," Laurie said.

Which, of course, we did.

"Anything you can tell us will help the police," Chris said, while I tossed "issues with money" around in my head.

"Kelly made some unfortunate choices in the men she chose to date. It has nothing to do with her passing."

In other circumstances, from someone else's lips, I might remind the person that KC did not "pass." She was murdered, and any connection she had, especially one that was intimate or even an unfortunate date, was relevant.

I began to say as much, but Laurie stood, a sign that we were done. Possibly for good.

We had at least gotten one thing we'd come for. The victim's mother and the security guard had identical timelines for the night in question.

I thought about Aly. How would a café owner's version stand up?

I thought we were about to find out when Chris's phone rang just as we buckled into my vehicle, possibly Annie and Wayne checking in.

"Chris here."

Since his phone was not synced to my car, I heard only his side of the conversation as we sat in the Pattersons' driveway. I hoped they wouldn't think we were staking out their home.

"Already?"

(pause)

"I didn't mean it that way. I meant I was glad about it."

(pause)

"It took longer than I thought."

(pause)

"Let me take care of it."

(pause)

"Don't do that yet."

(pause)

"Okay, see you tonight."

*Fascinating.* Something amiss in the part of Chris's life I wasn't privy to. Obviously not with Annie, who should be parading around the fairgrounds with Wayne at the moment.

It was a good thing I didn't have to stretch my imagination further.

"There's something I need to tell you," Chris said.

*Uh-oh. Here? In the driveway of a grieving couple?* I clicked on the button to lower my window. I couldn't decide whether the inside or outside air was more comfortable and settled on at least having fresh air make its way into the car.

"Old man Wally," he said.

One of the last people I had suspected to be at the other end of that phone call. He would be at the bottom of a list of all the single women of Elkview and environs. "That was your boss?"

He nodded, pushed up the sleeves of his new-looking army green sweater, and clicked open his own window. "The good news is that we have a lead on who made the phone call to security the night KC was having it out with the motorcycle guy."

"The lead is from Wally?"

"That's the first bad news."

I thought for a minute. "He got the information because you put an announcement in the *Bugle*." I felt my jaw tighten. *Without running the idea by me or the rest of the team* was what made it bad news.

"I know you hate it when we get ahead of the team and go to the public," he said.

*With good reason,* I thought, because it had happened before, with unfortunate consequences.

"But this time it was all Wally, okay?" Chris seemed to speak through a clenched jaw himself. "I asked him to hold off until I could bring up the idea at the meeting tonight. How to word it, and so on. And, believe me, I give him only the sketchiest of reports of our meetings. Just enough so I can keep my job."

"I understand. I need to remember your situation, which is entirely different from mine."

Chris shrugged and nodded simultaneously. "Then this morning I open the paper and there it is. The public announcement and hotline." He slapped his palm on my steering wheel.

I had a flashback to this morning. "Which is why you grabbed the newspaper from me at the Bear Claw."

"Yeah." Spoken softly. "Lame, huh? Chalk it up to cowardice."

And I thought I'd shed my reputation as a hothead a while ago. It wasn't a good look for the manager of a customer-friendly food establishment.

"It's okay," I said. "I appreciate the explanation." I took a breath. "And we have a contact for the phone call, which is great."

"Yes, it certainly is."

"But didn't you say there were two pieces of bad news? What's the other one?"

"The woman who answered Wally's request for information? She's a fruit vendor."

It took me only a moment to figure it out. I closed my eyes and blew out a breath.

"We're going to the fair, aren't we?"

This time Chris's nod was barely perceptible as he started the engine.

We were going back to the fair.

# TWENTY-SEVEN

MY FIRST CONCERN ABOUT MAKING A REPEAT VISIT TO
the fairgrounds was that my staff would think I was checking up on them, though I could think of no reason why I
would. I'd arranged for parking fees, entrance tickets, and
spending money for them. I genuinely wanted them to have
a good time without me and give them every reason to remain the loyal, hard workers they all were.

As for Annie and Wayne, I wouldn't seek them out, but
I saw no problem if we bumped into them. Annie would
probably call it a double date, but I could handle that.

According to the fair hype, the event covered three hundred acres, and I hoped that was enough to make it unlikely
for Chris and me to run into Victor or any of the crew. Why
would they be at the blueberry booth, where the lady who
had made the call to security on Friday night hung out?
Why would they be at any produce booth? Busman's holiday? That was what Victor had claimed, but I doubted they
would carry it out once they got caught up in the fair action.
I imagined them instead in line for the rides, concerts,
games, possibly even checking out the livestock, but not the

blueberries. I pictured them returning home with armloads of prizes, unidentifiable stuffed creatures of various sizes.

"Look at it this way," Chris said as we drove away from the Patterson residence. "We'll have a great lunch at the fair. What's your preference? Italian? Chinese? Mexican?" He smiled. "Diner?"

"Funny," was the best I could come up with. *Talk about a busman's holiday.*

"Okay, my treat," he said.

Chris was making it hard to remain grumpy.

Although we had agreed there was little advantage to stopping at Spencer's Hardware Store to question personnel about Tony Bellamy, we decided to do it anyway. It was on the way back to town, after all, and we might be able to pick up some gossip about Tony. The thought of meeting Tony himself at work was fading in light of Spencer's intimations.

"There could be someone at the store who might be willing to finish Spencer's explanations," I said, "since Laurie was set on interrupting him when he was about to get to the good part."

"Agreed."

I made a last-minute decision as we pulled into the parking lot.

"A couple of people in the store, a woman named Riley in particular, might recognize me from my trip here with Annie on Monday," I told Chris. "Why don't you go in alone and I'll slink down here in front."

"Making friends wherever you go, huh?"

I landed a fist to his shoulder, which was almost flirting, but too late to withdraw. I was glad he made no comment, nor did he bump me back.

I briefed Chris on the Employee of the Week sign, which Riley had removed from the bulletin board while Annie and I looked on.

Chris thought about his strategy, running ideas by me. "I can say something like 'A friend of mine said our buddy

Tony is Employee of the Week. Is that right?' Or 'Is he around today?'"

"You can try it with a clerk working the aisles, where they wear badges, or when you check out, or both," I suggested. "Riley could be anywhere in the store."

"Do you need any nails or a rake?" he asked.

"Not today. Just information."

"I'll collect a lot of little things so I can linger during the checkout process."

Chris left on his mission, and I did what everyone over the age of two did when there weren't physical toys nearby: I took out my phone.

I lowered my window and checked on Benny first. I found him snoozing in a beam of sunlight. Looking through the Bennycam, I realized I hadn't yet swept up the pieces of the I'LL BE BACK message. In the light of day, in a cone of sunlight myself, it seemed so silly of me to consider the words a threat from a killer.

Then I raised my windows and locked my car doors.

I blamed Mom and Willow for my reaction. I recalled a quote from somewhere in the complete works of Shakespeare. *I am as vigilant as a cat to steal cream.*

Not that Benny would ever have to steal anything.

I took a breath and closed the Bennycam app. My cat was not available to play. I kept my eyes on the wide automatic glass doors of Spencer's Hardware in case Chris came running out followed by the cops or the bad guys, assuming they were different. I was ready to be the getaway driver.

I checked my email and text messages and found a photo of my staff waiting in line for the fairgrounds to open at noon, which was twenty minutes away. I laughed and texted back.

Eager anyone?

And not that I was eager to have Chris return to the car with a report. What were the chances that Tony's coworkers would give away company secrets? Like embezzlement, if that's what Spencer had been hinting at.

I ran through the possibilities. Tony might have been stealing merchandise from the store. But who risks his employment, let alone his freedom, for a bucket of paint or a bag of run-of-the-mill tools?

Maybe there was a moral turpitude clause in Tony's contract—shades of my law school class coming through. That would include murder, of course, but I assumed the Pattersons wouldn't have simply hinted at murder, but would have brought that level of turpitude to the attention of the authorities, the ones above Chris's and my pay grade.

Thinking back to a money motive, I wondered how much profit there could be in embezzling from a small business like Spencer's Hardware? As far as I knew, this store was a one-off, not part of a chain.

My next attempt to distract myself was to FaceTime with my mom, designed to keep me from running into the hardware store and confronting Riley or anyone else in my way. But part of me argued with that. We were deputies, weren't we? With deputy privileges of asking questions, even tough or embarrassing ones. Even queries that might involve company secrets.

An image of my mom appeared on my cell phone. This time she was lounging by the side of a pool, as if she'd planned the scene as a way to calm me down.

"No sightseeing today?" I asked.

"Dad is golfing, and I'm reading"—she held up a magazine, the title of which I couldn't make out—"and this afternoon if it's not too hot, we're going to do the Portland Underground tour."

"A subway? Like San Francisco's BART?"

"No, they call this tour 'exploring the activities of Portland's shady past.' These tunnels weren't for regular public transportation but for the storage of illicit goods and for moving those goods around."

She took a sip through a straw of something chilled and orange that looked very appealing. I wondered if I could text Chris to buy some cold drinks. I was sure I'd seen a set of vending machines at the back of Spencer's store.

I tuned in to my mom again. "Of course," she said, "there's also lore that criminal activity thrived in the various twists and turns below ground, one of the worst being crimping. I can't believe I'm this old and didn't know about crimping. They used to kidnap people and force them into the military to work on ships."

"Just the kind of lore you like. I'll bet there's a crime novel or two set there."

Mom brightened. "I didn't think of that. I'm going to do a search and see if I can find one. Thanks, sweetie." She picked up what looked like a brochure, the kind that might be in a hotel lobby. "Listen to this. There's one story in here about how they grabbed up one man as he was walking down the aisle for his wedding."

"Heavy," I said.

"But that might be hearsay. It's all so fascinating, factual or not."

With that, we signed off. She was the mother I'd known and loved all my life, but retirement had brought out a whole new side of her. She'd found a long list of new interests, from historic sites to museums and parks, and now tunnels.

I was happy she and my dad were enjoying themselves. I found myself doing the math for my own retirement, when I saw Chris exit the doors of the hardware store.

He didn't exactly run toward the car, but he hurried, and I figured his aim was to get out of the heat. I had the fleeting thought that neither of us would be able to survive too long in the desert weather that prevailed in some of the lower forty-eight.

I unlocked the car so Chris could tumble into the driver's side, which he did, but only after placing one plastic logo bag on the back seat and the other on my lap.

"Cold drinks," he explained, concerning the bag on my lap. "The A/C is off in the store, and I figured you'd need something cold by now, too."

Excellent thinking, but I hoped that wasn't the only information that would be forthcoming.

He started the engine, but made no move to drive off. He opened a bottle of orange soda and handed it to me, then opened another bottle for himself. I thanked him for the drink, trying hard to be patient. "Did you know they sell mailboxes in there? Mine is all rusted out, and now I have a new one."

"Chris," I said. Was he hoping for another shoulder bump? I waited, finding it difficult to cross my arms in annoyance while also rolling a deliciously cold bottle of orange soda in the palms of my hands.

He laughed. "Oh, you want to know what else?"

I smiled. "Please?"

"There's always one, I swear. No matter the nature of the company, big or small. There's one guy who can't wait to break ranks and tell secrets. Most of the time it's some little guy who feels less respected, or even a middle guy who wants the attention."

"You would know all about that, wouldn't you?"

"I'll try not to take that as a disparaging comment on my profession."

"Not at all. I can hardly wait to hear about the secret."

He showed me his phone, where a slightly crooked, poorly shot photo of a guy in profile appeared. Not young. I looked again. Not old. A little too small for his apron.

"Meet Gus," he said. "Underappreciated, underpaid. Worth at least as much as Ernie and the other guys he works with, don't you think?"

"More," I said, glad to play along now that I knew there would be a payoff.

"In a word, embezzlement," Chris said.

"Really? I ruled that out because there would be such small pickings in a mom-and-pop, or only pop, store."

Chris pointed toward the back seat. "Can you guess how much that mailbox cost?"

"I don't know. Is it solid gold?"

"You'd be amazed at the places people see as worthy of embezzling from. In fact, you may have seen my article about the library, which shall go nameless, where the director was caught skimming off the top of library payments and purchasing expensive items for his library office that ended up in his condo."

"How low," I said.

He nodded. "A guy like Gus here found out and turned him in. When they went to his house, they found all kinds of things that the library had bought, but not really, because the stuff went right to this director. There was an office chair, a lamp, a couple of bookcases, that kind of thing."

"Things that looked like they could be for a library."

"Exactly."

"I still say 'low,' stealing from a public service."

"No one said criminals had a conscience or a sense of service to others."

I blew out an exasperated breath. "Back to Tony," I said. "Was it your new friend Gus who turned him in? And turned him in where? Is he in jail? On the run? How is this a motive to kill KC?" I was talking and thinking so rapidly, I answered the last question myself. "I guess if KC found out and threatened to turn Tony in, that would be motive."

"But it sounds as though everyone already knew. At least, Gus knew, and Tony didn't kill Gus. Or the Pattersons."

"But don't forget," I said, "Annie and I didn't talk to the Pattersons until after KC had been murdered. We don't know when this embezzlement issue came to light. The hesitation they had talking about him could have been just because they didn't like him. At least, Spencer didn't care for him, and Milo called him a jerk."

"I don't understand why the Pattersons are trying to

bury this. You'd think they'd want to help the police any way they can."

I nodded. "Maybe they did, and he's now on the run. If Gus doesn't know how it's turned out, like where Tony is, it could be because Spencer wasn't ready to confirm rumors."

"Either way, the sooner we talk to Trooper about this, the better."

I felt a rush of excitement that this could be the solution to the case. Sure, there were loose ends—like wouldn't KC go immediately to Spencer with information she had, as opposed to threatening Tony?

I imagined too many scenarios to count where KC talked to Tony first. Maybe Tony had left some ledgers or other clues around his apartment, and that's why KC knew about his embezzling before her stepfather was aware of the crime. Maybe she wasn't sure and wanted to get his version of things first.

Chris had his own maybe. "While I drive, maybe you can call Trooper and also the blueberry woman to find out what time she'll be at her booth? Assuming we still want to talk to her?"

"Good plan," I said.

Chris put the car, now considerably cooler, in drive and headed out of the lot while I clicked on one of my Favorites on my call list.

It seemed I was on my way to the fair for the second time in less than a week. As much as I'd have preferred to skip the return visit, I agreed that it would still be useful to talk to the woman who had made the phone call to the fair's security people. Besides, I had that photo of Tony, albeit a poor-quality one, that I'd taken while Riley was otherwise occupied checking us out. It was so poor I hadn't bothered to share it at our meetings. But then we didn't know about Tony's escapade then, either. It made sense to show it to the fair lady, however.

I tried to reach Trooper and got his voicemail. I figured

he was probably either listening to or giving a lecture at the conference. Not goofing off with Wayne, however, who was at the fair with Annie. I left a cryptic message and hung up.

The blueberry woman, listed that way in my Contacts when Chris had read it to me, was next. I smiled thinking of how Annie talked about the fair vendors that way. The quilt people. The watermelon people. The leather people. I wished she were with us, to prove the three of us could still work together as a team. Although it might be four now, with Wayne as her plus-one.

I called up the keypad on my phone, ready to call the woman, guessing at what she could tell us. She might have seen the whole fight. It was possible that someone other than the killer had picked that fight with KC a couple of hours before she was stabbed. I gulped and took a deep breath, not wanting that image. It was also possible that KC had instigated the fight, though I was doing my best to keep her free of any blame. Whatever the blueberry woman could tell us would be useful.

"Let's not call the blueberry woman," I said, surprising myself for a second. "Isn't it often better to give no warning? We can just walk up and introduce ourselves and start listening to her story."

"She already knows we want to talk to her."

"Still."

"Valid point," he said.

Chris drove the now-familiar route back to town and slowed as he was about to pass the strip mall on the left.

"Is that an ice-cream shop?" he asked.

"I believe it is."

# TWENTY-EIGHT

THERE I WAS SIPPING A CHOCOLATE MALT IN A PARKS Highway ice-cream shop.

*Déjà vu.*

Did that mean I should expect good or bad karma? The last time I was here, with Annie, the malt was delicious, but things didn't end well, and then they got worse.

*It's a good thing I'm not superstitious.*

"Excuse me, one minute," I said to Chris, taking out my phone. "I just need to check on Benny." I hit the Bennycam app before I finished my sentence.

"Is he sick?"

"Not exactly." *I might be, though.*

In fact, Benny had assumed one of my favorite poses for him, one I had a few dozen photos of: the sphynx position. Benny sat on the family room floor facing the window, his head erect, eyes straight ahead. His front legs were stretched out, paws together, and his rump was raised a bit. He'd wrapped his tail to align itself alongside his body. He looked like the poster cat for the Shakespearean quote about vigilance. I liked to think he was waiting for me. Most important, he was fine.

Since Chris had excused himself for the restroom, I took a minute and sent my mom a screenshot, captioned "Benny the Sphynx."

Chris was only slightly disappointed that he hadn't been the first to discover the ice-cream shop. He went for the coffee soda with vanilla ice cream, gave it rave reviews, and didn't seem to mind the shop's all-pink decor. I was sitting facing a different wall from last time—no sense tempting fate—and observed the variety of posters featuring menu choices from banana splits to triple-decker waffle cones. I could tell myself that I'd try something different next time, but I knew that one, I wasn't adventuresome that way, and two, I wasn't sure there would be a next time. It all depended on how today turned out, karma-wise.

When both our phones rang within seconds of each other, we figured it was an impatient Trooper, and we were right. Chris motioned for me to pick up, since I'd already polished off the first portion of my shake. I put my phone on speaker.

"We're on it," Trooper said. "I'll tell you more tonight, but it turns out the offended party decided to do some investigating on his own before reporting the incident."

"Are you talking about—"

"That's it for now. I'll tell you more tonight," he repeated. "Just go to the fair and see what prizes you can pick up for us."

I clicked off and looked at Chris. We gave each other quizzical looks.

"It's got to be about Tony," I said, "and the 'offended party' must be Spencer and his store."

"That was a lot of code. 'Incident' would be the embezzlement, I guess."

"And 'prizes' meaning 'information'?" I asked.

"He's probably just cell phone shy. A lot of people think they're not as secure as a landline. And phones in general are suspect as far as maintaining privacy."

"He hasn't been the same since Wayne came around," I said. "Do you think he's gearing up for retirement?"

"I don't like to think about that. He's been a great buddy, and a great resource for me."

We tried to come up with a good estimate of his age.

"He's in excellent physical shape," Chris noted.

"And I hardly remember his ever having a cold. On the other hand, he was coming into the Bear Claw when I was barely starting school."

Chris pulled a napkin from the metal container on the table and took a pen from his shirt pocket. "Let's do the math."

"You have to be twenty-one to enter the academy, I believe."

"But he spent a couple of years in the military first," Chris said. "Let's say you started school, what, Charlie? Thirty years ago?"

I cleared my throat. "Approximately."

He laughed. "Okay, I started school thirty-two years ago."

A couple of napkins later, we'd arrived at the conclusion that Trooper probably had thirty years of service, in which case he could retire no matter how old he was.

A sobering thought.

"That doesn't mean he's going to do it, though," I said.

"Not at all."

I stuck my straw into the metal container and downed the rest of my malt.

IT SEEMED LIKE A GOOD IDEA TO CHANGE CLOTHES. Chris and I were both in more or less suburban casual for our visit to the Pattersons, when what we needed for the fair was cowboy and cowgirl casual, to blend in.

Chris dropped me and my car off and picked up his truck, a routine that came about often, sometimes more than once a day. Today, he'd go home to change, then come back to my house and drive us in my car again.

*Off to the fair we'll go,* I thought.

I was glad to change into jeans and a light sweatshirt to meet the sunny, sixty-degree day, but what really mattered for this stop at home was a chance to visit with Benny. I couldn't decide what would be better for him. We could sit together on the family room rocker while I read aloud from one of his favorite stories, about an old man who finds comfort in a stray cat when he suffers losses in a severe storm. Or we could play the laser dot game, which would keep Benny running, jumping, and batting his arms around for a while.

I'd let him decide.

When I entered the house, Benny was walking lazily, sniffing here and there in corners of the rooms until he found his way around my ankles. I took this to mean he wanted exercise. The laser dot game won out.

I'd considered an update where the app would choose paths for the cat playing the game, but I preferred operating the laser dot manually—a slight misnomer since it was a virtual joystick.

We had worked out a rhythm such that Benny would be jumping up about as far as a doorknob and then racing around, sometimes sliding on the shiny wood floors. But articles had warned me about the frustration a cat could feel chasing the dot and not having anything to catch except an ungraspable dot of light. So my latest technique was to operate the beam with a collection of Benny's toy mice and other objects scattered on the floor. Thus, he could have the satisfaction of actually landing on something physical.

I made sure Benny's feeder and water were at maximum capacity and waited for Chris to arrive. Benny joined me on the rocker and listened to all the questions that needed answering before we could put a "case closed" tag on KC's file.

Maybe this visit to the fair would fill in all the blanks.

CHRIS AND I HAD A GOOD LAUGH AS WE SAW EACH other's outfits. Jeans, sweatshirts, and heavy-duty sandals for both of us. We looked like Ma and Pa Kettle, minus the fifteen children.

The trip to the fairgrounds was uneventful. Not a single moose wandering, lost on the wide shoulder; not a gang of elk crossing the road, both of which we'd experienced before. We never tired of "North to Alaska," and we sang along with satellite radio.

The unmusical clamor started in the parking lot and increased the closer we got to the action. We'd used an entrance that was different for me and ended up walking along a path with animal pens on both sides, housing pigs, sheep, cattle, dogs, and chickens, to get to the produce booths. Suffice it to say, the odors were unique and strong.

I stopped at the cardboard cows and horses designed for kids to "ride" them, within two feet of the animals themselves. They were the kind I'd see outside grocery stores in the San Francisco Bay Area, far from the real animals.

"Make sense to you?" Chris asked, indicating a small boy climbing on a cardboard boar.

I shook my head.

We passed a group of people cracking logs open, while others threw small axes at dart boards. There were guys climbing tall, stripped tree trunks and others rolling logs in a pool. There was no end to the creativity here. Any activity could be turned into a race to the finish, even if the finish was who had the biggest pile of wood chips.

We'd picked up maps at the entrance. I'd tossed the one I had used on Sunday, under the hopeful impression that I wouldn't be back.

The blueberry booth was number sixty-five. If the pamphlet was correct, we'd be meeting one Pauline Sims. And if my memory was correct, her booth would be directly across from KC's, number sixty-four.

We had only one more turn to take us to the blueberry booth, passing a clump of trees sprouting ruby red apples, which I knew resulted in a pink applesauce. I slowed down and checked out the barrelful that were for sale.

"Remember why we're here," Chris said. "We can come back tomorrow if you want to shop."

I immediately dropped the apple I'd picked up. I could always send Victor to shop.

LUCKY FOR US, IF NOT FOR PAULINE, HER BOOTH WAS not busy. A young man with a full array of tattoos along his arms was taking care of the lone customer.

Chris and I hung back a few feet and took seats on the ubiquitous bales of real or fake straw. I'd grown to love them on my last visit, but I was glad I'd changed out of my good pants.

We had a view of both KC's and Pauline's booths, giving me the creepy feeling that I was at a crime scene. It was easy to understand how Pauline could have seen and heard what went on in the area next to KC's booth: the infamous evening fight, preceding the fatal stabbing an hour or so later.

On one side of the wide path was the sign I remembered, KELLY CARSON'S CART, now staffed by a young woman I didn't recognize. Not Donna Madsen, for which I was grateful. She hadn't been very forthcoming with what she knew of KC's life and business, and I had no reason to think she'd be helpful today. We were here to talk with a woman who'd offered to help.

On the other side of the path, the side we were sitting on, was Pauline Sims's booth, called Very Very Berries.

A little people-watching was unavoidable.

I couldn't help wondering what was on the minds of the passersby. I would have bet that few if any were here to investigate a murder. Not the young couple who managed to eat ice-cream cones while gazing into each other's eyes. Not the woman who was eating a taco with one hand and pushing a stroller with the other hand. Not the baby who was sleeping in the stroller—how was that possible with competing music and thrill riders' screams all around? Not the man who was sweeping debris into an industrial-size dustpan.

"Ready?" Chris asked.

I nodded.

It was time to interview the would-be anonymous caller to Lee Hadley at the security building the night KC was murdered. I wondered if we'd finally learn whether the other party to the assault was also KC's killer.

Pauline's display was most appetizing. Of course she wore a blue apron and a blue beanie over her mostly gray hair, in keeping with the unstated theme, just as Steph, the young corn seller, had worn yellow, and so on. Clear plastic boxes of fresh blueberries in two sizes lined the table. Plus Pauline had found so many other ways to use and sell her blueberries—pie filling, jam, syrup, coffee cake, scones, and muffins, for starters.

First things first. Chris didn't stop me this time as I filled two blue plastic bags with fresh blueberries and those that had been baked into something. Pauline approached us as I placed the bags on the counter in front of her.

"Pauline?" I asked to be sure.

"Uh-huh."

"Full disclosure," I said. "We're here to ask you some questions about the call you placed on Friday—"

"Oh, sure," she said, looking back and forth between the two of us. "Which one of you is Chris? The person on the desk said someone named Chris would be stopping by."

I wondered what or who had persuaded Pauline to own up to making the call. I should have checked out the *Bugle* notice to see what the wording was. If I ever followed through on my plan to advertise the Bear Claw Diner, I'd need some help with salesmanship. Once I thought about it, however, I figured Pauline might have been inspired to do the right thing when she learned that KC had been murdered.

Chris introduced himself, and me, as troopers' deputies. "Thanks for answering our call for information," Chris said. "I see you have a clear view of the cabbage booth, where the incident took place last Friday evening."

"Oh, yeah," Pauline said. "I didn't know Kelly very well, but it's a small town, and we're in the same business. Plus, when you sit through vendor training and so on, you bond a little, and I had to say something. That's why I called, but I was alone in my booth and I didn't want to stay on the line long."

"Very understandable. We really appreciate your cooperation," I said.

"I was back there"—Pauline pointed to the rear of her booth—"starting to pack up for the night. Not too many people are around the produce at that hour, so I always start a little early. I heard this motorbike come through, and they're not supposed to, you know. But it came roaring through, and he left it where he wasn't supposed to park. They can park on that street." She pointed to where, as a matter of fact, the Jessups' stolen SUV had been left.

*Interesting,* I thought. *Steal a car, but be sure to leave it in a legitimate space.*

"Anyway, it was late, so I didn't say anything. But then when he started in on Kelly, I kind of panicked."

Pauline turned from us to speak to her helper, directing him to move to where several people had gathered to inspect the merchandise. I took the opportunity to call up the photos on my cell phone and scroll to the one I'd shot of Tony's poster appearance on the hardware store bulletin board.

Then I had an idea and scrolled past Tony.

I started by apologizing, a habit I knew they'd have broken me of had I gone to training camp for real deputies. "Some of these are poor images," I said. "But see if you recognize any of these men."

I scrolled through all the male photos I had on my phone, wishing I'd thought of this police procedure earlier. I did find a few men from the day I'd shot randomly, ostensibly for the *Bugle*. In between the photos of strangers, I had one of Roland, the dreaded one of Judd, and the one of Tony from the poster. I almost accessed the group photo of my staff, but thought better of it. This was no time for games.

When my finger landed on Tony, Pauline's eyes widened. "Oh, yeah," she said again, but this time I thought I detected an element of fear. "He walked right by me, you know, after he parked his bike. Very skinny face. And he had that same hair"—she stroked her own chin to indicate where his facial hair was. "Is he the man who—"

Chris jumped in, shaking his head. "At this point, we're looking at a lot of people," he said. "But you're pretty sure this is the man who fought with Kelly?"

"Of that I am sure," Pauline said. "And I was so glad that lady security person came by and shooed him off. I'm ashamed to tell you, I was hiding back here. I'd sent my son home, so I was by myself and I didn't know what to do."

"We're glad you made the call," Chris said.

"And that you were able to stay safe," I said.

Pauline nodded and pulled a non-blue sweater around her. I thought I heard a soft grunt and saw a slight shudder.

We switched to small talk to calm things down. How was the crop this year? How was business at the fair? Which berries did she recommend for the pastries, the larger sweet ones or the smaller tart ones? Did she think it was going to rain before the fair ended?

I felt a little better when I heard the young man call Pauline "Mom."

I figured she was not going to send him home early tonight.

**T**HAT'S THAT," CHRIS SAID. "ANOTHER DATA POINT."

"Trooper is already working on the incident, so we might not need to call him right away about our prize."

"Nice try, but you're not as good at code as he is."

"How about 'our photo shoot had positive results'?" I asked.

We'd been walking toward the food area, following the aromas—such a nice contrast with the animal area. Following the "eat dessert first" philosophy, we'd agreed that we might as well have lunch here. I'd forgotten the reason why, but I remembered Chris had promised to treat me.

"Hey, boss."

Victor's voice. And there was a table full of my staff.

# Twenty-nine

**W**HY DID I THINK I WOULDN'T RUN INTO MY CREW? They were food people, after all, and besides the thrilling rides and exciting prize-filled games, the fair was known for its wide variety of cuisine.

"Come and join us," Nina said. "Annie's here, too, with her friend."

Annie and Wayne, too? What happened to my carefully thought out statistics that made it near impossible that I'd bump into one or two of these folks, let alone all of them at once?

"They're getting food," said someone at the other end of the table from where Chris and I were standing.

It seemed to me there wasn't an inch of the wood-plank table that wasn't already holding up its fill of paper plates, white takeaway boxes, colorful cardboard bowls, plastic cups, and baskets with bread and rolls, with packets of condiments strewn throughout.

"There's plenty of room," Tammy said, moving closer to Bert on the wooden bench.

"You don't want me reminding you of your workplace," I said, turning to another table.

"We like you, boss," Victor said.

"Two words not often spoken together," Chris said. "'Like' and 'boss.'" He leaned in as we stood there. "You have every right to blush."

How could I refuse to join them, red-faced and all?

Annie and Wayne waved from the food line for gyros. Annie's wave was a beckon that we should jump the line and stand with them. I left it up to Chris, who was commissioned to surprise me.

"Only Trooper's missing," Victor said.

The idea of FaceTiming him got a brief mention, but died with a declaration that he couldn't be counted on to know how to use it.

It seemed everyone slipped in a few words about his or her favorite ride (the Megafall won over the Aerial Shoot), favorite game (popping balloons), favorite prize (bombed; they were all silly). The vote for favorite food was pending. I was rooting for the crepe Chris had brought me, stuffed with ham and cheese and a dozen other ingredients.

Plans were being made for catching as much of the free entertainment as possible and for following up on exhibitions and contests. The grounds closed at ten tonight, and I doubted this group would be leaving before then.

I still had most of my crepe and enjoyed eating it slowly. It seemed every bite had a different additional flavor. Peppers, arugula, avocado, even a bean or two. Everyone was generous, so we all got to taste the sides, too. Moose roll, mini pizzas, pork bobs.

Great food; sharing a fun time with people I felt close to.

Maybe the Alaska State Fair wasn't so bad after all. And next year maybe I'd come back, even if there was no murder to investigate.

* * *

ANNIE AND WAYNE SAT OPPOSITE CHRIS AND ME, AND eventually the four of us were alone at the table.

"We talked to Aly," Annie said. "She's very apologetic."

"Meaning?" Chris asked.

"Well, remember she said KC's mom, Laurie, was with KC the whole night, staying with her while she packed to go home?"

"Right, but Laurie said she left sometime before nine o'clock, before the attack on KC."

Annie was ready with the facts. Plausible facts, anyway. "Well, first, Aly and KC were kind of competing for Tony. Though don't ask me why. I thought he was kind of creepy looking."

"On the basis of that photo?" Chris asked, perhaps thinking of photos that didn't flatter him.

"Sometimes you can tell right away. Anyway, it seems it was Aly's turn for him, like, to date him, and KC told her, warned her, that Tony might be an embezzler. Aly didn't believe it and KC said she was going to tell her stepfather and then when KC died, Aly didn't want anyone to know that Tony might have been the one who fought with her, KC, I mean, so Aly said that KC hadn't been alone at all. Then Tony couldn't be blamed. See?"

Chris apparently didn't see. "But there was a call about the fight," he said.

"Aly didn't know there was a call."

Chris scratched his head, still not getting it.

I knew better and decided not to try to make sense of Annie's rendition of the story. For now, it seemed Aly herself was in the clear, and that was all that mattered. If I needed to, I could always ask Aly directly what her motive was for lying about Laurie's presence at the booth.

"Everything points to Tony," I said. "I wish we'd been able to talk to him at least once."

"And now he's in the wind," Chris said.

"We should ask his friends and coworkers if he ever mentioned a place he wanted to go to. Or maybe he has a cabin somewhere," Wayne said.

"Or more girlfriends," Annie said.

"We can sum it all up at the meeting tonight," Wayne offered. "I have a good lead on that boy Judd's juvie record. I might even know for sure tonight."

"Is it okay to have the meeting in the diner even though all your staff is here?" Annie asked, maybe holding her breath until she knew she was off the hook.

"Sure. It might be a different menu, but we'll be fine."

"Wayne and I are going to hang around here for a while. It's been ages since he's been, and we have some free time." Annie looked at me. "Don't we?"

"Of course."

"We'll be leaving though, right?" Chris asked me.

"Absolutely," I said.

Next year was soon enough for more fair for me.

I**T WAS ALL I COULD DO TO CALL UP THE LATEST MEET**ing's agenda and look it over with an eye toward updating it for tonight. I was ready to put the case to bed. As everyone had said at least once today, everything pointed to Tony, and as far as I was concerned, he could stay in the wind, as long as he never showed up again in Elkview. That wasn't the best outcome for KC's family, of course, who would want to see him brought to justice.

I supposed I could hang in there until we accomplished that. Or tried to.

Since Benny was napping, I did the same. All that fun at the fair had exhausted me, and I hadn't even been the one driving. Too much sun, too much food, too much thinking.

I didn't wake up until five p.m., giving me barely enough

time to edit the agenda, print it, and get to the Bear Claw to prepare for dinner.

I yawned and opened the last version of the agenda, summing up the investigation.

- The SUV. *On the agenda from day one. Trooper WAYNE is now on it!*

- The property lines. *Any word on Judge's ruling?*

- Plane crash. *Revenge re: losing lawsuit? WAYNE to check on current status of Meadows family.*

- Tony Bellamy. ** *Killer? In the wind!*

Down to four items. Maybe the shortest meeting in our history. Too soon to bake a celebratory cake?

I decided to be a good diner manager tonight and actually show up to do some work.

I changed into cooking clothes, which were even more comfortable than cowgirl clothes: a loose tunic over black leggings, and very flat, closed-toe shoes for safety. You never knew when knives might drop in a busy kitchen.

Alexandra and Drake were glad to see both me and the bags of blueberries. There had been a mild rush for early dinner, they said, and I was lucky enough to just miss it.

"It wasn't a problem," Alexandra said. "Victor and the regulars left things in amazing order. Lots of extras in the freezer, so we didn't have a single glitch."

"Glad you're here, though," Drake said. "Especially if you're going to have that meeting tonight. We don't know exactly what those folks like."

"They're easy," I said. "As long as there's dessert."

"On it," Alexandra said, smiling. "How about blueberry pie?"

"Make it two," I said.

\* \* \*

**W**HO DIDN'T LOVE A GOOD MOOSELOAF? VICTOR HAD prepared more than a dozen individual loaf pans. All that remained was to mash a few pounds of potatoes and toss a salad. Besides, it wasn't only about the food, was it? I yawned and smiled again.

When seven p.m. rolled around, there were still two booths with regular customers. Fortunately, they were fans of Victor's mooseloaf and seemed excited to order it as part of the special.

I set up the booth for the team at the other end, and Alexandra thought it would be good to have music in the background.

"White noise," she said, "so your meeting will be more or less private."

I'd put together an extra-large salad, enough for our team and the booth patrons, so I felt I could slip out to the back of the diner and read new texts from Willow and from my mom.

Good news. Property dispute settled. Milo OK.
Trooper knows.

I checked to be sure the text was indeed from Willow, and not my mom, for example, or even Wayne.

It seemed Willow had come through from five thousand miles away. I couldn't wait to see Trooper. He had a lot of explaining to do this evening, starting with the coded "incident" message on the phone earlier and ending with this text.

Mom's message was to remind me they'd be coming home this weekend, three days from now. I texted back.

See you at ANC!

I decided to give Alexandra a break. She'd prepared appetizers and met the team with nicely arranged platters, besides taking care of the booth people. The least I could do was assume the role of Nina and get the meal ready and serve the team. All anyone cared about were the blueberry pies anyway.

"Who's ready to work?" Trooper asked as I placed a plate in front of him. "It's a good news night."

"Before we eat?" Annie asked.

"While we eat," Trooper said. "It's too good to wait."

"The food or the work?" Annie asked, earning a smirk from Trooper.

I quickly distributed the agenda, in case Trooper needed it.

"Number one." He practically bellowed. "The SUV. Wayne, do you want to tell them?"

Poor Wayne had just inserted a healthy forkful of buttery potatoes into his mouth, but he managed to swallow quickly. Wayne's cheeks were so chubby in their normal state, it was hard to tell if he was in mid-chew.

"I had a hunch," Wayne said. "And some experience to draw on. Where I'm from, kids never steal a vehicle without stealing two of them." He had our attention. "Typically, a kid, or two or three of them, will steal a car, say, or an SUV to go somewhere. In this case, we had the fair, a perfect destination, which is what reminded me. When they're going to hang around for a while—"

"They're not sure if the vehicle has been reported, so they steal a different one to get home." That was Chris, slapping his forehead as if reprimanding himself for not thinking of it himself.

"Exactly," Trooper said.

"Doubling the chances of leaving a fingerprint or some little dab of evidence," I added.

"Wow," Annie said, which is just what I was thinking.

Trooper took the next segment so Wayne could get in another forkful or two. "Wayne went through the reports of other stolen vehicles from Friday night, focusing on the fair, and lo and behold, there was a usable print on the license plate frame of a motorcycle that was stolen from the fair and left on Main Street in Elkview."

"No answer yet from the lab," Wayne said, "but it's got a rush on it."

"Doesn't that mean the person—I guess it could be two for a motorcycle—lives near Main?"

"Not necessarily. In fact, not likely, or we'd be on him in a minute. Most likely someone would pick him up there and take him home, not too far away. Not as far as the fair, for example."

"Wow," Annie said again.

"Next up is Charlie," Trooper said. This time I was the one he caught with a healthy mouthful, but of mooseloaf, not mashed potatoes.

"Me? You mean Willow? I thought you knew more than I do about that. I just know that the dispute was settled and that 'Milo is OK,'" I said, putting the last phrase in air quotes.

"The judge gave me a heads-up that it was split down the middle, so everybody wins, in a way," Trooper said.

"And Roland is happy?"

"That's where your friend came in. She convinced him he did not want to prolong this and fighting it was going to eat into his profits, et cetera, et cetera. Milo, of course, is probably the happiest. He has no stomach for fighting right now."

"Just like Willow not to let a continent or an ocean get in the way of helping out," I said.

"It doesn't take Roland's motive away," Chris said.

"Not exactly," Trooper said, "And of course I'm going to interview him myself, but Ms. Yazzie, Charlie's friend, talked to him for a while, and I trust her judgment for now. Apparently his alibi is solid, in spite of the testimony of the flaky teens who work for him."

"I'm so glad all around," I said. "I'll make sure I take care of a proper thank-you for Willow."

"She really came through." Trooper addressed the rest

of the team. "This lady is in Paris for a conference and she bothered to set up a zooming thing so she could help us out. She's who gives lawyers a good name."

I was glad no one laughed at Trooper's reference to a zooming thing. He'd come a long way, technologically speaking, just in the last few months.

We were batting a thousand. Not that I was sure that was the correct figure of speech, but it felt good to be on the solving side of this case. I took great pleasure in checking off items on the agenda I'd printed out.

It was Wayne's turn again, as Trooper announced, "The plane crash."

Wayne was ready for it. He'd already cleaned his plate, and Alexandra was there to take it from him. "A little progress on the Meadows family search. They were the passengers in the plane Milo's father piloted, remember. At the time of the plane crash, there were grandparents, the husband's parents, in the Los Angeles area, and they took the child."

"That was when KC took Milo," I said. I remembered the sober note in the *Bugle*'s article at the time. *Each couple leaves behind a young child.* A wave of sadness washed over me, even though the incident occurred more than fifteen years ago.

"There doesn't seem to be anything about the family after a couple of years. The grandparents died, one of them not that long ago."

"Thank you, Wayne. Now, finally, we come to Tony Bellamy," Trooper said.

"We got your coded message," Chris said.

"And I got yours that the caller identified Tony from the photo."

"Charlie put together a photo array of men, Trooper. Right on the spot. You'd have been proud of her."

"I'm always proud of her," Trooper said.

This was my day to blush. I've had worse ones.

"But wait, there's more," Trooper said, bringing about a laugh as we all thought of late-night television shopping. "As soon as we got the word, we got a warrant to search his house. Guess what was in a vent in the hallway."

"A knife," Annie said, and grinned broadly as Trooper nodded.

"And now he's in the wind," I said.

"Good riddance," Annie said. "He's a creepy guy. I guess I've said that."

"It would be nice to find him and prosecute," I said.

"We won't quit on that," Trooper said. "It would have been a whole lot easier if the Pattersons had blown the whistle as soon as they knew they had an unscrupulous accountant."

"Technically not obstruction, though, if they claim they weren't sure, didn't have evidence, and didn't want to possibly ruin an innocent guy's reputation," Wayne said.

"I can check on things like property records to see if he owns anything in some remote area, and even go back to my new friend at the hardware store," Chris said. "I'll bet he'd love to tell us more. Whether it would be more than gossip is a question, but I can give it a try."

"That's great, Chris, but for now"—Trooper turned his head toward the through-window—"any chance of getting dessert to celebrate this team's work?"

Only a couple of blueberry pies.

I'D FALLEN ASLEEP ON MY BED, FULLY CLOTHED, WHEN Annie called. Apparently she could tell she woke me.

"Sorry," she said. "It's not even ten o'clock. Are you sick?"

"Just nodding off," I said. "I guess success is more tiring than failure."

I believed that we'd been successful at about the ninety percent level. I still wasn't happy that Tony Bellamy might have gotten away with murder. Plus, something was not right, and I couldn't shake it. *And by the way,* I said to Tony, whom I'd never met, in my head, *why didn't you take the knife with you and drop it in one of the many lakes and creeks and rivers you'd come to as you left town?*

"I know what you mean," Annie said, oblivious to what was in my head. "Can I come over?"

Dear Annie, a master at disconnected thoughts. "What's up?"

"I just want to see you to, you know, bc like we were, not how I was."

"You don't need to—"

"I'll be right there. I won't stay long. And I don't need any food."

Why argue? "See you."

Not fifteen minutes later, I'd brushed the wrinkles from my shirt and pants and was sitting with Annie at my dining room table, yearbooks and scrapbooks between us, Benny at our feet, looking through the memorabilia she'd brought.

It was as if she'd planned it—not typical of my BFF. She pulled out a photo of a cross-country ski meet, which was her first example of when things were normal, as she put it. In high school. And in fact, we didn't talk about "how she was" over Chris. This was Annie wanting to erase that phase of our friendship, short as it had been.

"Remember the Moose Club?" she asked.

We looked at a flyer we'd produced: "Tips for Dealing with Moose."

"We thought we were so clever, naming our hiking club that way."

Annie read aloud, "If a moose displays aggressive behavior—"

We read in unison, "Run as fast as you can."

"And try to put a large object between you and it."

"Like a car," she said.

We laughed, and the nasty phase was officially ended. For the second time, I thought, but Annie was worth however many times she needed.

I walked her to the door and waved as she got in her car, struggling a bit with all her props.

My choices now were to get into my pjs and officially go to bed, or make a cup of coffee and put a dent in Bear Claw paperwork.

A little of both, I decided. Make coffee, get in bed with paperwork.

I passed the family room, where we'd started out until we realized Annie needed a large surface for her displays. On one of the rockers was Annie's purse. *Bummer.* I'd heard her drive away, so there was no going after her. Hopefully she wouldn't be speeding home and be caught without her license. I texted her so she'd know her purse was safe and she could collect it in the morning.

Five minutes later, my doorbell rang. Annie must have decided she couldn't be without her purse. I understood that. Most of us women carried our lives there. Driver's license, credit cards—

I opened the door.

To Judd Waters.

Strangely, my first thought was: how many different black muscle shirts does this man have?

# THIRTY

JUDD FILLED MY DOORWAY, THEN QUICKLY PUSHED HIS way in.

I was tall. Judd was huge. I swallowed hard.

"You just won't quit, will you?"

He closed the door behind him, as gently as Annie had, but leaving no doubt about why he was here.

"I don't know what you mean, Judd," was my brilliant response as we did this crazy dance where he walked steadily forward as I walked backward past my family room.

I thought of running, back to my bedroom, where I could shut myself in and use my phone to call Trooper, Chris, Wayne, everyone. But as soon as I turned away, he grabbed my arm and pushed me back into the family room, where he shoved me onto a rocker.

He looked down at me, his eyes burning into my face, as if daring me to recognize him.

And suddenly I did.

"You're the child," I said. *Each couple leaves behind a young child.*

"I'm the child, the one who got the wrong end of the

stick. Milo's father killed my parents, and he got away with it."

I bit my lip so I wouldn't remind him that Milo's father died. Not what I'd call getting away with it.

"I came up here to settle things. Someone had to pay. I thought it would help me if I just chose one. I thought it might be Milo, but it turns out he's a nice kid. His aunt, however, she's the one who made sure my grandparents got no help at all to raise me. Not a cent."

"I'm sorry—"

"Shut up. I'm not finished. Did you know that Milo was sick that day? That's why his parents insisted on coming home. Milo was with his grandmother. And granny called to say she couldn't handle the sick kid, so they'd better fly home, no matter what the weather. And that was the only way my parents were going to get home. Smart, huh?"

Judd had taken a seat on the other rocker. He crossed one leg over the other, a relaxed pose except for his eyes. The same eyes that had stared at me as I captured that video at the fair. What did he want from me now? None of what he was saying was my fault.

Judd had no weapon that I could see. Was there a knife tucked away somewhere on his body? I realized now he must have planted the knife he used on poor KC in Tony's house. So why was he here making himself obvious as a killer? We had all thought Tony was the killer and Judd was out of the running. Why wouldn't he take that as a win and go back to LA as a free man?

And again, why me? My only guess was that he saw me as a threat, someone who might figure out that he'd framed Tony. That would be giving me too much credit.

But I couldn't ask if I wanted to. My lips and chin trembled. I felt every muscle tighten and my heart ready to explode. All I could do was wait him out, as frightened as I'd ever been. There was no car outside with Buzz and Fergie. I'd already said good night to everyone close to me.

Then my phone rang.

I made a move to grab it from the small table where I'd left it earlier, near Annie's purse.

"Ignore that," Judd said.

"Everyone knows I'm home."

"They can leave a message."

"They won't settle for that. They'll text to make sure I'm okay. And someone will stop by if I don't answer."

"Believe me, I know how much you're protected usually. I figured those rent-a-cops wouldn't be there tonight, thinking Tony had been the threat to you, and I was right."

Judd seemed pleased with himself, smiled for a second, then blew out an annoyed breath.

My phone hadn't stopped ringing.

Judd stood, his husky bulk overpowering my vision. "Okay. Answer, but put it on speaker." He shoved all the books and papers, the mug holding pens and pencils, my water bottle, and Annie's purse onto the floor, leaving only my phone, and pushed the table between us.

I saw Trooper's caller ID and had a split second of hope. I could simply yell into the phone and Trooper would come. But unless he was outside my door, which was unlikely, he'd never be faster than Judd could be with his thick bare hands. Which made me think of Benny and how vulnerable he was. I hoped he stayed in his condo. When I had checked on him before Annie arrived, I noticed him twitching and wiggling a bit, which meant he was in a deep sleep. I hoped he stayed that way.

I was happy to see Judd lean over and read the screen on my cell phone. CODY GRAHAM with the location under it: TROOPER STN.

I clicked accept and the speaker button. I cleared my throat.

"What's up, Cody?" I asked. "It's late."

He paused, processing my unusual greeting, I hoped.

"Just checking in. We got some news about the Meadows family I wanted to tell you about. Okay if I come over now?"

Judd shook his head. Hard. If he'd had any hair at all, instead of the shaved style I preferred to associate with Chris, it would have been blowing around his face.

"Sorry, Cody, I'm about to go to bed. Maybe tomorrow."

"Okay. You sure you don't want some company?"

Judd hovered over me.

"I'm sure, and there's no mincemeat pie left anyway, so don't even think about it."

"Okay, night, Charlie. See you tomorrow."

"Night, Cody. And don't call back." I chuckled nervously.

I hung up, hoping there were enough clues for Trooper to get the message. I never called him Cody. So, ironically, I was using code. He knew there was pie left, and besides, mincemeat pie was one of the few desserts neither one of us liked and was never made at the Bear Claw or in my kitchen. "Don't call back" meant we were at the front of my house. And he knew I'd never refuse a visit, no matter the hour.

The fact that Trooper had mentioned the Meadows family was, I was sure, his way of saying he knew who was in my house. It was also meant to convince Judd that Trooper didn't know he was there.

I'd done all I could do.

It was time to get Judd talking again, while Trooper Cody mustered the troops. I might as well ask the prime question on my mind, even though it might incite my unwelcome guest to real action.

"Why me, Judd?"

He sat down again. "I don't know exactly, except you've been snooping around. And then I learned it was your lawyer friend who got Milo that great settlement. There's no end to your reach when it comes to resources. Once again, Milo wins. He got a parent who wasn't a hundred years old like my grandparents and forgot how to handle a kid. Who didn't want a kid, as a matter of fact. He got insurance money from the destroyed plane." He waved his hand around. "Yes, I looked all this up. And now he has a house and farm."

As much as I feared for my own life, I hoped he wasn't rethinking his decision to leave Milo alone as "a nice kid."

I wished there were a clock in front of me so I could calculate the minutes, figure out when Trooper would be here. "One Mississippi, two Mississippi" wasn't doing it.

I had one more question. "The vehicles, Judd? The SUV and motorcycle?" I hoped he'd launch into a lecture about how a motorcycle wasn't technically a vehicle.

My intruder-captor shrugged. "Change of plans. I decided a big-deal state fair wasn't the place to get my revenge."

"You were going to kill KC during your fight?"

"Enough of this." Judd was angry now.

Not a good thing.

I tried to summon techniques I'd seen on television where cops were called in to defuse situations like this. But even better, I heard a car in the driveway. I hoped Judd, in his frantic state, did not hear it. I feigned a cough and knocked the table over to cover the sound of the car.

Judd turned red, angrier, if that were possible. He kicked the table out of the way.

"What's this about?"

It was about Cody, the Alaska State Trooper, and his civilian volunteers, who broke down my front door, rescuing me.

# THIRTY-ONE

SINCE THERE WAS A CHANCE OF RAIN (WASN'T THERE always, in Alaska?), we were gathered indoors, in the Bear Claw Diner, fully staffed.

My staff had found a way to print and frame a photo they'd had taken of themselves at the fair. They presented it to me on Friday, two days after Judd Meadows had been arraigned and charged with murder.

When Victor bargained to hang the photo on the wall in the Bear Claw, I said it would be fine as long as I had a copy for my house. The photo showed Victor in the center, between his sister, Nina, and his girlfriend, Rachel—"his girls" he called them, taking a big risk. The others were gathered around, and except for a clownish pose by Bert, everyone looked perfect. The best part? They'd found a way to include Benny, sitting at Victor's feet, in the sphinx pose. I could only guess that they'd involved my mom and gotten her to share that latest photo, the one I'd sent her.

There was a round of applause, also, that Benny had apparently slept through the entire takeover of my family room by Judd, never appearing until Trooper and his team came to the rescue.

Although this was a party, there was the usual debriefing.

"No wonder it was so hard to find a juvie record for Judd Waters. He was Judd Meadows at the time."

"I hear you used facial recognition in the end with Charlie's photo," Chris said.

"Finally," Wayne said, shaking his head.

"I should have given it to you earlier," I said.

And that was the end of the blame game. The rest of our time was spent congratulating ourselves.

"Nice work on sending code on that phone call," I heard several times.

Chris had found a property Tony owned, way past Denali, around Eureka.

"There's not much by way of law enforcement up there, but a plan is coming together," Trooper said. "You had a rough time of it, Charlie, with the threats and all, and especially the awful intrusion by Judd. How can I make it up to you?"

"Let's talk shirts," I said.

Trooper frowned. "Shirts?"

"And badges. I'll foot the bill. All I need is your permission."

"Hmm. I think I'll kick that to your new boss."

It was a bittersweet moment when Trooper tilted his head to where Wayne was helping Victor at the grill. "He doesn't know what he's in for."

My mom, who'd arrived home with my dad just in time for the party, took care of that one.

"Well, Wayne doesn't have to help Charlie with her math homework," she said.

"That was my pleasure," Trooper said.

"Mine, too," I said.

I didn't add how sad I was that Trooper would no longer be part of my daily life. I managed to join the well-wishers

and smile at the suggestions about life in retirement—
travel? fishing? or maybe taking up oil painting? All were
mentioned, but Trooper remained closemouthed. So did I,
since I couldn't bear to make his retirement real, as much
as I liked Wayne and knew that Trooper had paid his dues.

RIGHT UP UNTIL THE LAST MINUTE, I THOUGHT I'D MIS-
understood Chris. First that he had a new truck and could
drive us where he wanted to take me.

"New to me," was how he'd put it.

"We can take my car," I said. "Wherever we're going."

"Nah. I want this to be a real date."

I thought I managed to say "Okay" or "Fine." I hoped it
wasn't as lame as "Thanks."

I couldn't be sure, but it seemed we were at a landing
strip and there was a two-seater waiting for us.

"You know," Chris said, "there's a saying that flying is
the second-greatest thrill known to man."

I figured I'd oblige and play the straight man. "And the
first?"

"Landing."

The next thing I knew, I was looking down at what must
have been the world's most beautiful landscape. Low
enough to see a young girl fishing and brown bears making
their way across the river. High enough to clear the treetops.

It was the most date date I'd ever had with Chris.

# BEAR CLAW DINER
# FAVORITE RECIPES

## SLAW

MAKES APPROXIMATELY 10 SERVINGS.

### INGREDIENTS

- 8 cups red and green cabbage, shredded
- 4 medium carrots, shredded
- ½ cup parsley leaves, coarsely chopped

**DRESSING**
- ½ cup canola oil
- ½ cup white vinegar
- 1 T dry mustard
- 3 T sugar
- 1 tsp celery seeds
- salt and pepper to taste

## DIRECTIONS

Toss cabbage and carrots and parsley.

Mix all other ingredients to make dressing.

Pour dressing over cabbage and carrot mixture, wetness to taste.

Cover and refrigerate at least 1 hour.

# BOSTON CREAM PIE

*This is a three-recipe dessert,
but well worth the time and effort.*

THIS RECIPE SERVES 8, GENEROUSLY.

## INGREDIENTS

**CAKE LAYERS**
- 2 eggs
- 2 cups cake flour
- 1 cup sugar, divided
- 2 ½ tsp baking powder
- ½ tsp salt
- ⅓ cup vegetable oil
- 1 cup milk, divided
- 2 tsp vanilla extract

**CREAM FILLING**
- 1 ½ cups milk, divided
- 2 tsp cornstarch
- ¼ cup sugar
- 1 pinch salt
- 1 egg
- 1 T vanilla extract

**CHOCOLATE FROSTING**
- ¼ cup water
- 2 T sugar
- ½ cup semisweet chocolate chips

# DIRECTIONS

### CAKE LAYERS DIRECTIONS

Heat oven to 350 degrees. Grease and flour two nine-inch round cake pans, or line bottoms with waxed paper.

Separate eggs; place whites in a small bowl and set aside. In a large mixing bowl, combine cake flour, ¾ cup of sugar, baking powder, and salt. Set aside.

In a small bowl with an electric mixer, beat egg whites until soft peaks form. Very gradually beat in the remaining ¼ cup sugar; beat until stiff peaks form. Set aside.

Add egg yolks, vegetable oil, and ½ cup milk to flour mixture. With electric mixer, beat until smooth, scraping sides of bowl occasionally. Add remaining ½ cup milk and vanilla extract. Beat just until combined. Fold beaten egg whites into batter. Divide batter into prepared pans.

Bake cake layers 20 to 25 minutes or until centers spring back when gently pressed. Cool in pans on wire rack for 5 minutes. Loosen cake layers around edges and turn out onto racks. Cool completely.

### CREAM FILLING DIRECTIONS

In a one-quart saucepan, heat 1 cup milk to boiling. In cup or small bowl, combine remaining ½ cup milk, cornstarch, sugar, salt, egg, and vanilla extract until blended.

When milk comes to boiling, gradually stir in cornstarch mixture with wire whisk. Return to boiling, stirring constantly. Reduce heat and simmer 1 minute or until thickened to pudding consistency. Set aside to cool to room temperature.

## CHOCOLATE FROSTING DIRECTIONS

In one-quart saucepan, heat water and sugar to boiling.
   Add chocolate chips. Stir until glaze is smooth.
   Remove from heat. Cool 5 to 10 minutes or until slightly
thickened.

### ASSEMBLE

To assemble, place one completely cooled cake layer, up-
side down, on a serving plate.
   Spread with cream filling.
   Top with remaining cake layer, right side up.
   Spoon glaze over top; spread to edges of cake.
   Refrigerate until frosting appears set.

# ACKNOWLEDGMENTS

THANKS TO MY CRITIQUERS: GAIL ABBATE, SARA BLY, Nannette Rundle Carroll, Ann Parker, Susan Silva, Sue Stephenson, and Karen Streich. They are ideally knowledgeable, thorough, and supportive.

A special word of thanks to friends who also provided advice and pertinent photos throughout the project: Alaska resident Kris Hutchin; Ann Damaschino, Ellen Kirschman, Nancy Kors, Susan Lawson, Jo Mele, Gail Meyers, Judith Overmier, Lyn Roberts, Priscilla Royal, Leslie Rupley, and Sheryl Ruzek.

Thanks to Heather Haven for lending me the name of her late, beloved Yulie.

Special thanks also to expert ice climber and frequent Talkeetna visitor William McConachie, who showered me with information and outstanding photographs of the Last Frontier. Retired inspector Chris Lux has been another expert with endless patience as I ask LLEA questions, sometimes the same ones over and over.

My deep gratitude goes to my husband, Dick Rufer. I can't imagine working without his support. He's my dedicated webmaster (www.minichino.com) and personal on-call IT department.

Thanks to my agent, Lois Winston, for her hard work and welcome attention, and to the copyeditors, artists, marketing specialists, and other staff at Berkley Prime Crime for all their work on my behalf.

Finally, my gratitude to Jennifer Snyder, my dedicated, talented, and newest Berkley editor. I hope we'll have many projects together!

Ready to find
your next great read?

Let us help.

**Visit prh.com/nextread**